THE LIFE SHE COULD HAVE LIVED

LAURA PEARSON

B
Boldwood

First published in Great Britain in 2025 by Boldwood Books Ltd.

Copyright © Laura Pearson, 2025

Cover Design by Lizzie Gardiner

Cover Images: Adobe Stock

Interior icons: Adobe Stock

Every effort has been made to obtain the necessary permissions with reference to copyright material, both illustrative and quoted. We apologise for any omissions in this respect and will be pleased to make the appropriate acknowledgements in any future edition.

A CIP catalogue record for this book is available from the British Library.

Paperback ISBN 978-1-83603-475-9

Large Print ISBN 978-1-83603-476-6

Hardback ISBN 978-1-83603-474-2

Trade Paperback ISBN 978-1-80625-737-9

Ebook ISBN 978-1-83603-477-3

Kindle ISBN 978-1-83603-478-0

Audio CD ISBN 978-1-83603-469-8

MP3 CD ISBN 978-1-83603-470-4

Digital audio download ISBN 978-1-83603-471-1

This book is printed on certified sustainable paper. Boldwood Books is dedicated to putting sustainability at the heart of our business. For more information please visit https://www.boldwoodbooks.com/about-us/sustainability/

Boldwood Books Ltd, 23 Bowerdean Street, London, SW6 3TN

www.boldwoodbooks.com

For Joe, who made me a mum. Thank you. Here's a book you won't read.

PROLOGUE

Anna finished the wine in her glass and gestured for Nia to pour her another. 'I just don't understand...' she started to say.

'I know,' Nia cut in. 'You don't understand why he didn't call.'

'It was perfect, Nia. It was so perfect.'

'And that's why we're going to see Magda! We're going to get some answers.'

'I don't know... about Magda.'

Magda was Nia's next-door neighbour. She read tarot cards in her conservatory and had successfully predicted Nia's driving test fails (three) and her subsequent pass, Nia's dad's recovery from prostate cancer and Nia's appearance on a local radio quiz show. Nia believed that Magda could predict anything.

Four weeks and three days ago, Anna had met a man called James on the bus after accidentally poking him in the knee with the end of her umbrella, and they had got chatting, got off the bus together at Trafalgar Square and gone on a long walk that had led to coffee and then dinner and then a moonlit walk along the Thames. It had been the most romantic day of Anna's life. When James had kissed her, Anna had felt all those things you read about in books, the fireworks and the fizzing and the rush of pure joy. He'd taken her number and promised to call the next day, and it hadn't crossed her mind even once that he wouldn't.

But he hadn't. Not the next day, or the one after that. Not for four weeks and three days. Hence Magda. Nia knew that Anna was a sceptic. She'd lured Anna over to her house with the promise of wine and a video showing of *Point Break* (Keanu for Anna, Patrick for Nia), and then after a couple of glasses, she'd mentioned Magda. That she'd already made the booking. That it was in half an hour.

'Come on,' Nia said. 'I mean, what have you got to lose? We'll ask her to tell us about the loves of our lives, and then you can see whether it sounds like James is the one, in which case we need to find him, or whether you've just dodged a bullet.'

'I don't believe in "the one",' Anna said. 'And I don't believe in psychics, either.'

'But what if you're wrong?'

Anna let that thought settle. What if she was wrong? What if this woman next door, with her tarot cards and tea leaves and whatever the hell else these people used, could really see into Anna's future? She took another big gulp of wine, as if it might drown her doubts.

'Okay,' she said, smiling as Nia started to clap her hands and do a little victory dance. 'Okay, let's do it. But when we get back, we watch *Point Break*. Promise?'

1

MONDAY 5 JUNE 2000

When Anna reached the table where Edward was sitting, his face lit up. He was looking at her with the same expression he'd worn on their wedding day, a year before, when he'd stood at one end of the aisle and she'd stood at the other, waiting to walk towards him. Like she was precious. Like he couldn't quite believe it. He looked refreshed, no sign on his face or the drape of his suit of the long day he'd just put in at the office. He looked like a man who'd been waiting for his wife. She sometimes had to remind herself that that was her.

'Hello,' Anna said. She reached a hand out and Edward touched her palm with his, like a very slow high five. It was a thing they did. She didn't remember how it had started.

'Hello,' Edward said.

'So, year one, done.'

'That's right, just an eternity to go now.'

Anna laughed, then reached into her bag and pulled out a parcel. 'For you,' she said.

'For me?' Edward tore off the paper and pulled out the small notebook Anna had chosen. 'What is it?'

'Look inside.'

Anna watched his face as he began to turn the pages. It was a collection of photographs of the two of them. She'd had them printed off and stuck them in this book and written little joke-laden captions with reminders of where they'd been and what they'd been doing. One from their London wedding, one from the honeymoon in Rome, one from the first holiday they'd ever gone on together, to Majorca. She'd made sure that in every photo, it was just them. No friends, no family. While putting it together, she'd been flooded with happy memories.

When they'd first met, Anna had had a broken heart. She'd been cheated on by a boyfriend she'd thought she might be with forever, and Edward had been patient, understanding her need to take it slowly, reminding her that he was there, that he always would be. She'd found his solidness reassuring. He was loyal, to family, to friends, to his work, even. It was comforting, and at that time, comfort had mattered more than excitement. She hoped that it always would. She'd staked her life on it.

'Wow,' he said. 'This is wonderful. Thank you so much.'

Anna beamed. She'd taken a long time over the present, and enjoyed seeing how much he liked it.

'Happy anniversary,' he said.

Anna wanted to kiss him, thought about the way she would kiss him when they were alone.

'I still can't believe I finally persuaded you to marry me.'

They'd got married four years after meeting, which felt reasonable to Anna. The first time Edward had asked her, it had only been a year, and she'd said she wasn't ready. How could you know, after one year, that you wanted to spend your life with someone? How could he be so sure? Anna knew she had plenty of faults, from leaving her things all over the bathroom to being snappy and mean when she was tired. Edward always teased her about the fact that she struggled to make up her mind. That was another one. It baffled her, sometimes, that Edward felt so confident that he would always want to be with her. But he waited for her, asked again a year later, and again, another year after that. Anna had remained determined that she wouldn't say yes until it felt right. And that final time, it had.

When the waiter came, Edward ordered a bottle of champagne. A year before, they'd drunk champagne in a crowded room and kissed and danced until Anna felt dizzy. They clinked glasses, looked in each other's eyes.

'I love you,' Edward said.

'I love you, too.'

Over starters of grilled cod, Edward asked how her day had been. Anna had just started a new job as a publicist at the publishing house, where she'd worked on reception for most of the time they'd been together.

'Great,' Anna said. 'I have so many ideas. I mean, I've always had them, but it was never really appropriate to suggest them before. It's so nice to finally be in the inner circle, to feel like what I think matters. To be taken seriously.'

Anna's years spent working on reception had been a source of much frustration. Doing that kind of job in her late twenties had never been the plan. She'd decided at fifteen that she was going to be a journalist, and every step she'd taken had stemmed from that. An English degree, followed by a journalism course. Two years on a local paper. And then a little boy had been killed in a car accident and she'd been asked by her editor to go to the house, get a quote from the parents, and she'd known, ten years after deciding that this was the career for her, that it wasn't.

She'd walked out, moved back in with her mum for a bit,

while she tried to formulate a new plan. And then, in her haste to make a quick decision, she'd made a couple more wrong ones. When she'd first met Edward, she'd just abandoned a PGCE. By the time she'd settled on publishing, which seemed so right that she couldn't believe she hadn't realised it before, a lot of her friends were nicely settled into their careers. Edward, too. She'd made a few unsuccessful applications for editorial roles, and then applied to be a receptionist, determined to work her way up from the inside. The first step of which had taken longer than she'd expected.

'How was your day?' she asked.

Their starters had been cleared away and just then, a waiter appeared with their steaks. Edward cut into his to make sure it was medium, just how he liked it.

'Pretty good,' he said. 'I had a one-to-one with Holmes. He said he thought I'd be in his shoes this time next year. He's hoping to step up and he's told his boss that I'm the only one of his team in a position to take over his role. I'd have a team of twenty.'

'That's great,' Anna said.

Anna was proud of Edward, despite not fully understanding what he did. No matter how many times he tried to explain it, she felt no more informed. He worked for an investment bank, had joined on their graduate recruitment scheme and been promoted three times in ten years. It wasn't a meteoric rise, but it was significant. It was clear that he was going places, that he would be on the board by the time he was forty. A couple of times, recruiters had tried to lure him away, but he'd remained loyal and he told her, often, that the bank valued that loyalty in him, and would repay it. The money he made was approximately four times her salary, and she didn't much like to think about that.

'Anyway,' Edward said, 'that's enough talk about work.'

Anna was relieved. Edward worked hard and he deserved this success, but she wasn't all that interested in it. In the money or the steps that led steadily upwards to bigger offices and more sprawling teams and longer hours and probably an ulcer. It wasn't the side of Edward that she'd fallen in love with. She wanted to see the man who had made her laugh until there were tears streaming down her cheeks and her mascara was ruined on the night they'd met. The man who turned things she was saying to him into lyrics and sang them to her as soft rock ballads. The man who put his hand on the back of her head in public places and whispered in her ear about what he'd like to do with her.

'What shall we do at the weekend?' she asked.

'Stay in bed, eat Chinese food and watch documentaries about serial killers,' he said, as if he'd been waiting for her to ask exactly that.

Anna laughed. 'I think we might have watched them all. I was thinking we could go out on the bikes, maybe get out of the city.'

Edward sighed, pretending to be annoyed. 'Okay, we'll do your thing on Saturday and mine on Sunday.'

'Deal.'

'Can you believe the wedding was a year ago? I feel like it's flown. I'm still not used to saying wife instead of girlfriend.'

Anna thought back to that day. It had been so joyful. They'd pushed back against everyone's demands and done everything just the way they'd wanted to. An ice cream van outside the venue while the photographs were being taken, a Britpop disco, brightly coloured streamers everywhere in place of flowers, because of Edward's hay fever, and three choices of dessert at the dinner, because of Anna's sweet tooth.

'It was the best day,' she said.

He reached across the table and took her hand. 'Shall we skip dessert? Go home?'

Anna glared at him.

'Just kidding.'

They ordered a raspberry cheesecake and a crème brûlée to share, and Edward let Anna eat most of both, sitting back and sipping at his drink, laughing while she rolled her eyes to show how good they were.

This was happiness, wasn't it? This was what people searched for. How lucky they were, Anna thought, to have found it, to have kept it.

And then Edward launched into a story about his friend Rav at work and a senior manager who kept getting the two of them mixed up, despite them being different races and Edward being at least six inches taller, and Anna was laughing again, her sides hurting with it. They got up, walked out hand in hand, people turning to look as Edward kept up his impression of the manager, who had a strong Scottish accent.

'But didn't I talk to you about this last week? What do you mean that wasn't you?'

She suggested getting a taxi home and he agreed. Her feet were hurting and she didn't fancy the Tube and the walk up the hill to their flat at the other end. She hailed a black cab and they climbed inside, and she took her shoes off and he put his arm around her, pulled her in to his chest.

They lived in a two-bedroom flat in Clapham. It was a Victorian conversion, and they had the downstairs, which meant they had a garden, but it also meant they could hear their upstairs neighbours walking around at all hours. Edward let them in and Anna put the kettle on. When she brought the drinks through to the living room, he was looking at the door, as if waiting for her.

'Sit down,' he said, patting the space next to him. He reached out and took one of the mugs she was holding, and she put the other one down on the coffee table and sat. 'I want to talk to you about something.'

Perhaps he was about to suggest a holiday, she thought, or even a prolonged period of travelling. He knew that Anna regretted not taking a year out like so many of her friends had, that she'd never backpacked around Asia visiting temples and experimenting with Buddhism. Would she be a different person, if she had? Maybe he was going to suggest taking some time out of their lives and exploring. She pictured herself, barefoot on a beach.

Edward reached for her hand, took hold of it.

'I want us to have a baby,' he said.

A baby. Anna felt as though she'd been punched in the stomach.

It wasn't like they'd never talked about it, but it had always felt abstract, somehow. Something for the future. She hadn't expected to be making a decision about it yet. But she had to ask herself why not. She was thirty. She was married. She owned her home. Some of her friends were starting to have babies. Why did the suggestion come as such a surprise?

Anna closed her eyes and tried to imagine herself as a mother. A baby in her arms, in this flat. Edward a proud father. She could see it; of course she could.

When she didn't say anything for a few moments, he began to prod her with words.

'You know, I understand your reluctance,' he said.

Anna looked at him. Did he? She wasn't even sure she did.

'We won't be like your parents,' he said.

Anna felt rankled. She'd done her fair share of moaning

about her parents to him, but it felt different when he mirrored that back. Harsher, somehow.

'My mum did her best, she just had to work so hard, because of my dad leaving...'

Edward picked up her hand from where it was resting on her lap. 'But I won't leave, and you won't have to work hard, and it will all be so different for us. I promise.'

At the mention of working hard, Anna thought of another objection.

'I just started in my new role,' she said. 'What will they think?'

'Anna,' Edward said. 'That's your job, and this is your life.'

It was true. But it had taken her so long to get to this stage, and it was only the first step on the ladder she wanted to climb. She went back over his words. *It will all be so different.* Would it be different? Anna had sometimes thought that you must learn how to be a mother from your own mother. And she didn't feel like she'd learned so much. What if she made the same mistakes? Never saying I love you, never saying she was proud. What if that was just a pattern she was destined to repeat?

'Anna?' Edward asked. 'What do you think?'

* * *

'Talk to me,' Nia said.

Anna had locked herself in the bathroom to call her best friend. She kept her voice low, tried to remember how to breathe normally.

'Edward wants us to have a baby,' she said.

'And? What do you want?'

What did she want? When they'd been about fifteen, Nia sleeping over at Anna's house, both of them lying on Anna's bed at two in the morning, they'd talked about the future. About what they wanted, what they dreamed about. For Nia, it had been clear. She'd wanted a job in TV production (she had a cousin who did something similar) and a husband who was funny and rich (possibly the star of one of the TV shows she worked on), who had dark hair and blue eyes. She wanted children, a busy house, school photos on the wall and notes stuck to the fridge with alphabet magnets. Anna had struggled to articulate her own dream, which was fuzzier, more blurred. She'd talked about feeling content, secure, loved. She didn't know by whom. It was more a feeling than a vision. She wanted to be part of a team. She wanted someone who knew all her stories and still laughed at them, who made her feel like she was important. Who didn't try to change her into something else. Nia had listened and said that she could do all that, and didn't Anna want passion and everlasting love, too? And shortly after that, Nia had fallen asleep and Anna had gone on thinking about it.

'Remember when we were teenagers and we used to talk about what we wanted our futures to look like?'

Nia laughed. 'Anna, that is half our lives ago. And yes, of course I remember. You rambled about this feeling that you were looking for... and you had no idea what it should look like, in practical terms.'

'And I still don't, Nia. I still don't know what it should look like. I think that's the problem. I've always thought I would have children, because it's just what you do, but when Edward suggested actually doing it right now, I felt like I couldn't breathe.'

'Try to calm down,' Nia said. 'Close your eyes. Think of yourself holding a baby, with Edward next to you. Now, how do you feel?'

Anna shrugged, though she knew Nia couldn't see her. 'I don't know.'

'Not that elusive feeling?'

'I mean, maybe. I just don't know. I can't feel it. I can't tell.'

Anna paused, unsure whether she wanted to ask the question that kept coming to the forefront of her mind. 'Nia?'

'Yes?'

'When Edward and I first met, you said you didn't think we fitted. Do you still think that?'

Nia was quiet. Then, 'Did I say that?'

'You know you did.'

'Okay, I'm sorry, Anna. You know me. I was probably drunk. You fit. You totally fit. I think it was just because of what Magda said...'

Eight years earlier, Nia's neighbour Magda had read their tarot cards. She'd said Nia would have one big love and one child, and then they'd moved on to Anna. Magda had frowned, said that there would be some tragedy, but there would also be love. She had taken Anna's hand and said that the great love of her life would have a name that started with J (Nia had gasped and clasped Anna's arm, and mouthed 'James!') and that he would have something to do with food.

James, the perfect guy from the perfect date, hadn't worked in food, and he had never called. But Nia had taken it upon herself to lead a quest to find this man for Anna. So when Anna had brought Edward to meet her best friend, Edward, who worked in finance, Nia had been disappointed. When Anna had said she was going to marry this man, Nia had bitten her lip and nodded, looking like she was about to cry.

'Nia, I can't base my entire life around a prediction that some crazy tarot lady made when I was twenty-two!'

'Okay, first of all, Magda is not crazy. Magda is a genius.'

'And second of all?'

'I don't know. I didn't have a second of all. Do you ever think about him, still? James?'

'No,' Anna lied. 'Okay, maybe.'

'You chose Edward,' Nia said, gently. 'You married Edward.'

'I know that.'

'So what did you tell him?' Nia asked. 'He's not still waiting for an answer, is he? What did you say?'

2

YES

Tuesday 5 June 2001

Anna looked up at the clock that hung on the wall. Ten more minutes, and she could leave. All she wanted to do was go home, take off her bra, put her comfiest pair of pyjamas on and eat an easy dinner in front of the TV. But Edward had messaged her a few hours ago to say he'd booked a table at their favourite Greek restaurant. At least it was a five-minute walk from home.

'Anna?'

She looked up and saw that Ellie had approached her desk. She and Ellie had started as publicists just over a year before, and because of that, Anna always felt like she was in competition with Ellie when it came to any kind of progression. She looked down at her own protruding belly and thought, not for the first time, that Ellie had won, simply by not being pregnant.

'Hey, Ellie.'

'Anna, I need help.' She was shifting her weight from one foot to the other, and her face was all panic. 'I was supposed to send out two hundred proofs for *Wings of a Dove* yesterday, and I got my dates mixed up, and I need to do them before I go home tonight and preferably without Deborah noticing. Any chance you could give me a hand?'

Anna agreed but she couldn't hide her irritation. 'Okay, but let's get on with it. I need to leave in half an hour.'

When they were done, Anna went to the toilets and sprayed on fresh deodorant, retouched her makeup and brushed her hair. It would have to do.

She was about to disappear into the Tube station when her phone rang. Nia.

'Anna, I'm sorry, I know it's your anniversary. Are you out somewhere?'

'I'm on my way to dinner, but it's okay. Are you all right?' Nia sounded like she was out of breath.

'It's Charlie. He came to my office and tried to follow me home. I ducked into a pub and I'm just waiting for him to leave.'

'What?' Anna was on her feet. 'Where are you? I'll come.'

'But what about your dinner?'

'It's fine. Edward will understand.'

As she said it, Anna wondered whether that was true. Nia gave her an address, and Anna said she'd be there as soon as she could. While she walked, she called Edward.

'Hey, I just came out of the Tube. Where are you?'

Anna hesitated. 'I'm so sorry, Edward. Nia just called and she needs me.'

'Needs you for what?' His voice was light, like he was on the edge of laughter.

'You know her mad ex, Charlie? He's following her. She's hiding in a pub.'

Edward snorted. 'Convenient.'

'Look, I'm sorry, okay, but I need to go and make sure she's all right.'

There was a sigh. 'I'll cancel the booking and see you back at home.'

'You're the best, you know that? I'll see you in a while.'

As Anna approached the pub, she saw Charlie pacing up and down outside. She slipped past him and in through the double doors.

Nia was sitting at the bar on a high stool with a glass of red in her hand. She had her head leaned in close to the barman and when he finished speaking, she threw it back in laughter.

'Nia! You said you were cowering in the pub waiting for Charlie to leave!'

'Well, I might as well have a drink while I'm waiting.' She held out her hand. 'Look, shaking. Is he still out there?'

'Yes.'

'I'm so sorry about your anniversary dinner.'

'Yeah, whatever. Get me a drink, will you?'

'Are you still off the booze?'

'Yes,' Anna said, sighing. 'I'm pregnant. That's how it works. You stay off the booze until the baby arrives.'

'Another one of these,' Nia said to the barman. 'And a lime and soda for my friend here.' She turned to Anna. 'This is Josh, by the way.' She put particular emphasis on his name.

Anna rolled her eyes. 'Nia,' she said, in a low voice, 'I'm married and having a baby. When are you going to stop trying to find my perfect man?'

Nia shrugged. 'Just letting you know, that's all.'

'So, about Charlie. Do you think he's an actual threat?'

Nia looked grim and downed the rest of her drink. 'I don't know, Anna. I mean, he's here, outside. He's been here for about an hour now. And I couldn't have made it any clearer, could I? It's been over for months.'

'We'll face him, together, if he's still there when we've

finished these,' Anna said. 'And then I need to get home and give my husband his anniversary present.'

'Is it some form of sex?' Nia asked.

'No, it's a bread maker. Don't look at me like that. He really wanted one.'

'First a baby, now a bread maker. I feel like I hardly know you these days.'

Anna felt sure that Charlie wouldn't still be there when they got up to leave, but she was wrong. He was standing in the shadows, and Anna could see that there was no way to get past without him seeing them. But it seemed that slipping out wasn't Nia's plan, anyway. A couple of glasses of wine had emboldened her, and she called out to him.

'What the hell are you doing, Charlie?'

'Nia.' He stepped forward and put his hands on the top of her arms, and Anna didn't like it, the way it held her friend in place. 'I just want to talk to you.'

'Then call me on the fucking phone, don't wait for me on the street like a stalker!'

Charlie looked like he might cry. He turned to Anna. 'Anna, I don't know why she's being like this. We were good together.'

'Take your hands off her,' Anna said.

Charlie dropped his hands to his sides. He looked like a little boy.

'She doesn't want you,' Anna said, stepping a little closer to him. 'Just accept that.'

It was enough, to make him give up. He turned away, looking back once. Anna and Nia stood shoulder to shoulder, making sure he really left.

'He was always scared of you,' Nia said, once he had turned a corner.

'Scared? Of me?'

'Well, maybe not scared exactly. But intimidated. He said we were the loves of each other's lives.'

'And what did you say?'

'I said my name didn't begin with a J and declined to explain.'

They walked to the Tube arm in arm, and on the journey, Nia rested her head on Anna's shoulder.

'Will I see you this weekend?' Nia asked. They were standing on the corner where she went one way and Anna went the other.

'I can do Sunday,' Anna said.

'I'll buy ice cream and crisps and we can watch *Sex and the City*.'

'Perfect.'

Anna was starving, she realised as she opened the door to their flat. She found Edward in the living room, lying on the sofa, his eyes on the TV.

'How's Nia?'

'She's okay. Did you eat?'

'I got takeaway. Yours is in the kitchen.'

Anna kneeled down and kissed him. 'Thank you,' she said.

He sat up and pulled her onto the sofa, put a hand on her small bump. Whenever he did that, Anna felt a rush of excitement about how their lives were changing. She never forgot for long, but whenever she did, the realisation was like a jolt. Anna yawned.

'You stay here, I'll get your food.'

While she ate, he told her things. About his day, his work.

'Rav was in today, and guess what he told me?'

'What?'

'Him and Eleanor are having a baby too. Just a few weeks after us.'

When she'd finished eating, Edward went over to the stereo

and put a CD on. Anna heard the opening bars of the song they'd danced to at their wedding. '*Something Changed*'. She'd chosen it. It had come out a few years before they got together and she'd always loved the message of it, about the tiny decisions that took your life off in one direction or another. How every encounter with someone you end up loving could have never happened at all.

'Dance with me?' Edward asked.

Anna held out her hands and let him pull her up off the sofa. He held her close and she felt his pulse in his neck, kissed him there. He was warm and he smelled incredible and the steady beat of his heart was reassuring, the ultimate comfort.

It wasn't until later, when they were in bed and chatting, that he asked her about when she was planning to finish work.

'Go on maternity, you mean?'

Edward shrugged. 'I mean, yeah, I guess so. Although I thought you might just give it up, once the baby is here.'

Anna was shocked. She hadn't once considered leaving her job to be a stay-at-home mum.

'I mean,' Edward went on, 'I earn enough to cover the mortgage and bills and all that, so why not? You could stay at home and it would save us having to face the childcare nightmare.'

Why not? Anna had a hundred reasons. But they all came down to this. She didn't want to.

'I don't think that's the kind of mum I'm going to be,' she said. 'I like my job, I want to progress, to keep learning. I don't want to be at home all the time.'

Edward looked a bit pained, the way he did when things didn't quite go his way. 'Well, there's plenty of time to think about it, I guess. Just, keep an open mind about it, okay? We don't need to close off any options just yet.'

Anna mumbled an agreement because she didn't know how

to voice what she was feeling. Like she'd been backed into a corner, somehow. Edward was asleep within minutes, his breathing slow and steady, but Anna lay on her side for a long time, going back over the conversation, imagining relaying it to Nia. It was over an hour before she felt calm and settled enough to sleep.

3

NO

Tuesday 5 June 2001

'How is it six o'clock?' Anna asked.

She looked around her, saw that most people had left already. Her desk mate, Ellie, was still there. They'd had a sandwich together in the canteen at one, and since they'd got back, Anna had had her head down.

'It's almost quarter past, actually,' said Ellie. 'I'm heading out in five. Are you nearly done?'

'I'll have to be. Edward's cooking an anniversary dinner.'

'Ooh fancy, what's he doing?'

'I don't know. Probably pasta. And hopefully something decadent for dessert.'

'Nice,' Ellie said. 'I wish I had someone at home to cook for me. I'll be having toast on the sofa with my weird housemate who collects shoelaces, so spare a thought for me.'

They closed down their computers and were just about to leave when Deborah appeared by their desks.

'Just before you go, Anna, did those proofs of *Wings of a Dove* go out?'

Anna breathed a sigh of relief. 'Yes, two days ago.'

'Wonderful, thank you. Have a good evening, you two.'

'Wow,' Ellie said once they were out in the corridor. 'That's the first time she's ever told me to have a good evening. She loves you.'

Anna smiled. She knew Ellie was joking, but she did feel proud of how she was getting on at work.

'Enjoy your toast,' Anna said when they were outside the building.

'Enjoy your pasta. And happy anniversary,' Ellie called over her shoulder.

* * *

When Anna walked through the door, she was met with a loud blast of Oasis. She smiled. You wouldn't think it by looking at Edward, but he was obsessed with nineties Britpop. She went through to the kitchen. He hadn't heard her come in, and she watched him for a moment. He was standing at the hob, moving back and forth between two pans that both seemed to need attention, and singing 'Wonderwall' at the top of his voice. Anna waited until he'd moved away from the boiling water and then put her arms around his waist from behind. He jumped.

'Anna! I didn't hear you come in.'

'What are we having?' she asked, reaching over to turn the volume down a little. 'Can I help?'

'No, you go and sit down. I'll let you know when it's ready.'

She went into the living room, flopped down on the sofa and flicked through the TV channels. There was nothing on, but she left it on an old episode of *Friends* and let her mind wander until Edward called for her to come in.

He'd changed the music to Pulp, one of the few bands they both liked. He'd set the table too, and bought a nice bottle of red wine. Anna smiled at him.

'Thank you for this,' she said. 'It's lovely.'

He smiled back but didn't say anything, just gestured for her to sit down and put a bowl in front of her.

'Surely not pasta?' she teased.

'New recipe, though. Salmon and spinach.'

'Yum.'

'So how was work?'

'Good, busy. The afternoon flew by. I looked up and it was time to go home. You?'

Edward rubbed his forehead as if the very idea of work was bothering him. 'Yeah, not too bad.'

'Weren't you seeing Rav today?' she asked. 'How's he?'

'He's well,' Edward said, and Anna sensed that there was more there.

'And Eleanor?' Anna thought back to Rav and Eleanor's wedding, how beautiful she had looked, how elegant.

'Pregnant,' Edward said.

'Oh, that's lovely!' Anna exclaimed.

And then she saw Edward wince, as if the pregnancy, or her reaction to it, was causing him physical pain. He hadn't asked her, again, since she'd said she didn't want to try for a baby, but he made his feelings clear in other ways. And they were at that age, of course, when plenty of friends were announcing pregnancies.

'This is delicious,' Anna said, gesturing at her nearly empty bowl.

Edward smiled a little. 'I thought you'd like it.'

She noticed that he'd stopped eating and was looking at her. 'What?'

'This song, it's...'

It was their song, the one they'd danced to at their wedding. It felt like so long ago.

Edward stood up. 'Dance with me?'

Anna pushed back her chair slowly. They weren't a couple who did this, who danced in their flat. But she couldn't say no. He folded her into his arms and they swayed. She put her head on his chest, felt his heartbeat, its steady thunk. She'd always felt secure in his arms, but now, she felt sort of trapped.

When her phone rang, they both jumped a little.

'It's Nia,' she said, pulling it out of her pocket. 'I'd better get it. She's still having problems with that ex, Charlie.'

Edward pulled a face but didn't make a move to stop her.

'Hey, Nia.'

'Anna, I'm sorry, I know it's your anniversary...'

'It's okay. Are you all right?'

'Not really. It's Charlie. He came to my office and tried to follow me home. I ducked into a pub and now I'm standing in the doorway, waiting for him to leave.'

'Text me where you are. I'll come now.'

Anna hung up. She looked at Edward and he shook his head slowly, as if he couldn't believe what she had said.

'I'm sorry, okay? She needs me. Charlie's following her home.'

'I don't want you to put yourself in danger. She should be calling the police, not you.'

Anna sighed. 'I'm her best friend, Edward. Of course she would call me. And I don't think he's dangerous. He's just too persistent.'

She went out into the hallway, stepped back into her shoes

and picked up her bag. Just as she was opening the door, Edward called through.

'I bought dessert, you know. For you, Anna. I don't even like dessert.'

She didn't go back, but when she was on the Tube, she wondered what the dessert was. She would eat it when she got home, in bed. And then she'd make it up to him.

As Anna approached the pub, she saw Charlie pacing up and down outside. She turned her head away and slipped in without being noticed.

Nia was sitting at the bar on a high stool with a glass of red in her hand. She stood up when she saw Anna and took her in her arms.

'You're hardly cowering,' Anna remarked.

'What's a girl to do? You can't exactly wait in a pub and not have a drink. Speaking of which' – she turned to the barman – 'another of these, please, and one for my friend here. Thank you, Josh.'

She looked at Anna when she said his name and Anna couldn't help bursting into laughter.

'When are you going to stop with that?' she asked.

'I'm just saying. Works in food, too – well, sells crisps and nuts and stuff.'

'He's still out there,' Anna said, noting that Nia hadn't bothered to ask. 'Charlie.'

'Of course he is. He's obsessed with me. We'll just have to wait him out. Shall I ask Josh to make that a bottle?'

Anna laughed.

'I am sorry I interrupted your anniversary dinner, though. In all seriousness, I was pretty scared when I arrived. Wasn't I?' She looked over at Josh, who slid the drinks across to them and raised his eyebrows.

'She did seem concerned. I suggested she call the police rather than her friend, but...'

'That's such a man thing to suggest,' Nia said. 'So what did Edward cook? Pasta?'

'Yes, but a new one. A salmon one. It was really good, actually.'

'And did he make dessert?'

'He bought it, apparently. But we didn't get that far.' Anna smiled to show she wasn't annoyed. She tried to push aside the thought that she was glad Nia had called. She felt a hundred times happier and more relaxed here with her friend than she had at home with her husband. And that wasn't something she wanted to face up to.

'You'll have to be dessert when you get home, you lucky thing.'

'Maybe so. But shall we have another one first?'

'I can't believe,' said Nia, 'that you're a proper grown-up who's been married for... how many years?'

'Two,' Anna said solemnly. 'You were the maid of honour; you're supposed to remember things like this.'

'Oh whatever, the years go by like months now we're in our thirties. Anyway, two years, and I'm still having to call you with problems like being followed home by my ex-boyfriend.'

Anna motioned to the barman for more drinks and looked down at her bare legs and sandalled feet. 'I don't feel like a grown-up. Remember Edward's friend Rav, whose wedding we went to in the spring? They're having a baby.'

Nia narrowed her eyes. 'Already? What's wrong with just being married for a while?'

'Nothing, as far as I'm concerned.'

'But not Edward, right? Is he still putting pressure on you?'

Anna thought about this. He wasn't putting pressure on, was

he? He had asked her once, and she had said no, and he hadn't mentioned it again. But he'd made it clear in a thousand ways that his feelings on the matter were unchanged. And that was a kind of pressure in itself, wasn't it? And the thing that Anna hadn't told him, that she'd barely told herself, was that she wasn't sure it was just a no for the time being, either. She wasn't sure whether she wanted to have children at all.

'He wants what he wants,' Anna said. 'And I just don't. Not yet, anyway. We should have talked about it before we got married. I think I was putting it off, because I didn't know how I felt, and he just assumed I felt the same way he did.'

'Kids, though,' Nia said. 'I don't feel old enough.'

'Me neither. And yet we're thirty-one, and I think we would officially count as old mums these days.'

'No way. Although I have resigned myself to the fact that if I told my mum I was pregnant now, she'd just say congratulations.'

Anna laughed. 'We've gone way past the point of scandalous pregnancies. Remember how terrified we were of getting pregnant when we were in our early twenties?'

'I do,' Nia said. 'And I still am. I haven't grown up like you have. And yet here we are, drinking wine together on your second anniversary.'

'Yes,' Anna said. 'Here we are.'

Charlie was long forgotten. They had another two glasses, and when they got up from their high stools, Anna felt suddenly and overwhelmingly drunk. They left the pub arm in arm, and there was no sign of Charlie anywhere, not that they really took the time to look. They shared a taxi. It was almost midnight by the time Anna crawled into bed. Edward had left her bedside lamp on, and she was annoyed by this thoughtful gesture, just when she was feeling guilty for being so thoughtless. He was snoring gently. The present she'd meant to give him – a book of essays by authors and musicians and actors about the one day that had changed their lives the most – was on her bedside table. When she'd first seen it in the bookshop, she'd thought of him, of how he talked about the day they met as a turning point for him.

She would tell him in the morning, she decided. She would say she wasn't sure about children full stop. She would get it out in the open, and see where it left them.

4

YES

Wednesday 5 June 2002

Anna looked at Thomas, who was sitting in front of her in the highchair, refusing to eat the carrot she'd peeled and chopped and cooked and blended for him. The preparation for this one tiny meal that he wasn't eating had been ridiculous. This was her third attempt, and Thomas was yet to swallow anything. She went back to the fridge, cut a long finger of cucumber, ran it under the tap and handed it to her baby. He put it straight to his mouth and sucked, and Anna took the opportunity to drink some of her lukewarm cup of tea.

She thought about sending a message to Edward, telling him that it was a hard day, but thought better of it. It sometimes seemed like every day was a hard day. Edward was sympathetic, but there was only so much he could do. Every morning, when he dressed and prepared to leave the house, she wanted to beg him to change places with her. And every morning, she said nothing. But when he told her to have a nice day on his way out of the door, she felt like pulling the carving knife from the block on the kitchen side and stabbing him in the heart. Now, he was on his first work trip since Thomas had been born. New York, all week. Anna had been terrified when he'd first mentioned it, and in time some of that terror had turned to jealousy. She knew, when she was being rational, that he'd spend the week in the airport and the office and his hotel room, but her more unhinged self imagined him seeing the sights she'd always longed to see, soaking up that city she'd always been desperate to visit. The one they'd said they would visit together, and never had.

It was nothing like she'd imagined, being a mother. What had she imagined? It was hard to separate it out, now that she was living this life that was definitely not it, now that she hadn't had more than a few hours' sleep in one go for months. Had she given it much thought at all? She'd imagined a baby, curled in her arms and sleeping, and not much else. How foolish she'd been. She looked at Thomas. He was perfect. Doing all the things he should be doing and always causing old women and quite a few young women to squeal and coo in the street. He had Edward's dark hair and eyes but otherwise he was all her. She adored him, could lose hours just watching him sleep, his eyelids flickering and his fingers gripped tightly around hers. The first time he'd rolled over, she had cried with pride.

The day he'd been born, the midwife had put him gently into Anna's arms, and she had waited to fall in love. It hadn't come at once, in a rush, like everyone said it did, and she'd been disappointed. But then a few days later, she'd been lying beside him in bed, Edward snoring, Thomas looking up at her with those big eyes and her looking back, and she'd just known that this was a love more powerful than anything else. Through her bleary eyes, she'd smiled at him, knowing he couldn't yet smile back. She'd whispered her love into his soft hair.

Thomas started to wriggle and squirm, the cucumber long forgotten, abandoned on the highchair tray.

'Let's get you out of there,' Anna said, and her voice sounded loud in the quiet room.

She unstrapped him and lifted him into her arms, caught a hint of that smell he had, the one that made her want to hold him tight to her chest forever. She kissed his forehead and sat him on the playmat, built a wall of cushions around him. He was sitting pretty well, but he still had the occasional tumble. Imagine, Anna thought, not being able to sit on your own bum. She handed him a block for each hand and he tapped them together and smiled up at her. There were times, like this, when he was ridiculously easy to please. And yet so many more when he was screaming and angry and she didn't know what to do. And she hated all the books that talked about recognising your baby's different cries, because when Thomas cried, she never knew what he wanted.

Anna's laptop was open on the coffee table, the cursor blinking. She sent a quick email to Ellie, asking how things were at work. She wanted them to remember that she existed. And another to Nia, trying to sound casual, saying they hadn't caught up for a while and could they arrange to go for a drink or something. And then she refreshed her emails a couple of times, hoping one or other of them would be quick to reply. On a whim, she called her mum, not really expecting an answer. Her mum worked as a cleaner, in homes and offices, and Anna could never keep track of her hours.

'Hello?' Her mother's voice sounded muffled, as if she was at the bottom of a well or had her hand across the phone.

'Hi, it's Anna.'

She always announced herself like that and thought it probably wasn't normal. She'd overheard Nia and Edward on the phone to their own mothers enough to know what normal was. Edward always did a lot of laughing and 'remember whens', and Nia just started each conversation like it was a continuation of the last, like she did when you saw her.

'Anna,' her mum said, her voice now clear. She sounded surprised to hear from her.

'How are you?'

'Oh, you know.'

I don't, thought Anna. Why was it like this? Why was it always so hard?

'Work okay?'

Work was her mother's favourite subject. Always had been. She always had a story about one of the other cleaners or someone who lived in one of the houses. Her stories ran the full gamut from cancer survival to losing luggage on holiday. She launched into one then, and Anna zoned out a little. When there was a pause, she willed her mother to ask about Thomas. He cried out then, and she picked him up.

'How are things there? How are Edward and Thomas?'

Anna let out a big breath and felt grateful, and then she was sad for the fact that this was such a small thing, and it wasn't guaranteed.

'Edward's in New York with work this week. It's hard.'

'Oh, New York. It's all right for some, isn't it?'

'Well, he'll be working long hours, but yes, it's a nice trip.'

Anna felt like she was always defending her mother to Edward or defending Edward to her mother. It wasn't even as if they actively disliked one another. They barely had a relationship.

'Thomas is starting to sit up,' she said, trying to change the subject.

'He will be, I suppose.'

Anna wasn't sure what she meant by that. That he was the right age for it, she supposed. And he was. But that hadn't stopped her from hoping for something approaching enthusiasm. It was clear that the conversation was over, but Anna knew from experience that she would have to be the one to end it. If she didn't, they'd sit there in near silence for hours.

'I'd better go, I guess.'

'Yes, I'm sure you have plenty to do.'

There was silence where there might have been a 'thanks for the call' or 'have a nice day'. Anna ended the call, wishing she'd never made it. It was a little after twelve. It felt like a lifetime since she'd been woken by Thomas that morning, and the hours to go before his bedtime stretched ahead. They would have to go out, she decided. They would have to do something. She grabbed the changing bag from the hallway and checked she had all the essentials. Then she did a quick nappy change and put Thomas in his buggy. It was a warm June day, but she stashed a blanket in the basket underneath him just in case. And just like that, she was ready to go. She thought back to the early days, when it had been winter and she'd needed to dress him in so many layers just to leave the house. And then she thought of the even earlier days, before she'd had him, when she could just grab her purse and her keys and go.

She'd only got as far as the end of the street when she saw Steve, a stay-at-home dad from a flat across the street who she knew a bit from playgroup. She thought about turning back. Had he seen her? Was it too late? It was. Steve made her feel a bit uneasy and she wasn't sure why. Or she did know why but was pretending she didn't. She felt pulled to him, in a way she hadn't experienced since... Since when? Edward? That long-ago date with James? Steve had sandy hair and a beard and he was always dressed in jeans and t-shirts that hinted at a great body underneath. He was the opposite of Edward, with his dark hair and sharp suits. And yet. There was something that made Anna feel light and a little scared whenever she was with him. He looked like a man who knew how to put up a shelf, give you an orgasm and then make dinner. Sometimes, when they were drinking bad coffee and chatting about the babies with other mums at playgroup, Anna found herself fantasising about him. And she was always certain that he'd know. That he'd sense it, somehow.

She put up a hand to greet him. He was pushing his buggy too, and when she crossed the road, she peered inside and saw that his son Luke was fast asleep.

'Hey, Anna,' Steve said. 'Where are you heading?'

'I'm not sure,' she said, and all at once she found she was fighting back tears.

'Just had to get out of the house?' he asked. 'I know the feeling. We're not going anywhere either. Fancy coming with us?'

Anna nodded, not sure that her voice would hold. What was this? Her emotions were so close to the surface these days, and she sometimes worried that she'd forever be in tears when she went back to work. Once she'd blinked a few times, she felt a little stronger.

'Sorry about that,' she said. 'I don't know what's wrong with me.'

Steve stopped for a minute and turned to her. 'There's nothing wrong with you,' he said. 'You're doing a bloody tough job and sometimes you need a minute, that's all.'

She was so grateful to him then that she wanted to throw her arms around him. Why couldn't Edward ever say anything like that? When she cried in front of him, he never seemed to know what to do or say.

'Tell me something funny,' Anna said.

And then she wondered whether she'd overstepped a mark. That was the kind of thing she might say to one of her friends, but she didn't know this man very well. They weren't close. Might they be?

'Okay, here's something. My wife, Theresa, started a new job recently. She's a solicitor. She kept talking about me and Luke, saying her partner was at home with the baby. And yesterday she found out that the whole firm thought she was a lesbian. She was absolutely baffled about it, had no idea why they might think that. And her boss clued her in that it was just because of me being the one to stay at home. They couldn't conceive of a man doing that job.'

'That's kind of more sad than funny,' Anna said, but she did laugh a little as she said it.

'You're right. I'm the only man at every group I've been to. You've noticed that at playgroup, right?'

Anna laughed again. 'Yes, I've noticed. I can always hear your voice when we sing "The Wheels on the Bus". Plus I've heard a few comments about your arse.'

As soon as she'd said it, she was embarrassed. And she could see that she'd embarrassed him, too.

'My arse?'

Anna couldn't look at him. 'Yeah, you know, you have a few... admirers.'

'Bored mums, I expect.'

Anna felt like she was suddenly walking a tightrope, where before she'd just been chatting to a friend. Was that what she was, a bored mum?

'Well, anyway, for us it just made sense to work it this way. I was doing building work and I earned a fraction of what Theresa does.'

'Will you go back to it?' Anna asked. 'At some point, I mean?'

Steve seemed to consider this. They were walking through the common now, having not discussed where they were going, and Anna looked around at the games of rounders and dog walking that were happening around her.

'I'm not sure yet. I liked my job, but I like being at home with him too. And the cost of childcare would mean that I was doing it for basically nothing. Plus, I think we'll have another one in a couple of years. What about you? What were you, before you were a mum?'

That was almost enough to start Anna crying again. What was she? She was rarely asked these days. When she'd been in her twenties and she'd met new people, the first question they'd asked, after her name, was what she did. And now, no one asked her name, they just called her Mum or Mummy. 'Give that to that mummy over there.' 'Ask that mum if her little boy would like a rice cake.' 'And would Mummy like a cup of tea?' Now, she was asked what Thomas's name was, and how old he was, and whether he was starting to crawl yet, and whether she was breastfeeding, and how the birth had been.

'I'm in publishing. Publicity,' she said. 'I didn't earn much either, but I liked it. I'd only been in that role for a few months and I'm hoping there'll be an opportunity to step up at some point, when I'm back.'

Steve nodded. 'It's not straightforward trying to make those decisions. And it's not an easy ride, being at home, is it?'

'No,' Anna said.

Nothing she'd ever done had been harder than this. And she couldn't quite explain it. Because she did watch daytime TV sometimes, or go on nice walks like this one, through the pretty area of London where she was lucky enough to live, or sit with her feet up while Thomas napped on her, taking in the magical scent of him. And she'd been there when he first clapped, when he first laughed, all those milestones Edward had missed because he'd been in the office. And yet. She felt like she'd forgotten who she was. And worse than that, she felt like she'd stopped being herself entirely.

Anna's phone rang, and she pulled it out of her pocket, and they both stopped walking. It was Nia.

'Hi,' Anna said.

'Hey,' Nia said. 'I got your email. You sounded a bit low. Shall I come over after work?'

'Yes please,' she said. 'I would really like that.'

It was so good to hear her friend's voice.

'Edward's still away, right?'

'Yes, he's in New York until Friday.'

'Okay. I'll bring food. See you at about seven or so.'

Anna slipped the phone back into her pocket and they set off walking again without a word. They were heading for home now.

'What do you have planned for the rest of the afternoon?' Steve asked.

'I'm not sure. We might play in the garden.'

Steve nodded. 'I love June, when the summer is ahead and it's starting to warm up.'

Anna felt something tugging at her. 'What's the date?'

'Fifth, I think. Why?'

Anna shook her head. 'It's my anniversary,' she said. 'I'd forgotten.'

* * *

Nia turned up with a bottle of wine, a bunch of bright tulips and a bag of Chinese takeaway. Anna had just got Thomas off to sleep and knew that, if she was lucky, she might have four or five hours before he woke again. Sometimes, she'd go straight to bed after putting him down, knowing that she'd be up feeding him in the night and wanting to get some rest while she could, but tonight she couldn't think of anything she'd rather do than see Nia.

'Thank you,' she said. 'For knowing.'

They were in the kitchen and Anna was opening the bottle and getting glasses and plates while Nia cut the stems of the flowers and filled a vase with water.

'Knowing what?'

'That I needed you.'

'Oh, that.'

Nia carried prawn crackers and fried rice over to the table. Anna brought the rest of the food: duck in plum sauce for her, beef and mushrooms for Nia. Anna thought about what she would have eaten if Nia hadn't come. Probably toast or a bowl of cereal. There was never any time to make something proper. Never any time to take care of herself.

'So what's happening?' Nia asked once they were sitting down, facing one another.

'I just feel really lost,' Anna said. 'It's so hard to explain. I don't know what I'm doing, and I feel like I'm getting it all wrong.'

'With Thomas?'

'Yes. And with me. Edward wants me to stay at home now, like a 1950s housewife...'

Nia snorted.

'And it's not what I want. But I feel guilty for that. And I just feel like my whole life is about him now, and I've lost sight of me. But is that selfish? Don't all mums do this without complaining?'

Nia held up both hands. 'That's a lot of stuff,' she said.

'Firstly, going back to work, if that's what you want to do, is absolutely fine. Thomas will benefit from being with other babies, I'm sure. Plus, when he's a bit older, he'll see that this is how the world works. Men and women bringing home the money, sharing the load. It'll be good for him. Then maybe when he's an adult, he won't have quite such dated views as his father.'

Anna was never sure whether Nia really liked Edward. Nia often mentioned how attractive he was, and she wondered, now, whether that was a cover, because she didn't really have anything else nice to say about him. It hurt, that worry. Like everyone, she wanted the different people in her life to like one another.

'Secondly, I bet it's really common to feel the way you do. Your whole life has changed and you're having to put Thomas's needs before your own and you're alone with him all day every day and he doesn't even speak! So I think you're probably fine, but I also think you should go to see your GP in case you have post-natal depression. My sister had it, and none of us knew, and I felt awful afterwards.'

Anna hadn't considered this. Could there be a chemical, medical reason for the way she felt? She thought about all the crying she did, in the shower, into her pillow, sometimes when she had Thomas in the sling and was out walking. Maybe it was more than just a really tough period of adjustment. She smiled at Nia, grateful.

'Thank you,' she said again.

'What for?'

'Just... everything.'

Nia put down her fork. 'Listen, Anna, whatever this is, whatever you're going through, we'll sort it out, okay?'

'Okay,' Anna said.

She felt stronger just having Nia there.

'Me and Edward, we'll get you through. And Thomas, of course.'

The sound of his name was enough to make Anna smile. She thought of him, fast asleep in his cot, the way his arms would be flung above his head, and the love she felt was almost painful in its intensity.

5

NO

Wednesday 5 June 2002

Anna sent Edward a text as she walked from the Tube to the office.

> Happy anniversary. Let's celebrate when you're home.

He wouldn't get it for a while. It was still the early hours of the morning in New York. She slipped her phone into her bag and flashed her security pass to get into the building.

Deborah was already at her desk. It didn't matter how early Anna got in, she never beat her boss. However, she knew that Deborah noticed what time she got there, and how late she stayed, and she knew it wouldn't do her any harm when a promotion opportunity came up. Deborah equated working long hours with working hard, and Anna was happy to prove herself.

'Coffee?' she asked.

Deborah held up her cup to indicate that she already had

one. 'Come over to my desk once you've got yours and settled in. I want to talk to you about *Wings*.'

Anna made an instant coffee in the kitchen area. *Wings of a Dove* was one of the first books she'd been really involved with. It had come out in hardback last year and been a smash hit, and the paperback was due in a couple of weeks. Anna had been working hard on it, and they'd secured reviews in some great magazines and newspapers. She hoped whatever Deborah wanted to discuss, it wasn't bad news.

She pulled her chair over and sat opposite Deborah, the desk between them. 'So,' she said. '*Wings*?'

'Yes.' Deborah finished typing something and fixed her gaze on Anna. 'I want this book to go stratospheric, you know that. And you know there's a tour of bookshops?'

Anna nodded. She had organised the bookshop tour. Liaising with the shop managers and with the author, Katy. Sorting out train tickets and accommodation.

'I was planning to accompany her,' Deborah said, 'but my husband's been on a waiting list for an operation on his foot and he's got a date now and, long story short, I can't do it. And I'd like you to go in my place.'

Anna widened her eyes. 'Me? On the tour, with Katy?'

Deborah nodded. 'It was you or Ellie, and I think you've really proven yourself lately. I'm confident that you can do an excellent job.'

Anna smiled. 'Thank you,' she said. 'I'd love to.'

Back at her desk, Anna started composing an email to Edward. But what had seemed like such exciting news when she'd been at Deborah's desk a couple of minutes ago suddenly lost its shimmer when she tried to explain it in writing. Edward got to travel all over the place, and she was pretty sure he wouldn't be impressed by her two-week trip around the country.

In fact, he was likely to say it was an inconvenience, or to ask if they were going to put her up in nice hotels, maybe suggest he could come and join her for a couple of nights if they were. She deleted what she'd written and minimised her emails. Then opened them up again. She'd tell Nia instead. She fired off a quick, excited email and two minutes later, Nia responded.

Sounds great! Well done, Mrs. You rock. Fancy a celebratory lunch at The Dog?

Anna beamed, sent back a reply suggesting a time, and sat back in her chair, drinking her coffee.

Four hours later, Anna walked into The Dog, a fairly dingy pub that she and Nia had been frequenting for lunch for years, after discovering that it was pretty much exactly the midpoint between their offices. They did great sausage sandwiches at a fraction of the price of the more upmarket cafés and bars in the area. Plus, the landlord, Kev, knew their names and their order.

'Usual, Anna?' he asked. 'Nia's over there.'

Anna smiled. 'Thanks, Kev.'

Nia was sitting next to the window, but she stood up when Anna walked over. 'Congrats on the book tour!'

'It's not really a big deal,' Anna said, failing to hide her grin.

'It is a big deal,' Nia said. 'And it just goes to show that those long hours and all that hard work really pays off. What did Edward say?'

'I haven't told him. He's in New York and' – she glanced at her watch – 'he'll only just have woken up. Plus he goes on all these fancy trips. Mine's to places like Sheffield and Watford.'

Anna laughed, but Nia furrowed her brow. 'So what? He should still be happy for you.'

'He will be, I'm sure. I'll just... tell him when he's home.'

Kev brought their drinks over, a tea towel thrown over his shoulder. Lemonade for Anna, Diet Coke for Nia. 'Sandwiches are on their way, ladies,' he said. 'Oh, and we've got a new lad on the pot wash. His name's Jason.'

'How old is he?' Nia asked, while Anna looked on in amusement.

'Seventeen.'

'Ah okay, not for us. But thank you!'

They both laughed, Anna giving Nia a soft punch on the arm.

'Is everything all right?' Nia asked once the laughter had tailed off.

'Sort of. I mean, yes. It's just...' Anna thought back to the conversation she'd had with Edward the night before he left for his work trip. How could she frame it, so Nia would understand?

'It's our anniversary today,' she started. 'Which means that it's two years since he said he wanted to try for a baby. And it seems like everyone in our lives is announcing a pregnancy, and every time, I feel so tense...'

Nia raised her eyebrows. 'No baby here,' she said.

'You know what I mean. Not everyone, but enough people. Last year, I told him that I wasn't sure it was ever on the cards for us, but it's like he doesn't take it in. He just keeps asking. Before he went to New York, he asked. And when I said no, he asked whether I was ever going to change my mind.'

Kev came over again then and placed a plate down in front of each of them. White baguette, with halved sausages stuffed inside, grease dripping down the side of the bread. Anna realised how hungry she was, realised she hadn't had any breakfast, and thanked Kev enthusiastically. Nia waited while Anna took a big bite.

'And what did you say?' she asked eventually. Her voice had changed a little. She sounded worried.

'I said I didn't think I would. That I didn't see myself having children. Ever. I think in the past I haven't been clear enough. He needs it to be black and white.'

Nia said nothing, and Anna loved that her face didn't twist into an expression of shock. That she just took Anna's words and stored them away, that she understood.

'And what did he say?' Nia asked.

'Well, he was upset. Angry. He really wants a family, Nia. And I was basically telling him that that won't ever happen for us.'

For a few moments, they ate and drank in silence.

'Do you know?' Anna asked. 'I mean, I know you're not with someone right now, but do you know whether you want to have a child someday?'

'No,' Nia said. 'I don't have a clue. But Magda said I'd have one, remember? I trust her.'

They were thirty-two. When she'd been a teenager, Anna had imagined she would have children by now. Things had seemed more straightforward, more cut and dried. She'd never imagined this.

'I don't know whether I'm enough for him,' Anna said.

'Did he say that?' Nia looked furious.

'No, it's just something I wonder about. He thought he was marrying me and children would follow, automatically. But what if we tried and we couldn't, or what if we had one and it wasn't how we imagined it?'

'Or what if you just didn't want to?' Nia said softly.

'Yes, or that.' Anna's voice was little more than a whisper now.

'If he made that assumption without ever having a conversation with you about it, that's not your fault.'

'But it's just what people do, isn't it?' Anna asked. 'They have children. Almost everyone.'

'It's not the only path,' Nia said. 'It's not the only thing you can choose.'

'You're right,' Anna said, but inside, she wasn't sure. If they never had children, she thought, what else was there? There was work. She loved her job, and she was good at it. Deborah's faith in her hadn't come from nowhere. There was each other. Lazy weekends and carefree holidays and dinners out and trips to the theatre. That was all good, wasn't it? That was the kind of thing her friends with babies said they missed, that they longed for. She could have that, without it being a compromise. It could be her normal. Was it enough, to fill a life?

Anna wasn't sure she could talk about it any more. She changed the subject, asked Nia to tell her something, and Nia launched into a story about her colleague who was going through a divorce and spent, according to Nia, at least 50 per cent of her working day doing things to express her anger at her soon-to-be-ex-husband.

'This morning,' Nia said, 'she printed about a hundred of their wedding photos off on the office printer. Full colour, the works. Then she sat there at her desk, cutting his face out of them. Humming. When the boss came prowling round to check up on us, I had to create a diversion so she could get all the photos off her desk. I had to pretend I had an Excel question. He bloody loves Excel questions, he thinks he's the only person in the world who knows how to use it, so he was in his element. Leaning over my desk and breathing all over me. And all the time, I could see Ellen out of the corner of my eye and she was checking the printer and sweeping masses of paper straight off her desk and into a drawer and I could see that there were two little husband heads on the floor but I couldn't alert her to it without Mr Excel noticing.

'So after he'd finished showing me how to insert a row or some such thing, he went over to her and he bent down to pick up one of the husband heads and I felt like everything was changing to slow motion and I saw her noticing and her face falling and I had to do something, because last time, when he caught her making one of those ransom note things using letters from different newspapers telling him exactly what she thought of him – the ex, not the boss – he said she was on her last warning, and I could tell he meant it. So I launched myself out of my seat and took the husband head out of his hand and said it was mine and I must have dropped it, and they both stared at me for ages until I said that I was on a dating website and I liked to carry pictures of my next date around with me so I could work out whether I was interested. And we all looked down at this tiny picture of Ellen's husband, who's about fifty and has a porn-star moustache, and then the boss slunk off back to his office without saying anything else. And then – get this – later, Ellen came up to me and asked if I was really going on a date with her husband. Tears in her eyes and everything!'

Anna laughed. She loved Nia's work stories, even though she suspected they were massively embellished. She'd met Ellen and Nia's boss in the pub a couple of times and they both seemed quite normal to her.

Before she knew it, it was time to go back to work. At the door of the pub, Nia wrapped her in a hug and kissed her cheek.

'Happy anniversary,' she said. 'What were we doing this time two years ago?'

Anna looked at her watch. One thirty. 'Photos?' she said, unsure.

'God, you looked amazing.'

'So did you.'

'You know, you said earlier that you might not be enough for Edward. But I think the question is more whether he's enough for you,' Nia said.

Anna was surprised. She looked at her friend, and Nia met her gaze and didn't smile or frown. Just showed that she was serious.

'I've always felt lucky to be with him,' Anna said. 'He has this great career and he looks like he should be modelling suits or something. I've always wondered why he chose me.'

Nia rolled her eyes. 'You're the shit. He's the lucky one.'

Anna tipped her head to one side slightly, as if it might help her see the world, and her relationship, a different way. Was Nia right? Was Edward lucky to have her? Nia started walking away. They never said goodbye. It was a thing of Nia's, that every meeting was just a continuation of the last. All the way back to the office, Anna tried to make herself see things the way Nia saw them.

6

YES

Thursday 5 June 2003

'What shall we do?' Edward asked.

'Nothing,' Anna said.

They were lying on their backs, fully clothed, on a bed in a hotel room in Brighton, their eyes closed. They'd arrived ten minutes before and had collapsed there.

'If we were going to do nothing, we could have stayed at home,' Edward said. But it didn't sound like he was trying to persuade her into anything. He wasn't standing up.

Anna opened her eyes momentarily, to check that Edward hadn't opened his. He hadn't. 'That's not true at all,' she said. 'If we were at home, we wouldn't be able to do nothing. We'd have to do everything, like we always do. That's precisely why we've come away.'

They'd sold their flat, bought a house. It hadn't needed loads of work but there was always something to be painted or tidied up or cleaned, and that was on top of them both working and looking after Thomas. Anna felt exhausted all day, every day.

'What do you think he's doing?' Edward asked. He turned on his side, to face her.

Anna opened her eyes again, met his gaze. 'He's probably terrorising my mum. She'll never offer to have him again.'

'We've only been gone for a couple of hours.'

'Still, I wouldn't be surprised.'

Anna hadn't told Edward quite how much work it had taken to get her mother to agree to this. His parents adored Thomas, and if they didn't live up in Scotland she was sure they'd offer to have him all the time. With her mum, she'd had to introduce the idea slowly and fabricate a story about Edward being stressed at work and on the verge of collapse.

Thomas was one and a half. It seemed like all the other mums gave their children's ages in months, but Anna refused to. She'd done the weeks thing for a while, then switched to months, but once he turned one, she told people he was one. She didn't mind adding a half, but she felt fourteen months or twenty-one months was unnecessary. He was one and a half. He could do all kinds of things now, like running very fast away from her in car parks and climbing onto dangerous objects. He could sniff out anything inedible and slip it into his mouth when her back was turned. He could launch himself into her legs when she was carrying a just-boiled kettle. Anna wasn't bored any more; that boredom of the early days felt very far away. Now, she was terrified. Constantly on high alert, constantly checking his small mouth for foreign objects and prising tiny pieces of plastic from his surprisingly strong grip.

He could cuddle, too. For months, he'd been putting an arm loosely around her, but it was only recently that he'd gripped her tight, pulled her close. It had made her gasp, the first time. He only did it to her, and while she longed for Edward to experience it, she secretly thought it was sort of lovely, too, that he'd singled her out for this expression of affection. A few days before, she'd rushed to nursery from work to pick him up, hoping like she did every day that she wouldn't be the last one there. When she'd arrived, he'd been sitting with his key worker, Carly, looking at a book. There were two or three other children still there. Anna had watched him silently, grateful for this chance to see how he behaved there without her. He'd traced the picture on the page with his finger and dissolved into giggles when Carly had pretended to be a monster. And then he'd looked up without warning, spotted her watching. She'd expected him to smile, but instead he'd pressed a hand to his mouth and then thrust it towards her.

'We learned to blow kisses today,' Carly had said, shrugging.

And Anna had reached for him, lifted him over her head, and he'd done the throaty chuckle she loved so much.

'Shall we call?' Edward asked, dragging Anna back to the present.

'It's too soon,' she said. 'It would be pathetic to call so soon.'

Anna thought about the story her friend Steve had told her last week. He and Theresa had gone to Paris on the Eurostar for Steve's birthday but had spent half the time on the phone to Luke because they missed him so much. And just like that, she was thinking about Steve, imagining being in Paris with him, her hand folded in his. Nothing had happened between them, at least outside of her head. But she'd found that she liked talking to him as much as she liked looking at him. He seemed to understand her without even really trying.

'I miss his face,' Edward said. And Anna snapped back to the present, to Edward, to talking about Thomas.

Edward pulled his phone out of his pocket and scrolled through some recent photos, and then he played a video of Thomas giggling while Edward danced just out of shot. Anna moved across the bed until her head was resting on Edward's chest, and indicated for him to play it again.

She felt a pang, thinking of Thomas. That was natural, she supposed. Her love for him was all physical. All that agony when she'd pushed him out of her body, the toe-curling pain of early breastfeeding. And now, this dull ache when she wasn't with him and she thought of him. 'Did I tell you what he did when you were out with Nia last week?' Edward asked.

'No,' she said, although she thought he probably had. She was hungry for new stories.

'He took a photo of you to bed,' Edward said.

Anna felt her heart clench, and if he'd suggested getting in the car and going back, she would have done it. His little face. She wanted to squish his cheeks between her fingers. But, she reminded herself, that was something she could do every day. And lying in the quiet on a bed in the middle of the afternoon was not.

'I'm going to read for a bit,' she said. She got up from the bed and went over to her suitcase, pulled out a slightly battered proof copy of the novel *Wings of a Dove*. She opened it up where her bookmark was and checked the page number. 'Do you know, Ellie at work gave me this proof when I was pregnant with Thomas. Two years, and I'm still only on page sixty-eight. And I work in publishing!'

When Anna had got back from maternity leave, Ellie had been promoted. Senior publicist. It wound Anna up because she knew she was better at the job than Ellie, or could be, given the chance. But Ellie was the safer bet, still in her mid-twenties and probably years away from having a family. Years away from being called urgently in the middle of a meeting because her child had stuck something up his nose at nursery.

'Don't beat yourself up,' Edward said. 'You can't read every book.'

'I can't read any book!' she said, but she was on the edge of laughter, thoughts of work starting to melt away, and Edward saw that and began to tickle her ribs. He kissed her open, laughing mouth and stopped moving his hands, letting them rest on the sides of her ribcage, and she let herself go, let herself stop thinking. Edward pulled her onto his lap and Anna became fixated on the places where their bodies were touching. He reached up and slipped one strap of her vest top off her shoulder, then buried his face in the side of her neck, and Anna groaned a little. She could feel him getting hard against her. With one index finger, he traced around her left nipple in small circles. He didn't kiss her mouth. Sometimes he didn't kiss her mouth until she felt like she would die from the lack of it.

Their sex life had been whittled down to its bare bones, to the essential elements. They were masters at making each other come in a matter of minutes. But this, this was like the old days. When there was so much time to tease and play, and no chance of the sound of little feet padding along the landing. Anna turned her head to kiss him and he pulled away, a smile playing at the corner of his lips. She tried again, and again he pulled back. Meanwhile, his hands were inside her top, inching their way up her sides. She felt her nipples harden, waited impatiently for him to touch them, to pull her top off and take one of them in his mouth. She wrapped her legs around his back and put her own hands inside his T-shirt, ran them over his smooth chest. And then he was pushing her backwards, so that she was lying back and he was on top of her, and then he did kiss her, and she didn't expect it, and she let go of everything she was holding on to in her brain and let the joy of it all wash over her.

A little later, Edward sat up. 'Shall I book us in somewhere, for dinner?' he asked. 'What do you fancy?'

Anna thought about that. It was true that they didn't have the opportunity to eat out very often, and it was something she missed. But she felt so relaxed, lying here on the bed, that the thought of having a shower and doing her makeup and squeezing into the black dress she'd brought – the one that had never quite fitted her since she'd had Thomas – was exhausting.

'What I really fancy,' she said, 'is going to a supermarket and buying whatever we feel like that you don't have to cook – cheese, bread, crisps, pastries, chocolate – and then coming back here, getting in our pyjamas and eating it all with the TV on.'

Edward looked at her, and she thought he was going to screw up his face, but then he broke into a smile. 'Can we get a jar of Nutella and stick our fingers in it?'

'Whatever you want. It is our night.'

'It's oooooooooooour night,' Edward sang, like he was an eighties crooner.

Anna slapped his arm. 'Come on.'

They were like teenagers in the shop, giggling and slipping things into the basket without the other one seeing, so that when they got back to the hotel room, Edward pulled out a box of two chocolate eclairs that Anna didn't know were there. She screeched, grabbing for the box.

'I wish we were in France,' she said.

'I know,' Edward said. 'Because the eclairs there have custard inside instead of cream...'

'Yes! And they don't only come in chocolate. You can get coffee ones, or vanilla...'

'Strawberry?' Edward asked.

'I don't know. Who would want strawberry?'

'Er, me.'

Anna bit into one of the eclairs and Edward took a bite from the other end and she pushed him away, playfully.

'Get your own!'

'These are my own. I put these in the basket!'

* * *

Anna was on the edge of sleep when the thought crept in. She had to ask Edward straight away. She put a hand out and touched his shoulder. 'Are you still awake?' she whispered.

'Just.'

Anna sat up, pulled him up a little too. 'Three years ago,' she said, 'on our anniversary, you asked if I wanted to try for a baby.'

'I did,' he agreed.

'And I did, and we did, and now we have Thomas.'

'I know all this,' Edward said, rubbing his eyes.

'Well, I was wondering how you'd feel about having another one?'

Edward looked at her, checking that she was serious. 'I didn't think you'd want to, so soon.'

'Well, in for a penny and all that,' she said. 'I mean, he's our life now, isn't he? And I'd like him to have someone. And I think I might be better at it, second time around.'

'You're good at it,' he said. 'Don't think you're not good at it.'

Anna smiled. 'I've found it hard,' she said. 'There's no denying that. But I think it was partly the shock of it, and I know what it's like now. I think we should do it again.'

Edward lay back down and smiled. 'Yes,' he said. 'You know how I feel about kids. I'd have a whole bunch of them. Yes.'

Anna kissed the tip of his nose, and a second later, he was asleep. He always found it easier than her, in new and different places, to rest. She lay awake for a little longer, thinking of the way Thomas's face had looked on the screen when they'd called him earlier, the way he'd tried to put his arms around them, the way it had made her feel. Loved, in love. Why did she always doubt herself? Maybe if they had another one, her confidence would kick in. Maybe she would find her stride, and be the together one. She tried to imagine another baby, a girl, perhaps. Or a second boy. Tried to imagine Thomas as a big brother. She felt a little fizzy with the excitement of it, and it was a long time before she relaxed enough to sleep.

7

NO

Thursday 5 June 2003

'New York?' Anna repeated, making it a question.

'New York,' Deborah confirmed.

'As in...'

'As in the Empire State Building and the Statue of Liberty, yes.'

'As in Carrie Bradshaw and yellow cabs and massive pretzels?'

'I don't know how else to say it, Anna,' Deborah said, a smile in her voice.

They were in a coffee shop in Soho, where Anna thought they'd come to talk about a new campaign she'd been planning.

'But why me?' Anna asked.

Deborah sat forward in her chair, drained her coffee, and fixed her steely gaze on Anna. 'It's a programme we run; anyone's eligible to apply. I just think you'd be great for it. Or maybe it would be great for you.'

Anna remembered hearing about it when she'd first started.

Whispers of some people getting to go to New York for a year. She'd ignored it; thought it was an urban myth. Like the rumours about bosses sometimes letting you go home at lunchtime on Christmas Eve that had circulated at every single office she'd ever worked in. She realised Deborah was still speaking and tuned back in.

'He was so impressed with you when he came over. With the campaign for *Wings of a Dove*. He contacted me a while ago asking if I thought you might give it a go...'

Who? Was she talking about David? David had come over from the New York office in the spring and Anna had thought he was so handsome she'd found it hard to look directly at him, and had spent at least one full evening describing his face to Nia in graphic detail.

'But what about...'

'Your husband? I did say that might be a sticking point. We'd be able to get him a working visa, but I don't know whether it's something you've ever considered, the two of you. What is it he does again?'

'He works for an investment bank,' Anna said.

She was stunned. The whole time she'd been with Edward, it had been his career that had mattered the most. It was unspoken, understood. He earned all that money, and she'd often thought that if he had to move with his career, she would go too. But they were in London, so where would he possibly have to move to? Nothing like this had ever come up. She thought about telling him, about asking him whether he'd be prepared to take a year so that she could... what? Follow a dream? But it wasn't even a dream of hers, was it, to go to New York? It was somewhere she'd always wanted to go on holiday, but living and working there was something that had never entered her head before Deborah had suggested it.

'I just don't know,' Anna said.

Deborah shrugged her shoulders. 'Well, you need to think about it. Talk to your husband. I certainly won't be upset if you turn it down. And of course, no one's expecting a decision straight away. I'll get David to email you all the details. He wanted to ask you himself, over the phone, but I persuaded him to let me do it. Anyway, shall we head back?'

Deborah stood up, all calm and composed, as if she hadn't just put out a hand and rocked the boat of Anna's life, which until then had been sailing on reasonably still waters. Anna drained her coffee and stood up. Her legs were a little shaky. She was glad they were only minutes away from the office. It took all her composure to make small talk about the weekend with Deborah as they made their way back, and as soon as she was safely behind her desk, at her computer, she started typing a flustered email to Nia. Just as she was about to hit send, she realised she hadn't even told Edward yet. She deleted the words on her screen, watching them disappear. Then she picked up her mobile, slipped it into her pocket and left the office. In the hallway that no one ever used, because it just led to the first aid room and a meeting room that had been locked for over a year, she dialled his number with shaking fingers.

'Anna? Is everything okay?' he asked.

She never called him during the day. Sometimes they sent each other messages, but they never spoke. 'Yes, I'm fine. Do you have time to talk?'

He didn't speak straight away and she knew that he was checking his watch. She heard him sigh. 'I've got a call in five, but I'm fine until then.'

'Okay. I just had coffee with Deborah and she asked me if I'd like to move to the New York office for a year.'

Silence. Then, 'New York?'

'Yes!'

'As in, Central Park and the Rockefeller Center?'

'The very same.'

'I don't understand. Why?'

Anna had asked this question herself, but that didn't stop her from wishing that Edward hadn't. Couldn't he conceive of her just being very good at her job, so good that someone from another office might want to offer her a role? Couldn't he just believe in her?

'It's this thing the company run, and they think I might be a good candidate. I can fill you in later,' she said, trying to keep her voice bright. 'I just wanted to let you know. So you can, I don't know, think about it.'

'You mean you want us to consider this? Moving to New York? Me leaving my job?'

Anna was leaning against a wall. She sank down then, until she was sitting on the floor. 'I thought we might,' she said. 'It's just a year. And I mean, if you were offered this kind of opportunity, I think we'd consider it, wouldn't we?'

'But that's completely different,' he said. 'I mean, unless they're talking about significantly increasing your salary?'

'No,' Anna said. 'No, there's been no talk of that.'

'No, I'm not surprised. What I mean is, I'm the main breadwinner, so if it was my job that was moving to New York, it would make more sense to give it serious consideration. Hang on, what happens if you say no? Is your job here safe?'

'Yes.'

'Well, there you go then,' Edward said, as if the whole thing were settled. 'Listen, I need to dial in to that call. We can talk about it more tonight, if you want to...'

He didn't say that there wasn't really any point, that he'd decided for both of them. He didn't need to.

'Okay,' Anna said, holding back tears. 'See you later.'

And even after he'd ended the call, and there was silence, she held the phone in her hand, because a part of her still believed that he would call back, that he would remember to say well done. To say I love you, and you're brilliant, and well done.

* * *

That evening, by the time she heard Edward's key in the door, Anna was standing in the kitchen with a glass of wine in her hand. She hadn't stopped thinking all afternoon, hadn't got any work done. Part of it had been daydreaming about New York, but most of it hadn't. Most of it had been running over that phone call she'd had with Edward, and other conversations they'd had, and trying to come to some sort of decision.

'Hey,' he said, putting his head around the door.

'Hi.'

'I got held up, my meetings all ran on. And then Rav caught me just as I was trying to leave – can you believe his son is eighteen months old? He was asking if we want to sort out a weekend away with them. Anyway, what do you fancy doing for dinner? Shall we order something?'

'I'm not really hungry,' Anna said. 'You go ahead.'

Was she waiting, to see if he brought it up, to see if he was taking it seriously? Or was she just putting it off, because she was a coward, and she knew this was going to come out of nowhere for him, and she didn't know how to start?

'Are you okay?' he asked, reaching into the drawer where they kept takeaway menus.

'I don't think I am,' she said. She pulled a chair out and sat down at the kitchen table. 'Can you sit for a minute?'

Edward pulled out the menu he'd been looking for. Chinese.

He would order that prawn thing he always had. Would he, still, after what she had to say? He sat down, reached across the table for her hand. 'Is this about the New York thing?'

'Kind of. Did you think about it any more?'

'Not really. I mean, it's not really feasible, is it? I can't just throw away my job and follow you to New York...'

Anna wondered, for a minute, whether he was jealous that it wasn't him who'd had this offer. His company had New York offices.

'I feel like you should have at least asked me some questions. Like whether I wanted to do it, whether it was important to me. I feel like you should have taken it seriously, not just dismissed it. I mean, you keep asking me to have a baby, and you expect me to take a year out of my career for that, and yet you're not prepared to do the same, for me.'

Edward dropped her hand. 'What is this?' he asked, an edge of anger in his voice. 'Where is this coming from? You can't compare a job opportunity to a baby!'

Anna took a sip of her wine. 'When Deborah said it,' she carried on, 'I was so shocked. I mean, me? In New York? I was just a receptionist until a few years ago and now, suddenly, I'm someone who other people want in their publicity team. I couldn't believe it. But then I called you, and you couldn't really believe it either, and that made me realise something.'

Edward swallowed. 'What?'

'That you don't believe in me at all. That you were hoping, after we got married, that I would give up work and have babies and...'

Edward stood up, his chair scraping across the tiles. 'I did think we might have babies, yes! Is that so wrong? Is that so unusual?'

'No, it isn't. And you still want that, and I still don't. And now there's this, and the thought of it is terrifying but in that good way, you know, like when your stomach's in knots every time you think about something. Like when you're falling in love.' Anna trailed off. It wasn't until then that it hit her. That it had been a long, long time since she'd felt anything like that when she thought about Edward.

'What are you saying?' Edward asked. 'I didn't realise how important it was to you...'

'You didn't ask.'

Edward was standing behind the chair he'd been sitting on, his hands balled into fists and pressing down on the back of it. Anna kept her eyes on his hands. His wedding ring was a thick platinum band. Hers was much narrower, white gold. They'd chosen them together, and Anna had asked whether he thought it mattered that the rings were nothing like each other, and Edward had said that of course it didn't, that they were nothing like each other and they were still perfect together, weren't they? And right there in the shop, he had kissed her and she'd felt the whole world melt away, the way she always had. She couldn't look at his face. If she looked at his face, she would see how he felt about this. He might be crying. Or worse, he might be just fine.

'I'm going to go,' Anna said. 'To New York. It's the kind of opportunity I won't get again, I think, and I just want to give it a go.'

'What about me?' Edward asked.

She wanted to ask him not to make her say it. Hadn't she made it clear? Hadn't he realised where this was going? But that wasn't fair. Just because this had been pushing its way to the forefront of her mind all day, all year, even, it didn't mean his thoughts were keeping pace. On their wedding day, when she'd sat on her bed for half an hour before getting up, asking herself over and over whether it was the right thing, perhaps he'd just been sure.

'You're going to stay here,' Anna said. 'You're going to stay in your job, because it's important to you.'

'Anna, you're my wife! That isn't how it works. You don't just have jobs thousands of miles away from each other. You find a way to be together, no matter what.'

Anna felt a tiredness like nothing she'd ever experienced. There would be so much to do, she thought, so many people to tell. There would be forms to fill in, explanations to be made. And yet. The fact that it was those things that she was focused on told her everything she needed to know.

'It's not working,' she said. 'I'm sorry, but it's not.'

And she did look up and into his eyes then, and she couldn't quite read them. If he was sad, it wasn't clear-cut. He was annoyed, she thought. None of this had gone to plan. First she had said she didn't want to have children, and now she was saying she didn't want to be with him at all. It was messy, it was difficult. It was a failure. It didn't fit with his idea of how his life should be. She stood up and left the room, and he didn't call her back, and she wouldn't have gone if he had.

Upstairs, in their bedroom with the door closed, she called Nia.

'I think I'm leaving Edward,' she said.

'Fuck.'

'You were right. We don't fit.'

'Fuck.'

'And there's something else. I've been offered a placement in New York for a year.'

Anna heard Nia's intake of breath, listened out for what she would say. 'Christ. Congratulations! Do you want to go?'

'Yes. I really do.'

'Wow. Big day.'

'Can I come over? Can I bring some stuff, stay on your sofa?'

'You can sleep in my bed,' Nia said. 'I'll open a bottle of wine. See you in half an hour. If you're not here, I'm coming to get you.'

'I'll be there,' Anna said, taking a shaky breath. She hung up. She opened her wardrobe door to pull a suitcase out, and in doing so, she caught a glimpse of her watch, of the date. She sank down on the bed. Four years ago, they'd been cutting the cake, dancing under a mirror ball with a hundred pairs of eyes on them. And now, four years to the very day since they'd promised to be together forever, it was over.

8

YES

While Anna played with Thomas, she was watching the clock. She'd planned a lunch with Nia, and was excited about it. A childfree weekend lunch was such a luxury these days.

'What are you boys going to do while I'm gone?' she asked while she was hunting around for her sunglasses and her purse. It felt like a long time since she'd taken her handbag out rather than the changing bag.

Edward shrugged. 'What do you think, buddy?'

'Thomas!' Thomas shouted.

He was obsessed with Thomas the Tank Engine. He thought it was named after him. All he wanted to do was watch episodes of the programme and then try to recreate elements of them with his own track and engines. Anna found it soul-destroying, but Edward quite liked it.

'You heard the boy. We're playing Thomas. Now go, and have fun.' Edward pulled Anna in for a quick hug. He put his hand up and she touched it with hers.

She took the Tube to Soho, revelling in her freedom. She'd put a book in her bag but she just spent the journey looking around, watching people, like a tourist in her own city. And when she emerged into the clear day, she put her sunglasses on and walked up and down the narrow streets, looking for the place Nia had suggested. She was first to arrive, and she took a seat in the small, busy restaurant, feeling like, by being here alone in the middle of the day, she was managing the impossible.

And just then, Nia burst through the door, all colour and light.

'Anna!' She descended on her friend, hugging her. 'You haven't been here long, right?'

Anna put two fingers on her glass to measure how much she'd drunk. 'Only this long.'

Nia sat and shrugged off her cardigan. 'It's kind of hot in here, isn't it?' She reached for the glass of water Anna had poured her from the jug in the centre of the table and chinked her glass against Anna's in a half-hearted cheers. 'So what's the emergency?'

Anna took a deep breath. Where to begin? With the facts, she decided. With the beginning. 'I'm pregnant,' she said.

Nia looked straight at her, unflustered. 'Okay, and is that a good thing?'

'It should be, right? Having another baby was my idea. But all I've felt since I've known is panic.'

Again, Nia didn't react strongly, and Anna loved her for it. This was why she could tell Nia almost anything, always had been able to. Nia had always known the black corners of her heart. How she'd kicked Julia King during a hockey match when they were at secondary school and then sworn it was an accident with the hockey stick, after Julia had kissed the boy Anna longed for. How she'd felt more than a little relief mixed in with her grief when her elderly grandmother had died after a long descent into dementia. How she'd wondered what the hell she'd done after Thomas was born; how she still did, sometimes.

'Do you know why?' Nia asked gently. 'You always seemed disappointed when you told me you'd got your period, that it hadn't happened again.'

Anna put her head in her hands. Just then, a waiter came over.

'Everything okay over here?' he asked.

Nia nodded. 'Have you looked at the menu? Shall we just get the sharing platter and then dessert?'

'Yes,' Anna agreed.

'Could I have a glass of Riesling and can we have the sharing platter, please? And then we definitely want to see the dessert menu, even if we say we don't later.'

Anna laughed. 'I won't say that.'

'Are you feeling sick?' Nia asked, once the waiter was gone.

'A bit, but nothing I can't handle. I just have to keep eating. But, I don't know, I just keep lying awake at night, thinking about being at home with two of them, about leaving work again and then going back, never progressing, and I just feel scared, and sad. It's partly about work, I think. Ellie, the girl who joined as a publicist at the same time as me, is Deborah's favourite. And it sounds so braggy, but I know I am better at the job than she is. But she's the safer bet, because I'm part-time and sometimes I get called away, if Thomas is ill or whatever. It's like you choose – kids or career. Still, in the twenty-first century!'

'What does Edward say?'

It was a reasonable question. She and Edward were in this together, of course. Except that they weren't, not yet, because she hadn't told him. In fact, when he'd asked when her period was due a few days ago, she'd said that it had started that morning, and he'd pulled that face he always did, and said that maybe it was time for them to talk to a doctor about it.

'I haven't told him,' Anna said.

She expected even Nia to blanche at that, but she didn't. She just nodded. 'Because you're not sure what you want to do?'

Anna didn't need to consider that for long. No, she had no plans to end the pregnancy. She just wasn't quite ready to face his uncomplicated joy at the news that had so thrown her.

'No, I'll tell him. I'm just not quite ready.'

There was silence, and Anna took a sip of her drink.

'Is there something wrong with me?' she asked. 'I mean, Edward's great and he looks after us, and I have Thomas, and he's wonderful and exhausting and all those things a toddler should be, and we've been trying for a year to have another one, and this should be the best news I could possibly get, and yet...'

'It isn't,' Nia finished helpfully.

'I mean, it might be. I just don't feel quite how I expected to.'

'Maybe you just don't feel how you expected to yet,' Nia said. 'And you shouldn't feel bad about it. How you feel is how you feel.'

She always knew, Nia, how to say just the right thing. Anna wondered whether it was a skill she had with everyone, or whether it just worked with Anna because they knew one another so well.

'Thank you,' she said.

'For what?'

'God, for everything. There's no one else I could admit all this to, you know? Also for not asking the waiter whether any of the staff are called Joe or John.'

Nia laughed, reached out a hand and put it on top of Anna's, on the table. 'There's a time and a place,' she said. 'Even I know that.' Then her voice turned serious when she spoke again. 'I love you. And we'll work this out.'

And after days of worry, Anna believed they would.

The food arrived then, and they began to eat.

'Try the prawns,' Nia said, pushing the dish a little closer to Anna.

Anna took one. 'So good,' she said. And then she was crying without knowing she was going to.

'Anna,' Nia said. 'Anna, come here, it's okay. It's going to be okay.'

Anna moved across to sit next to Nia and let herself be wrapped up in Nia's arms. She was vaguely aware of the waiter coming over and then backing away again when he saw they were having a moment.

'I don't know what I'm doing,' Anna said. 'Do you? I'm so tired every minute. I'm either working and feeling guilty about Thomas being at nursery or I'm with Thomas and feeling guilty for not enjoying it enough. It's like I'm trying to do everything and not getting anything quite right. It was so important to me to have a career, and now I'm in my early thirties and I'm still just a publicist and—'

'Stop,' Nia said.

Anna did. She took some deep breaths and brushed away the tears with the cuff of her cardigan.

'You're not "just" anything,' Nia said. 'Let's get that straight, for a start. Your job is not you. Yes, you're a publicist, but you're also a bloody good mum, a loving wife, a fabulous best friend. You're good and kind and funny and about a thousand other things that so many people aren't. So don't do that. Don't put yourself down.'

Anna smiled shakily. 'Thank you.'

'Tell Edward,' Nia said. 'Talk to him. Work it out.'

* * *

That evening, Anna thought, she would do as Nia had advised. She would tell Edward. What was she going to do, she reasoned, just keep it to herself as the baby grew inside her? Edward was the father. He had to know. But all the time they were bathing Thomas, reading his story, brushing his tiny teeth, Anna was struggling to find the words.

'One more story?' Thomas asked.

Times like this, when he was sleepy and sweet and wanted to cuddle, she could imagine doing it all again. But there were so many other times that weren't like that at all.

'One more,' she said.

Edward leaned over and kissed Thomas. 'Night, buddy,' he said. Then to Anna, 'I'll go down and make a start on dinner.'

Anna read a story about snow bears, and when Thomas asked for one more, she laughed and shook her head. 'But in the morning, when the sunshine on your clock comes up, you can come in our bed for cuddles, okay?'

He laid his head down, and she turned out his main light, put on his nightlight, kissed him. She went downstairs to the kitchen.

Edward was standing in front of the hob, giving a sizzling pan a quick shake. Fajitas. 'Okay?' he asked.

He meant with Thomas, she knew, but it was as good an opportunity as she was going to get to say something. 'I need to talk to you about something.'

Edward's face dropped, and Anna saw at once that he was expecting something different from the news she was about to impart. What was it?

'Okay,' he said, his face drained of all colour.

'Do you know what it's about?' Anna asked, unsure where this was heading.

'Is it about Fran?' He reached over and turned off the hob ring, and the room suddenly seemed eerily quiet.

Fran? Fran was a woman Edward worked with. Anna had met her at a couple of work events. She was a few years younger than them, pretty in a birdlike way. Anna had never once considered her a threat.

'You tell me,' she said, and suddenly the conversation wasn't about the baby any more and Anna wasn't sure it would move back in that direction.

'Oh fuck,' Edward said. 'It wasn't that, was it? It's just, I saw a receipt I'd left in my pocket on the bathroom windowsill the other day and I've been waiting for you to bring it up...'

Receipt? Bathroom windowsill? Anna cast her mind back. When she did the washing, she always checked all the pockets, and took out anything she found. She did remember taking some paper out of Edward's trouser pocket but she hadn't looked at it. She must have forgotten to put it in the bin.

'What was it a receipt for?' she asked, putting everything she had into keeping her voice steady.

'A dinner. I took her for dinner, Anna. That night last week when I said I was having drinks with Rav. I don't know why, but I...'

'But what?'

Anna felt like she'd walked into the wrong house, like she was at the centre of someone else's marriage drama. This wasn't how she'd expected the evening to go at all. By now, she had thought they'd be caught in a little celebration. Her biggest worry had been faking her own enthusiasm, not her husband admitting to dinner with another woman.

'Anna,' Edward said, stepping in front of her and taking both her hands in his, 'I don't know what the hell I was thinking. Things have been a bit strained lately, haven't they? I feel like all we are is parents sometimes. I feel like we've lost our own relationship in the middle of it all. It's such a cliché. And Fran was flirting with me and it just seemed so easy, and I lost my mind. I temporarily lost my mind.'

'Do you think I never think about other men?' Anna asked, and out of nowhere, she pictured Steve. 'Do you think I don't notice people, that men don't sometimes flirt with me? The reason I don't act on any of those things is because we promised to stay together and we have a child.'

Edward was nodding, as if to show that he agreed and understood. But as she finished speaking, he stopped. 'You don't cheat on me because we promised not to? Not because you want to be with me?'

'Don't you dare turn this around on me! You are the one who did this. And what did you do, exactly? Did you sleep with her?'

Edward looked at her, his eyes never leaving hers. 'We kissed. I promise that's all. I told her I couldn't do it.'

Anna made a sound that was half laugh, half groan. Tears threatened, but she didn't want him to see them. She wanted to wait until she was behind a locked door. She went upstairs to the bathroom and shut him out. She ran the bath so hot it scalded her when she stepped into it. And then she lay there, her skin reddening and her face flushed, her hair piled on top of her head. When she looked down at her stomach, she imagined she could see a little protrusion. Life was growing. How the hell had it turned out like this?

When she'd been lying there for half an hour or more, there was a soft knock on the door.

'Anna?' Edward asked. 'I don't know what you wanted to talk

to me about, but I'm ready to listen, when you come out, okay? And dinner's ready whenever you want it.'

Anna didn't answer him. She thought about the connection they'd always had, physically. Her skin had always felt like fire the second he touched her. Was that just a gift he had? Did he make every woman feel that way? She had thought it was chemistry, that it was something between the two of them, that they were just the right fit. But perhaps she'd been foolish. She pictured Fran, her long, wavy hair that looked effortless but which Anna knew must take a lot of upkeep. Her tiny frame. She closed her eyes and imagined Edward putting his arms around her, kissing her.

When she was dry and in her pyjamas, she went downstairs. She couldn't face eating anything, so she left the food he'd prepared on the kitchen side and wandered into the lounge, where he was eating. She picked up the remote control and muted the TV.

'I was going to tell you that I'm pregnant,' she said.

And then she turned and left the room, went up to bed. In a moment, Edward was beside her, his hands on her body, on her stomach, tears running down his cheeks.

'I'm so sorry, Anna. Please tell me I haven't broken this. I'm so very sorry. I love you, Anna. I love our family. You've made me so happy. Please forgive me.'

'I think you should leave,' she said.

9

NO

Saturday 5 June 2004

It struck Anna, when she first woke up, that it might have been her fifth wedding anniversary. What would that have been like? Instead of waking up next to Edward, she was in New York, city of her dreams. And it was Saturday, the best day of the week. She missed Nia, but that was the main sticking point. She didn't miss Edward the way she thought she might have. The early weeks had been bleak – getting drunk with Nia and crying, saying it had been a mistake and she was going to call him, Nia confiscating her phone. She'd called in sick to work more than she should have, sometimes spending the entire day in bed staring at the wall opposite her, feeling nothing but empty. And then she'd left, flown to New York, and her brain had been caught up in the excitement and fear of all of that, and by the time she was settled, she knew for sure she'd done the right thing. This morning, though, she'd woken up with Edward on her mind. She checked her watch. It was just after nine in the morning, which meant it was two in the afternoon in London.

She picked up her phone and called Nia, hoping she'd have time for a quick chat.

'I was just thinking about you,' Nia said.

'Really? How come?'

'I have something to tell you. I was thinking about when I could call. I was going to wait until it was at least ten your time, in case you were having a lie-in.'

'What is it?'

'Well, you know I've been seeing that guy, Jamie?'

'The one you said looked a bit like Peter Andre? And who you weren't sure about dating just in case he was my J man?'

'I said that about Peter Andre once, after our first date. I can't believe you're still going on about it.'

Anna laughed. 'Yes, you can. You still talk about the guy I kissed who looked a bit like a young Phillip Schofield and that was last century.'

'I haven't mentioned him for at least three weeks. Anyway, now we've established that you know who I'm talking about...'

'Yes, sorry. What's the news? Are things getting serious?'

'Pretty serious. I mean, about as serious as things can get, actually. We're...'

The line dropped out and Anna said her friend's name a couple of times. When it came back, Nia was still speaking.

'Aren't you going to say anything?'

'I missed it, Nia. The line dropped. What did you say?'

'Oh, thank God. I thought your silence meant you disapproved. I said we're going to have a baby.'

Anna felt sick for a second. A baby? Nia? And this guy Anna had never met who might or might not look like Peter Andre?

'Wow,' she managed to say. 'That's amazing, Nia. How do you feel?'

Nia let out a sound that might have been a groan. 'So sick. I've been dying to tell you. I'm only a few weeks pregnant, so no one at work knows yet and I have to keep running off to the toilet to retch.'

Anna felt like the worst kind of friend. This was the biggest news Nia could have come to her with, and Nia had been waiting to tell her, and Anna didn't know how to respond properly. She wondered whether it was because she wasn't there, because she couldn't grab hold of Nia and hug her and tell her she loved her and she couldn't wait to meet her baby, but she wasn't sure. A part of her, a bigger part than she wanted to admit, felt a bit cheated. She'd said no to having a baby with Edward, but maybe it would have been different if she'd known that Nia would get pregnant so soon afterwards? Maybe they could have done this together. But then she shook herself, reminded herself that her marriage to Edward hadn't been right, and you couldn't just have a baby because your friend was having one. She'd made the right decision. Still, she felt as if she was losing Nia. Which was ridiculous, given that she'd been the one to move away.

'I wish I was there,' Anna said when the silence had gone on for too long.

'I wish you were here too,' Nia said. 'You've always been the best person when it comes to holding my hair back.'

Anna laughed. 'Listen, I have eggs boiling, can we talk about it properly next time?' It was a lie, and not a good one. Would Nia be able to tell?

'Of course. And what were you calling for, anyway? Anything in particular?'

Anna paused. Was it still okay to bring it up? To say that she'd been feeling a bit sad about Edward? She decided to go for it. She'd never held back when it came to Nia.

'It's my anniversary, mine and Edward's. Or it might have been. You know what I mean.'

'Oh. Anna, I'm sorry, I totally forgot.'

'Oh, don't be silly. I wouldn't expect you to remember. I mean, what is an anniversary when you're not even together any more? It's nothing, is it? It just feels a bit...'

'A bit what?' Nia asked.

'Funny. I don't know.'

'Do you miss him?'

Nia had asked this a lot in the early days. In the days of crying and packing up boxes of things and sorting out paper-work to do with the house and all of that. But she hadn't asked it for a while.

'I don't miss him, as such,' she said, then, 'it's just, sometimes I wonder about the life I didn't have. The one I could have had with him, if I'd agreed to having a family.'

Nia was silent, but Anna knew it wasn't judgement. She was just giving Anna the space to say what she needed to say.

'Listen, Nia, I have to go,' she said.

'I don't want you to be on your own over there and feeling sad,' Nia said.

'I'm not, honestly. I have a date tonight.'

'Oh good. Listen, let's talk properly tomorrow. I'm free all day.'

'Yes,' Anna said.

'Have a good morning.'

'Have a good afternoon.'

Anna ended the call feeling a little churned up. She ate a bowl of cereal, flicked through the TV channels. And then she called Lee. She'd met Lee on her second day in the New York office in a marketing meeting and had known immediately that she wanted him for her friend. She'd felt pretty lost up until that point, finally understanding that thing she'd heard about Britain and the US being divided by a common language. She got funny looks whenever she attempted something funny or sarcastic. Lee had lived in London for three years as a student, and he claimed that was why he 'got' her, but Anna secretly thought he was just one of those people she would have clicked with no matter what.

'What's up?' he asked.

'Do you have time for lunch or a drink or something later?'

'Sure.'

Anna was tempted to let the morning drift past her but instead she had a long shower and then got ready to go out. When she'd first arrived in New York, she'd bought a map and just walked around the city for hours. The apartment she shared was in Brooklyn, and she liked to walk across the Williamsburg Bridge into Manhattan, to really take in this insanely busy island that she'd once known only from films and was now starting to really feel a part of. The map, worn and tatty from being folded and refolded, rarely came out of her bag now. She made her way to McNally Jackson, her favourite bookshop, and browsed for half an hour. She saw one of the books she'd worked on recently and felt the rush she always did when she spotted them out in the world.

It was a warm day with a slight breeze, and Anna bought a sandwich from a deli and ate it wandering around, window-shopping in the tiny boutiques she was too scared to step inside. It was the kind of day she loved, just mooching around with no destination in mind. She imagined being able to go back in time to her teenage years, to tell herself that this was what her life would be like, that she would be living in New York, working with books, carefree. But she wasn't sure quite what her teenage self would make of it all. She'd be impressed by the New York thing, for sure, but she'd probably ask why Anna was single and childless. Back then, it had all seemed much more straight-forward.

When it was almost time to meet Lee, she walked back across to the Lower East Side, to the bar they liked there with its mismatched sofas and 90s posters that always reminded her of a sixth-form common room. Lee was there already, halfway through a muddy orange cocktail that had been served in a tumbler.

'So, what's up?' he asked as soon as she'd ordered a drink and sat down next to him on a low, creaky sofa.

'I feel wobbly,' Anna said.

'Wobbly how? Like, sick? Or shitty and you don't know why? Or about to burst into tears?'

Anna gave it some thought. 'It should have been my anniversary today. Five years. And I called Nia to talk about it and she told me she's having a baby. And I want to be happy about it, and I am, but not as happy as I should be. I feel like she's leaving me behind or something. There, I said it. I'm the worst friend in the world.'

'Nia, with a baby?' Lee asked, and just that asking made Anna feel a bit better.

Nia had come over for a visit in the run up to Christmas and made it her mission to ask the staff of almost every Manhattan bar and restaurant their names, still looking for Anna's mysterious 'J' man. Anna, Nia and Lee had gone ice skating at the Rockefeller Center, although Lee had said he would die if anyone he knew saw him. Afterwards, they'd had cocktails (served by a Brad) on empty stomachs and three drinks in, Lee and Nia had declared themselves lifelong friends. They even thought they might just have met once, back in Lee's London days, although they didn't know how.

'Exactly!' Anna said, a little too loudly. 'That's exactly what I thought, and then I felt horrible about it. Do you know that when we were fifteen we did that flour experiment, you know, the one where you have to look after a bag of flour for a week?'

'Er, no,' Lee said. 'That must be a weird British thing. Is it to prepare you for having a baby?'

'Yes. Anyway, on the very first day, Nia wanted to go to the park because this boy she liked was playing football there, and she tried to convince me to just leave the flour babies in my bedroom. I ended up staying in and looking after both of them while she went to the park with our friend Rachel.'

'Did anything happen, with the football boy?' Lee asked.

'Oh, probably. But the point is, she left her baby to die, because she couldn't be bothered to look after it for one day.'

A woman at the next table looked over with a horrified expression and Anna realised how loudly she was speaking. When the woman looked away, Anna started to laugh, and it set Lee off, and for a couple of minutes, the two of them were uncontrollable, brushing away tears and clutching one another's hands. The woman from the next table didn't look over again. She probably thought they were genuine psychopaths.

When Lee had gathered himself, he spoke. 'I don't think that's going to happen with her actual baby.'

'I know that,' Anna said, suddenly serious. 'But I just wasn't prepared for her taking this step. I think part of the reason I didn't want to take it was because I was so sure she wouldn't.'

Lee had heard all about Edward, and Anna's reluctance to have a family.

'I don't believe that,' he said. 'If you'd really wanted to have a baby with Edward, you would have done it regardless of what Nia was doing. Just like she's doing now. She hasn't consulted you; she's just doing what feels right for her. That's how it should be.'

Over the years, Nia had consulted Anna about all sorts of things. Whether she should lose her virginity to Dean O'Leary or hold out on the off-chance that Luke Shears would change the habit of a lifetime and show an interest in her. How she should word her break-up text to Alex London after she found out he was cheating on her with Lucy Mason. What she should say her greatest weakness was in job interviews. But not this. Anna wondered whether the baby had been planned. It couldn't have been, she decided. Nia had only been seeing this Jamie guy for about four months. No one talked seriously about having a baby at that point.

'I guess it's nice that you'll be back before the baby's born,' Lee said.

Anna realised she hadn't told him her news.

'David's asked me to stay for a while,' she said.

'How long is a while?'

'I'm not sure. I mean, it's permanent, so as long as it's working out, I suppose.'

'Do you think he fancies you?' Lee asked.

David was the subject of much office gossip. Anna still couldn't believe he was an actual living, breathing man. He looked like he'd been cut out of a catalogue and stuck to the wall of the office. Sometimes, she found herself staring at his lips in meetings.

Anna gave Lee a sharp look. She was pretty sure he was joking, but she hoped it wasn't what people thought.

'No, I think he thinks I'm good at my job.'

There had been the occasional look, between her and David. She had allowed herself to wonder, sometimes. But no. He was her boss. And besides, she didn't want to have been asked to stay for any reason other than her work.

'Shall we go out tonight and get wasted?' Lee asked.

Anna considered this and was on the verge of accepting when she remembered she had plans.

'I have a date,' she said.

'You sound really happy about that.' Lee laughed.

'Well, I quite liked the getting wasted idea.'

'Maybe you'll get wasted with your date.'

'It's not the same, though. You're my favourite person to get wasted with. This side of the Atlantic, at least.'

'Is it the rich guy?' Lee asked.

Anna had made the mistake of letting Lee look through the dating site she was on with her one weekend. It had been him who had persuaded her to get in touch with this man, Brandon, after seeing photos of him on yachts and at extravagant-looking parties.

'That's the one.'

Anna sipped at her cocktail and thought that there'd be no getting wasted with Nia in the near future. They had a long history of drunkenness, starting with cider in the park at fifteen and continuing with vodka in water bottles on the way to house parties on the Tube. Plus pubs, the endless pubs they'd drunk in together before first dates and after breakups and over Sunday lunches that stretched from afternoon to evening. And now Nia was pregnant and wouldn't be drinking, and then she'd have a baby and wouldn't be able to go out much. Anna caught herself. They didn't even live in the same city, or the same country. The impact of Nia's pregnancy on Anna's social life was not the main issue here. It was about growing up, wasn't it? They were thirty-four, and it was finally happening. Nia was growing up without her.

When they'd finished their drinks and were standing outside the restaurant, about to walk off in different directions, Lee pulled Anna in for a hug.

'I know what it's like, to feel like you're losing someone,' he said, his voice low, as if he was afraid that someone else would hear. 'People move away, move on, like you did. It's almost always okay, in the end. It works out.'

'Thanks,' Anna said. She meant it. Lee made her feel better about things. It was a skill he had.

'Anytime,' he said. 'Good luck on your date. Imagine, this time next year you could be a lady of leisure, if you play your cards right.'

Anna laughed. 'Imagine.'

10

YES

Sunday 5 June 2005

Anna stood in the doorway, surveying the damage.

'I made Sam into a snowman,' Thomas said earnestly.

Sam was covered in Sudocrem from head to toe. He was dressed in just a nappy, and Anna wondered briefly where his clothes were but then reminded herself that that was really the least of her concerns. Thomas was covered in patches of the stuff, too. He looked like a painter who'd got carried away. It was on his cheek, his top, in his hair. A quick glance around the room confirmed that the worst of it was confined to the two boys. She couldn't see any Sudocrem on the walls or the furniture or the carpet. That was something. She reached out and picked Sam up, holding him at arm's length and carrying him into the bathroom.

'Come on, Thomas,' she said, 'let's have a bath.'

'But it's still the morning,' Thomas said.

He was a stickler for rules and routines. If only she'd made it a rule not to cover his brother in Sudocrem, he probably wouldn't have done it. But how could she possibly pre-empt all the ridiculous things they might do when her back was turned? She'd only left them for about five minutes. It was quite impressive, when you thought about it.

'It is still the morning,' she said, 'but you two need a wash, don't you?'

Sam started to cry, then. He was sitting on the bathmat and he'd wiped his arm across his face and must have got some of it in his mouth. Plus, it was nearly time for a feed. Anna felt exhausted. How many times had she been up in the night? Three? Thomas had been sleeping better at this stage, she was sure. But then, she couldn't really remember. How were you supposed to remember every little thing when you hadn't slept properly for months or years? She sat down on the lid of the toilet and put her head in her hands for a minute. She would bath them, and then she would feed Sam, and then she would drink a lot of water and it would help her stay awake.

A thought flashed up: this would be easier if Edward was here. It was a thought she had a lot. More and more. And through the fog of tiredness, it was hard to tell whether it added up to wanting him to be here. Since the revelation about Fran, he'd been living with a friend. He hated it, and never wasted an opportunity to let her know that. He was meticulous about his time with the boys and she was pretty sure nothing further had happened with Fran, or with any other woman. Some days she was ready to take him back, and others she just wasn't, quite. Being a single mum, though, was so different to what she'd planned. She supposed it was that way for everyone. Very few people set out to do it alone. Occasionally, she felt like perhaps that was why she'd felt so worried when she'd first found out she was pregnant with Sam. Like somehow her body and brain had known that she wasn't only going to be stepping up from one child to two, but that she was simultaneously going to be going from two parents to one.

'Mummy?' Thomas asked.

She looked at him, at his soulful brown eyes which looked full to the brim of sadness.

'Yes, Thomas?'

'I shouldn't have turned Sam into a snowman, should I?'

'No,' she said. 'You shouldn't.'

He looked like he might start to cry and she pulled him into her body. 'But it's okay, because it will come off. Don't be sad, come on. Clothes off.'

Sam was still wailing, and as much as Anna tried to block it out, it tugged at her. Thomas lifted his arms and she pulled his top over his head. She thought of him as being so grown up now that she had Sam, but when he was in his vest and pants she was reminded of how little he still was. Sometimes she wanted to hold him tight and not let go, and other times she wanted to leave them both and run from the house as far and as fast as possible.

The bath took forever, because the Sudocrem was reluctant to wash off, but once they were finally clean and dressed, and she'd fed Sam and given Thomas some biscuits, they went to the park. Anna had learned that, hard as it was sometimes to go out with the two of them, she always felt better when they had. When they arrived, Thomas ran over to the climbing frame and Anna freed Sam from the buggy and sat him in a baby swing, gave him a little push.

Five minutes later, she heard her name being called and turned to see Steve with his little boy. Luke was holding the soft toy rabbit he carried everywhere by one ear. He'd spotted Thomas and raced to join him, and Anna knew that they would be caught up for ages, pretending they were pirates or fire fighters. She raised her hand in greeting and Steve walked over to join her. She felt the gentle clenching and unclenching she always felt in her stomach when she saw him. She was used to it by now.

'No Theresa?' she asked.

It was as much to remind herself that Steve was married as anything else.

'She's working. Big case. She thinks she'll be in the office until about eight. So it's just like any other day, for me.' He laughed, but Anna thought she sensed some bitterness in it. Theresa's hours were long, and Steve had said before that sometimes he felt like a single parent.

'Well, we had a great start to the morning,' Anna said, to change the subject. 'It involved half a tub of Sudocrem and an unplanned bath.'

'Oh, been there. But only with one, so I take my hat off to you.'

Sam started to fuss and wriggle, so Anna lifted him out of the swing.

'I've got a blanket under the buggy,' she said, gesturing.

Steve fetched it and laid it out on the grass, and the three of them sat down. Anna took a few toys out of her changing bag and handed them to Sam. Straight away, he put a plastic ring in his mouth and tried to bite it.

'Teeth?' Steve asked.

'I think so. Awful night. How long does it last? Do you remember?'

'About twenty years,' Steve said, smiling.

Steve looked at her, and his eyes were sad. 'I miss it sometimes, the baby years.' They both looked over at the two older boys and Anna waited for him to go on. 'I always thought we'd have another but it's looking less and less likely.'

'Oh?'

Anna had wondered about this often. When she'd first known Steve, he'd always talked as if he thought Luke was the first of possibly many children, and then, sometime before she'd had Sam, he'd just stopped.

'Things are... shaky. With Theresa.'

'Oh.' Anna hadn't expected that. 'I'm sorry,' she said.

'Yeah, well. It is what it is.'

Anna felt like something had shifted between them, like she was scared to breathe, almost, in case it shifted back.

'Do you think it's salvageable?'

'I don't know. I'm not even sure I want it to be. Before we had Luke, we used to stay up all night talking or decide on a whim to book flights to, I don't know, Switzerland. But now it's like we don't even have anything left to say to each other. I feel like I have more meaningful conversations with you than I do with her...'

Anna looked at Steve as he rubbed his jaw. He didn't meet her eye. The draw she felt to him was physical, she knew that. But it had deepened the longer she'd known him. He was so different to Edward that he provided a glimpse of another life. Some days, she really wanted to know more about what that life might be like. With Edward, it had been fun, mostly. Shared jokes and lazy weekends and comfort. She had felt like she was in the right place, until she hadn't. Steve's life looked more chaotic, less steady. Somehow, despite being an at-home parent like her, he made life feel like an adventure. He was always doing last-minute camping trips with Luke or being invited to glamorous events by his rich clients. And Anna wouldn't mind a bit of adventure, now and again.

If she were with Steve, would another side to her come out? A more impulsive, slightly messier side? How much of who she was, was tied to who she was with? Anna wanted to believe that her personality was strong; that her essence was rigid. But how could you know, really, without testing it out?

Anna felt like she needed to say something, to steer them back. 'Do you want a coffee?' she asked, jerking her head to indicate the café across the road.

'Yep, that would be good. I'll keep an eye on Sam.'

Sam was one of those babies who would go to anyone, so Anna headed off without worrying about leaving him. And all the time she was crossing the road, queueing up, giving her order, she was thinking about what Steve had said. That things were rocky, that he didn't know whether he wanted to salvage them. When she got back, she handed a cardboard cup to Steve and sat down.

'Sam okay?' she asked.

'Well, he got into a bit of trouble with a gang but I set him back on the straight and narrow.'

'And the other two?'

'Over there.' Steve pointed, and Anna saw that Thomas and Luke were still lost in a world of make-believe. But then, as if they'd known they were being talked about, the two boys thundered over and said they were hungry.

'You've had your morning snack. I haven't brought anything with me,' Steve said.

Thomas looked at Anna pleadingly, knowing she always had something stashed in the changing bag.

'It's too close to lunch,' she said. She looked at Steve. 'What are your plans?'

Steve shrugged. 'Cheese sandwich?'

'Do you fancy heading back to ours? I mean, it'll be one of those whatever's-in-the-fridge lunches. I think we've got some ham and cheese, carrot sticks, bread...'

Thomas and Luke gave a little cheer, and Anna smiled.

'That would be great,' Steve said.

So they walked back together, Thomas and Luke going ahead, holding hands. Anna pushed the buggy with a sleepy Sam inside. And she realised, because of the absence of the feeling, that she'd been feeling lonely lately. It was strange, to feel lonely when you were never alone. But you couldn't have a proper conversation with children so young, and they had so much need, it was overwhelming. It was nice to walk beside Steve, to chat and joke about their day-to-day and the programmes they watched endlessly on CBeebies.

When they were all inside the house, Anna left Steve watching the kids in the lounge while she pulled things out of the fridge. She cut up some bread and put it on the table along with the butter. Grated cheese. Sliced some cucumber and pepper. Opened bags of crisps.

'This looks great,' Steve said, coming into the dining room.

'I'm letting everyone fill their own plate,' she said. 'I know what Thomas can be like if I dare to put something he doesn't like on his. Taking it off later does not make up for the offence.'

'Yes, I can be like that,' Steve said, and Anna laughed.

'Come on, guys,' Anna called, and the older boys came into the room. Anna went to get Sam and lifted him into his highchair. He was just starting to eat solids, and Anna had a sudden memory of how stressful she'd found this stage with Thomas. This time around, she was hardly pureeing anything. She put a carrot stick, a slice of cucumber, a finger of cheese and some bread on his tray and let him get on with it. Back in the kitchen, she ran the tap and reached for the bottle of orange squash.

When she turned, Steve was behind her, a little closer than she was used to. Anna was overly aware of her body, of her lips. She met Steve's eye, and it was like he was asking her a question.

'Steve,' she said, her voice a little croaky.

He reached out a hand and brushed her hair from her face. 'Yes?'

And just when she was sure he was going to kiss her, or at least try to kiss her, there was a cry from the dining room and they both bolted in there and found Thomas lying on the carpet, his hands clutching his head, which looked to be bleeding.

'What happened?' Anna asked, feeling hysterical.

She knew what had happened. He'd been swinging on his chair, like he did every mealtime, and he'd fallen, like she always predicted he would. But it felt like a punishment for what she'd been about to do.

'I don't know what to do,' she said, turning to Steve.

She'd attended a baby first aid course when Thomas was six weeks old. They'd covered cuts and bumps and burns and falls, and more serious stuff like choking and the recovery position. But Anna didn't remember any of it. She had thought at the time that she wouldn't. Her brain was mush from lack of sleep, and Thomas breastfed through about 80 per cent of the two-hour course.

'Grab a tea towel to hold on the cut,' Steve said. 'Then I'll look after Sam while you take him to A&E.'

Anna fetched a clean tea towel and pressed it to Thomas's head. He was wailing. She sat him back on his chair and gave him a big cuddle, got him to hold the tea towel in place while she started to gather some things together, shouting instructions at Steve as she went.

'He might take a bottle, worth a try. And then he'll go down for a nap. His sleeping bag is in his cot, upstairs. Are you sure you and Luke don't mind staying here?'

'It's fine,' Steve said. 'There are plenty of toys and it's easier than packing up all the stuff Sam needs. We'll be absolutely fine here, won't we, boys?'

Luke and Sam were both still eating, apparently oblivious to Thomas's fall.

'Okay,' Anna said, 'thank you. I'll keep you posted.'

She lifted Thomas into her arms. He was too heavy to carry for long these days, but she somehow always managed to find the strength when he was upset. How long until she wouldn't be able to? Another year or so, perhaps. Or maybe forever. You heard those stories, didn't you? Mothers lifting up cars to save their children. She took him out to the car and strapped him in, kissed the tip of his nose. 'You'll be okay, Tom-Tom. Just keep holding that towel there, okay? Don't forget.'

He nodded, tears still falling from his long eyelashes onto his cheeks. Anna got into the driver's seat and set off for the hospital where she'd given birth to both of her boys. It was twenty minutes on a good day, but good days were rare when it came to traffic in London, and the journey took more like forty. She played nursery rhymes and sang along with them, and asked Thomas questions to make sure he was awake and alert, and every time the fear and panic threatened to overwhelm her, she pushed them down.

She wished Edward was here. It was always in these moments of crisis and fear that she questioned what she was doing, keeping him at a distance. Not only in those moments, but most acutely then. When one of the boys was feverish and sleeping beside her in bed, or when they fell and she wasn't sure how serious it was. Her mind flitted from Edward to Steve. They had nearly kissed. If Thomas hadn't fallen, they would have kissed. She was certain of it. She wouldn't have stopped him, despite knowing he was married and having been on the other side of that sort of betrayal. She had been sure, in that moment, that it was inevitable. And now, what? She wanted to rush back to the safety of her marriage just because Thomas was hurt? She missed Edward, she did. Life was hard without him. But Steve. That look he'd given her, the way her tummy had flipped. That was worth examining too, wasn't it?

When they got to the hospital, when they were called, Anna felt a great weight lift as she handed her boy over to the experts, who were gentle and kind and showed him soft toys they kept in their pockets to distract him from any pain while they glued him back together. All the time, she held his hand and talked to him and made sure he felt as safe as possible.

By the time they were home, it was almost tea-time and Anna felt wrung out. It was strange, coming into the house and Steve being there, holding the fort. Holding Sam. It was like a look into a possible future, and there was no denying that she liked it. It felt comfortable and somehow right. Steve looked up and saw her in the doorway, her hand on Thomas's shoulder, and Anna felt herself redden, imagining he might be able to read her thoughts. Thomas ran into the room, and that sudden movement was like the bursting of a bubble.

'All fixed?' Steve asked, pretending to inspect Thomas's head.

'Fixed,' Anna said, reaching out to take Sam from him.

'You look like you could do with a glass of wine.'

'I could. I might see if there's some in the fridge.'

'Sit down with Sam,' Steve said. 'I'll look. Unless you want me to go home?'

'No,' she said. She didn't. She didn't want him to go. 'Was everything okay here?'

'Fine.'

Anna noticed that the lunch things had been cleared away and everything looked pretty neat and tidy. Sam's playmat was out with a few toys and his wooden blocks, and Luke was dressed as a firefighter and putting out imaginary fires. Thomas joined in, and she wondered at the ability of children to recover from things. Whenever either of her boys was hurt, it was her who took the longest to get over it. Steve appeared with two glasses of white wine and handed one to her, and she took a sip, feeling it warm her.

They ordered a pizza, put a film on for the boys. Anna put Sam to bed, and then she and Steve stood in the kitchen while the older boys stared at the TV.

'About earlier—' Steve said.

'Yes?'

'I'm sorry, if I was out of order. I mean, I was out of order. I'm married.'

Anna didn't know what to say. They were standing close together and her body felt a little loose from the wine and she wanted more than anything to look up at him, to put her hands on his face, to kiss him. There had been no one since Edward had moved out. But there was Theresa, and no matter how rocky he said things were, they hadn't called it a day, had they? Still, she was tired of worrying about everyone, taking responsibility for everyone's actions. She was single. She looked up, locked eyes with him, and felt her insides turn to liquid. He leaned down, and she knew he was going to kiss her and she was going to let him, and the anticipation was exquisite. And when their lips touched, and his hands were in her hair, she forgot about everything else.

11

NO

Sunday 5 June 2005

All the way from Heathrow in the taxi, Anna swore to herself that she wouldn't do it. But then as they approached Clapham, she leaned forward and told the driver she'd changed her mind. Not Cathles Road, after all. Hazelbourne Road. She had him pull up a little way away from the flat she'd shared with Edward, and then she paid him and stepped out onto the street. It was cooler than it was in New York, but she'd expected that. She pulled her case behind her and walked past her old flat on the opposite side of the street. Edward didn't live there any more. They'd sold it and he'd bought himself something smaller, something further out. They were still in touch, but not often. He had a new girlfriend, Anna knew, and she sometimes wondered what she was like. What she looked like, how pretty she was. But also whether she made him laugh. And whether she brought out a side to him that Anna had never managed to find.

Anna stopped for a moment and looked. The new owner

had changed the curtains, and the hedge was more neatly trimmed than it had ever been when she lived there. She tried to imagine crossing the road and going inside, letting herself in. What would her life look like now, if she'd stayed?

A man with a little boy walked past her. He was on the phone, and she heard him say 'you're always working' in an irritated voice, saw the boy look up at him, his eyes full of worry. Just a little way up the road, the boy dropped his toy rabbit without the dad noticing.

'Excuse me,' Anna called, and the man turned. When he looked at her, Anna felt all churned up and she wasn't sure why. Did she know him? She didn't think so. And there was clearly no recognition from his side.

'Can I help you?' he asked, and Anna realised she'd left it too long without explaining why she'd called out to him. She was embarrassed, felt herself flush.

'I think your son dropped his soft toy,' she said.

He ended his call and came back towards her. 'Thank you so much. We'd have had a nightmare at bedtime if this was missing. Luke, you need to be more careful.'

The little boy grabbed for his rabbit and they walked on, chatting now, the dad's head angled down towards his son. And as they walked away, Anna had the strangest feeling that she was the one who was losing something. She shook her head as if to dislodge her thoughts.

She could have a child that sort of age by now, if she and Edward had started trying for a baby when he'd first brought it up. She couldn't imagine it. And yet, here she was, back in London to meet Nia's baby. Was it something in her, some reluctance to grow up and accept adult responsibilities? Was she somehow abnormal? Her friends were having children left and right and she felt like she was forever buying new baby cards and gifts, and yet she still didn't feel any closer to wanting that for herself. With one last look back, she carried on down the road, heading for Nia's.

Nia opened the door with her baby daughter attached to her breast and tried to give Anna a hug, but Anna was scared the baby would suffocate.

'Come in,' Nia said. 'I probably shouldn't flash the whole of Clapham.'

They went into the living room and sat down, and Anna really looked at her friend. Nia's daughter, Cara, was eight weeks old. Nia looked tired; more than tired. She looked almost broken. And then Cara pulled away from the breast and Nia adjusted her clothes and beamed at her little girl and Anna saw that she was transformed, in that moment. She was a mother.

'How is it?' she asked. 'How are you?'

Nia gave her a wobbly smile. 'I can't stop crying,' she said. 'Thanks for asking. Everyone just wants to look at her. No one cares how I'm doing.'

'I care,' Anna said.

'It's so weird,' Nia went on, 'I feel like my body isn't mine. My tits are huge and they go from being quite normal to being rock hard with the milk, and my tummy's all saggy and I just don't feel like me. Do I look like me?'

'Not quite,' Anna said, truthfully. 'But I think you will, in time.'

'God, it's so bloody hard. People tell you about the sleep deprivation, but they sort of talk about it as if it's a joke. They don't tell you that you feel like you're going to die from it.'

Anna thought that perhaps spending time with Nia wasn't going to change her stance on wanting children any time soon. 'What can I do?' she asked. 'I want to help. I'll get up in the night, anything.'

'Trouble is, I'm the only one who can feed her,' Nia said, and she looked miserable. 'I think that's the hardest bit. Jamie's brilliant but he can't help with that.'

'Then I'll get up and keep you company,' Anna said. 'Get you water. Change her nappy.'

Nia smiled gratefully.

Anna looked around. Jamie had moved into Nia's flat shortly after they'd announced the pregnancy to everyone, but there wasn't a great deal of evidence of him. There was a book on the coffee table that Anna was pretty sure wasn't Nia's – something about the history of film – but she couldn't immediately spot anything else.

'Where is Jamie?' Anna asked.

'Oh, supermarket. We run out of nappies or wipes on an almost daily basis. He won't be long. I keep forgetting you haven't met.'

'I can't wait to see whether he really looks like Peter Andre. Anyway, while we wait, let me make you tea.'

Nia smiled gratefully.

In the kitchen, in the fridge, Anna could see Jamie's influence. Gone were Nia's out of date yoghurts and bottles of beer. The fridge was full of cheese and meat, a veritable rainbow of vegetables and, in the door, nestled next to the milk, all sorts of sauces and condiments. What was it Nia had said about Jamie's job? Didn't he work in finance?

'Is Jamie a foodie?' Anna asked once she'd made the drinks.

'God, yes. Didn't I tell you? I've never eaten so well, or so much. You'll see, while you're here. He has this dream of opening up a café but I'm not sure it's ever going to happen. How long are you here, by the way?'

'I'm over for five days but I'm going to go to my mum's for a night. Is that okay?'

'Of course.'

Cara was asleep in Nia's arms, and she stood and laid her gently in the Moses basket at her feet. 'That's better,' she said.

'Can I have a hold, when she wakes up?' Anna asked.

'Of course you can! I try not to thrust her on people too much, in case they don't want to hold her.'

'I've brought you things,' Anna said. She fetched her suitcase from the hallway and opened it, pulled out the clothes she'd bought for Cara, which Nia exclaimed over, and the scarf she'd chosen for Nia at a flea market, supplemented by the big Toblerone she'd picked up at the airport.

'We'll open that right now,' Nia said. 'Thank you, really.'

'Is it what you imagined?' Anna blurted out. It was the question she'd most wanted to ask but she hadn't known quite how. She didn't want it to sound like she was asking if Nia had any regrets, not with her beautiful baby daughter lying there, fast asleep with her tiny chest rising and falling almost imperceptibly with each breath.

'Nothing like,' Nia said, and Anna couldn't determine what emotions lay behind those words. She'd always been able to read Nia, but Nia was changed. Anna felt as though she was looking at her friend through a shower screen, or an obscured window.

'It's harder,' Nia continued. 'It's really fucking hard. Did I mention that? And I don't fully understand why, because there is a lot of sitting around. I think it's hard emotionally. And there's all the stuff about never getting to eat a meal without being disturbed. That's hard too. And Jamie and I are never together, because I sleep in the evenings and then I'm up with her half the night while he's asleep. And we hadn't been together that long, had we? It's quite a jolt to go from that honeymoon period to talking about how to get shit out of a cot sheet.'

When Nia stopped talking, Anna wasn't sure it was because she'd run out of things to say. She gave a slight nod, to show that Nia should go on, but she didn't, at first. Anna let the silence settle, looked down in case her eye contact was preventing Nia from being able to speak.

'You know that you can tell me, don't you?'

'Tell you what?'

'I don't know,' Anna said. 'Just... anything. If there is anything. You don't have to feel like I won't understand, because I haven't been through it. Even if I don't, I'll listen. I'll do my best.'

There were tears in Nia's eyes. 'I haven't said this to anyone, but sometimes I feel like I've made a huge mistake. I can't unmake it, of course. I can't go back. But I feel like this is it now, for the rest of my life, and I don't know whether I like it.'

'It won't stay the same,' Anna said. 'Nothing does.'

'That's another thing, I go to playgroups and these women with older kids say stuff about how they miss the newborn stage because the baby slept all the time and stayed still, and I want to strangle them. I want to say that if it's going to get harder than this, I can't cope with it.'

'I bet they've just forgotten what it's really like. They say your brain does that, don't they? It blocks out trauma. Like childbirth. If your brain didn't forget, no one would do it again.'

Nia shuddered. 'I'm not doing it again any time soon.'

'Well, no,' Anna said. 'I mean, you're all set now, aren't you? One big love, one child.'

It was what Magda had predicted for Nia all those years ago.

'So now we need to concentrate on you,' Nia said. 'Met any J men lately?'

Anna batted the question away, as if she didn't always feel a twinge of hope when she was introduced to someone she liked the look of that they might fit the bill.

'Let's go out for dinner, you and me. Your J man can have Cara, can't he? If you feed her just before we go and we stay local...'

Nia looked uncertain. 'I've never left her. I don't know.'

Anna shrugged. 'It's up to you, of course. Let's see how you feel a bit later.'

When Cara stretched and woke, Anna lifted her carefully from the basket and held her for a minute or two, but then she started to root around and cry and Anna had to pass her over to Nia for a feed.

About twenty minutes later, she heard a key in the lock. Anna felt oddly nervous. Usually she met Nia's boyfriends after the first couple of dates, and her approval was one of the hoops they had to jump through to be in Nia's life. But this was a done deal, wasn't it? Jamie and Nia were living together. They had a baby, they were a family. Where did Anna fit into this picture? What did her approval matter, now? God, she hoped she would like him. She looked over to Nia and saw that Cara had finished feeding and they'd both fallen asleep. Nia was sitting up on the sofa, her head slightly back. Anna stood and took Cara from her arms, and then went into the hallway.

Jamie was locking the door, but when he turned, Anna found herself taking a sharp breath in.

Because Jamie was James. The James she'd met on the bus almost a decade ago, who'd promised to call, but hadn't. The James she'd held every first date up against since. Wasn't it? It was. How had she not seen this in the photo Nia had sent her of the two of them together? Perhaps it had been a strange angle or something. Perhaps she'd been blinded by how happy Nia looked. She saw him recognise her, saw his expression change.

'You're Jamie now,' she said. It was all she could think of.

'Anna?'

How was this possible? She had quietly hoped to find this man, and then she'd left the country and her best friend had stumbled across him.

'I didn't realise...' he started to say.

'Of course,' Anna said. Why would he? It was one date. One magical, totally perfect date.

'Where's Nia?' he asked. He looked worried, as if he thought perhaps Anna had done away with her best friend and stolen her baby.

Anna jerked her head in the direction of the living room. 'Asleep on the sofa. That's why I came out, to warn you.'

Jamie pulled a face. 'She's so tired,' he said. 'I don't know what to do to help more. Come on, let's go through to the kitchen.'

They snuck past Nia and went into the kitchen, and Jamie pulled the door closed.

Anna couldn't stop looking at him, couldn't believe he was here, in the flesh, after all the years she'd looked for him in crowds and in bars and on streets. He was Nia's, she reminded herself. The love of food and the name starting with J, it was all a coincidence. She let her brain adjust to the fact that the thing she'd dreamed of was never going to happen. Set fire to that dream. Stamped on the embers.

'That time we went out—' Jamie said.

'Yes?'

'I had a good time. I wanted to see you again. I lost your number.'

Anna had wondered about something as simple as that. She hadn't had his number, so she hadn't been able to call him.

'It doesn't matter now,' she said.

'No. Do you think, I mean, what should we say to Nia?'

Anna thought about her friend, struggling with her changed life and new to this relationship that seemed so right. She thought about the times they'd discussed James over the years, jokingly, and sometimes more seriously. Nia knew what Anna had built that night up into. She didn't need to know that the guy Anna had always held up as her dream man was her own boyfriend.

'Nothing,' Anna said. 'I mean, don't you think?'

Jamie looked relieved. 'I think so. It was so long ago, right?'

Anna nodded. It was. She tried not to be hurt by how quickly and easily he'd agreed with her. It had been her suggestion, after all. A memory came to her, of kissing him. Of the way he had held her face in his hands, the warmth of his body against hers. And then she pushed it out, swearing it would be the last time. A dream she'd carried through her adult life was dying – was dead – and she couldn't let Nia or Jamie know how much it meant. She'd been ridiculous, she knew, to have built all she had out of one encounter. Nia had encouraged it, the way friends did. But she could see now how silly it had been.

Nia came into the kitchen, looking creased and sleepy and entirely at ease.

'So you two have met,' she said. 'Sorry about the impromptu nap. I was so looking forward to introducing you.'

Jamie smiled. 'Pretend we haven't. Met, I mean.'

He caught Anna's eye and she looked down at her feet.

'Okay,' Nia said. 'Jamie, this is Anna, the only woman for whom I would genuinely jump in front of a bus. Other than Cara, of course. She's brave and brilliant, and she lives in New-fucking-York, where we're totally going to visit her one day, when I feel brave enough to take this one on a long-haul flight. And Anna, this is Jamie, the love of my life, or something like that. He makes the best scrambled eggs in the world – I have no idea what he does to them, and I don't care – and he made me feel butterflies even after I'd had seven awful dates in a row. You have to like each other, because I can't choose between you.'

While she'd been talking, Jamie had taken a bottle of white wine from the fridge and was pouring three glasses. He handed them one each.

'Thanks, N,' he said, leaning across to kiss her forehead. 'And it's so good to finally meet you, Anna.'

Even though they'd both agreed it was the right thing, Anna felt uncomfortable about the lie being cemented like that. There was no going back on it.

'Listen,' she said, 'I was trying to talk Nia into the two of us going out for dinner. What do you think?'

'I think it's a great idea,' Jamie said. 'Me and Cara will be just fine here. You get about three hours between feeds in the evening, right?'

'Exactly,' Anna said, although she had no idea how long Nia got between feeds. 'And there's that Italian just down the road – is that still there?'

'That Greek place is better,' Jamie said.

Anna shuddered involuntarily.

'She used to go there with her ex,' Nia said, and Jamie put his hands up, as if in surrender.

'Nothing fits me,' Nia said, but Anna could tell that this wasn't a real excuse. She was almost persuaded.

'Go in your maternity jeans,' Jamie said. 'Who cares? Just go and have a nice couple of hours with your best friend, who's flown a long way to see you.'

'Okay,' Nia said. 'Okay.' She smiled. 'Give her to me, then, and I'll feed her.'

* * *

As soon as they were seated in the Italian restaurant, Nia smiled brightly.

'So what do you think, of Jamie? I mean, I know you're always honest but I'm sort of tied to this one, so if you could stick to the positive, that would be appreciated.'

'He seems perfect,' Anna said.

It was the truth. It was clear to Anna how caring Jamie was, how he wanted the best for Nia, and wasn't that what every woman wanted? Someone who had her back, who supported her and gave her space and time to be the best person she could be? And it didn't hurt that he looked the way he did. She thought about going against what she'd agreed with him, just throwing the fact that she'd once gone on a date with him into the conversation. *Funny thing*, she'd start. But no, she couldn't. They'd acted like they'd never met. She had to stick to that. It felt uncomfortable, because it was the first big secret she'd ever kept from her best friend. Nia had been the first person she'd told when she got her period and her GCSE results, when she lost her grandfather and her virginity. Now, something had changed between them, and Nia didn't even know.

Nia took a long drink from the water the waiter had just poured for them. 'That's it? I mean, I know I asked you to be nice but no criticism at all? It feels a bit weird. Remember when you first met Charlie and said you thought he had the capacity to become a psychopath?'

Anna laughed. 'And look how that turned out! You calling me from a bar because he was waiting for you outside like some kind of stalker.'

'I'd forgotten about that. Doesn't it seem like a lifetime ago?

You know, when we were carefree and you lived round the corner.'

'It does.'

They ordered pasta and wine, ascertained that the waiter's name was Will, and Anna felt herself relaxing, but she could see that Nia was on edge. She kept looking at her phone. Anna wanted to reassure her, to say that Cara would be fine, but what did she know about how it felt? This separated them, she realised. It put them on either side of something huge, something insurmountable. And they might always be on either side of it, she thought. It might change them fundamentally.

'So, are you happy?' Anna asked. 'I mean, with Jamie?'

'Yes,' Nia said, and Anna noticed that she didn't pause, or qualify it in any way. 'Jamie is a good thing in my life. Thank God it was him I got pregnant with.'

'Could have been Charlie,' Anna said.

'Imagine. He'd probably have ditched us by now.' Nia smiled. 'What about you? Is there anyone?'

Anna shook her head. She'd thought dating was dating everywhere, but she'd found it hard to establish the rules in New York. Men loved her accent, like everyone said, but after a couple of dates they seemed to freak out, as if she might want to marry them to stay in the country.

'Nothing to report,' she said. 'But it's really okay. I love it there, I'm happy exploring.'

They both ate for a couple of minutes, and didn't speak. When they'd finished, the waiter cleared their plates and offered them the dessert menu, and Anna looked at Nia, ready to take her cue from her friend. Nia looked uncomfortable, like she couldn't quite settle in her chair and she didn't know what to say or do about it.

'Shall we just get the bill?' Anna asked.

'But you love dessert,' Nia said.

'I can pick up a Dairy Milk from the corner shop,' Anna said, and Nia smiled gratefully.

'I don't remember how to do it,' Nia said, on the short walk back to the flat. She put her arm through Anna's. 'I don't remember how to be a normal person, to go out for dinner or relax. It's not even that I miss her, you know. I'm desperate for the time away, to feel like myself again. But then when I get it, I can't enjoy it. I feel like I'm doing something wrong, letting her down somehow. If she starts crying and won't stop until she's fed, I'm the only one who can help with that.'

'It's early days,' Anna said. 'Just follow your instincts.'

She wondered whether that sounded trite. It was the best she could do.

Nia let them into the flat and they found Jamie and Cara asleep on the sofa, daughter lying on her father's chest, her head to one side and her lips pursed.

'They look pretty content, don't they?' Nia whispered.

'They do.'

'Shall we sit outside while we eat this?' Nia asked, waving the bag of chocolate they'd bought on the way home.

They stepped into Nia's small garden, sat on her garden chairs. And for half an hour, it was like it had always been. The miles swallowed up, Nia's baby asleep. Nia had relaxed, now that she was back home and ready to take care of her daughter. She seemed like the old Nia again.

'How's that hot boss of yours?' she asked.

Anna groaned. 'So hot. And, you know, my boss. So I have to pretend he isn't. Hot, I mean.'

'Isn't that always the way?'

'Yes,' Anna said. 'Isn't it?'

12

YES

Monday 5 June 2006

Anna woke and turned on her side and Edward was propped up on his elbow, watching her.

'Happy anniversary,' he said.

She smiled. 'What time is it? Are the boys still asleep?'

Most nights, one or other of their children ended up in their bed in the middle of the night. Thomas came in of his own accord and they didn't always realise until they woke up and found him there. Sam was in a cot, so he called for them, and if they had the willpower for it, they would try to get him back to sleep in his own room. But if they didn't, they would carry him in his sleeping bag into theirs and lay him down between them.

'It's six-fifteen,' Edward said. 'Both asleep. I have to get up soon. But I wanted to make it up to you, for not always being great at the anniversary thing.'

Anna rubbed her eyes. She wasn't awake enough for this kind of conversation. But her instinct was to say that they hadn't been together the year before, and she couldn't really remember the year before that. But before she could speak, the door creaked open and Thomas stood there, his panda toy in his arms.

'Do you want to come in?' Anna asked him.

He nodded and did a sort of half-run into the room, launching himself onto the bed. Anna pulled him to her, breathed in his sleepy smell.

'Any dreams?' she asked him.

He nodded again. 'About a big, green monster eating Sam,' he said.

Anna and Edward exchanged a look.

'You know that's not going to happen, don't you?' Edward asked.

Thomas shrugged his small shoulders, and Anna pulled him closer still.

'I'd better get in the shower,' Edward said. 'But I wanted to say, I've booked us theatre tickets for tonight.'

'What about the boys?' she asked, surprised. It wasn't like him to spring something on her. But then, he'd been making an effort since she'd asked him to come home just before Christmas. He'd been trying to show her that she'd made the right decision. And she had, she thought. She'd made the right decision for their family. And for her. That kiss with Steve had been a one off. She'd stopped it before it had gone any further, unable to get past the fact that he was married. One afternoon when the leaves were turning red and gold, they'd almost kissed again. And despite her body screaming yes, Anna had pushed him away and told him that he owed it to Theresa to really decide whether what they had was worth saving. That night, she'd called Edward and asked him to come home. She was scared of the way she felt about Steve, in truth. She was terrified of him turning her down, deciding it was over, so she pre-empted him.

And once Edward was back, it felt like he hadn't been away, and she choked back her feelings when she saw Steve, and they didn't talk about what could have been.

'Keira from nursery is babysitting. It's all sorted.' Edward came around to her side of the bed on his way to the bathroom and leaned down to kiss her.

'Thank you,' she said.

She heard the shower start up, heard Edward step into it. Thomas wriggled his body until it was touching hers at the shoulder, hip and knee. He clung to her in a way that Sam never did. Just then, Sam shouted out and Anna peeled Thomas off herself to go to him. Sam was standing up in his cot, his dark hair in disarray, his eyes huge. He looked at her and raised his arms and she lifted him, carried him through to her bedroom. She had ten minutes before she needed to get up, and while she knew there was no hope of going back to sleep, being horizontal was enough. The boys lay beside her, Thomas close and Sam rolling around on Edward's side, and when Edward came through, wrapped in a towel, he got back in for a couple of minutes and Anna felt so content she thought for a minute she was going to cry.

This was it, wasn't it? This was why everybody did it. Why they put up with the sheer hard work of it and all the juggling of childcare, work and endless washing. They did it for moments like this. Four in a bed, everyone happy. A family.

Too soon, her alarm cut into her thoughts and she stood up, knowing that if she snoozed it, she would never win her morning battle. It was time to get everyone ready and break-fasted and out of the door. Each morning, it took every ounce of patience she had.

It wasn't until she was leaving the house with the boys, Sam strapped into the pushchair and Thomas on the buggy board, that she thought to ask Edward about the arrangements for later.

'Where shall I meet you?' she asked. 'What time?'

'No need to come home. Keira's bringing them back here after nursery closes. I've given her a spare key. Just meet me at seven at that cocktail bar in Covent Garden, the one with the tree inside.'

'Okay, see you,' Anna said, kissing his cheek.

And on the walk to nursery and the Tube to work, she smiled. It was a long time since she'd had a night out to look forward to, something that was just for her.

* * *

Edward was standing at the bar when she arrived, one cocktail in his hand and another on the bar.

'For me?' she asked.

'For you.'

She smiled and picked up the delicate glass. 'What is it?'

'Something with vodka and pomegranate juice. Same as mine.'

Anna took a sip and put it back. 'So what are we seeing?'

'*Blood Brothers*,' Edward said.

It was her favourite show. Edward knew that, but he'd never agreed to see it with her before. Musicals weren't really his thing. Edward didn't know that she'd last seen it with Steve, almost a year ago. It was the closest they'd come to having a date. He'd come over to the house and said that a friend had given him tickets and Theresa didn't like theatre, and he remembered her saying she liked *Blood Brothers*, and did she want to go with him? Theresa had offered to have the kids. Anna had thought that Theresa probably wouldn't have offered to babysit while Anna went out with her husband if she knew the contents of Anna's brain when it came to Steve. She'd also thought that she had no recollection of telling Steve she liked *Blood Brothers*. But they'd covered a lot of ground in conversation while the kids played on the floor over the years. And so they'd gone. They'd drunk slightly warm white wine in the interval and then sung the songs on the way back to the Tube. And Anna had tried not to think about kissing him, or about reaching out for his warm hand.

In the theatre, Edward went to find the toilets and Anna tried to decide whether she should order interval drinks. In the end, she bought a big bag of Minstrels instead. They had good seats, in the stalls, and when they were sitting down waiting for the show to start, Edward took her hand in his, lifted it to his mouth and kissed it.

Anna leaned closer to him and whispered. She couldn't help herself. 'What is all this?' He'd clearly gone to some effort. Booking the tickets, finding a babysitter.

Edward looked a little hurt. 'I just wanted to treat you. I know how hard you work, you know, with the boys and your job. I know you bear the brunt of it.'

Anna was surprised. They had settled into their own routine, as all parents did. There were things she did, things he did. She often felt that she did more, but she hadn't realised Edward was aware of it. When he'd come back, she'd thought it was a chance for them to reset, to start again from scratch. But they hadn't, of course. They'd fallen into the same patterns, the same routines. She leaned in to speak again, but just then the curtains swept open and the show started. She didn't think about what Edward had said again until they were walking out at the end.

'What did you think?' she asked.

'It was okay.'

Anna smiled. He was incapable of lying convincingly.

'Did you hate it?'

'No, I didn't hate it. It's just... you know it's not really my thing. But I did enjoy seeing how much you loved it.'

Anna felt a flip inside when he said that. A couple of times, he'd taken her to football and she'd been cold and not really understood or cared what was happening on the pitch, but she'd loved seeing his enthusiasm for it, seeing the way he came alive.

'So, about what you said just before, about me bearing the brunt?'

They were outside then, carried along by the crowd and pushed out into the warm evening.

'Yes?' Edward said.

She pulled him round a corner, away from the crowds, so they could talk. 'I never felt like you noticed. It's so hard, you know, trying to fit in work and the boys...'

'That's why I think you should give it up,' Edward said.

'Give what up?'

'Work. It's too much. You're going to burn yourself out.'

Anna didn't say anything. She had hoped he was going to offer to take on more of the domestic drudgery. But they were back to this, his preference for her to stay at home and be a wife and mum and nothing else. Internally, she examined why she was so reluctant. There were parts of her that loved being a mum, and sometimes she wished she didn't have to go to work, wished she wasn't always rushing. When she dropped the boys at nursery, sometimes they cried and asked her not to go. Those mornings she could see a different life, one in which there was time for second pieces of toast and slow games of snap.

And in September, Thomas would go to school and everything would change again. She'd already signed up for the school's breakfast club and after-school care with a heavy heart, thinking of how long the days would be for him, and she kept meaning to talk to her boss about cutting down by another day. Wouldn't this be the answer to so many of those problems? She could spend her days at home with Sam, and they could take Thomas to school and pick him up. She could be one of those mums at the gate, who she imagined chatted and swapped stories and always had time to go to the park.

But it came down to this: she didn't want that. She wanted to work, to feel she had a purpose beyond being a mum. She wanted her boys to grow up in a house where both their parents worked, so that they might expect that when they settled down themselves. She wanted to feel a part of something, a useful cog in the machine. She wanted to have something for after they were grown up and gone, something more than an empty house and regrets.

Edward had taken her hand and they were walking towards the Tube, quiet.

'It's not what I want,' Anna said eventually.

'What, us?' Edward stopped and turned to face her, panic written on his face.

'No, of course not. Being at home, I mean. It's not for me.'

Edward sighed. Anna wondered whether he ever thought he'd married the wrong woman. Whether he ever went back over the other women he'd known, the ones he might have chosen, and speculated about whether they would have made better at-home wives. Better mothers.

'I was hoping—' he said, but then he broke off.

'What?' Anna genuinely had no idea what he was going to say.

'I was hoping we might try for another.'

Another child. Anna had never seriously considered it. Two was plenty, she'd always thought that. And the way she felt, like she was barely making it work, barely giving her existing children what they needed. It was laughable. But Edward wasn't laughing. He clearly didn't feel the way she did, constantly pulled in so many different directions, always feeling like she wasn't doing anything well enough.

'I don't want to,' she said.

She didn't sugarcoat it, didn't see that she should have to. It was her body, her family, and she didn't want to.

Edward nodded tightly. He'd been careful not to upset her, since coming back. She wondered whether he felt like he was walking a tightrope even bringing this up.

'It's not so long since you came back,' she said. 'I don't want to rush into anything. And besides, I just don't feel like I could manage, with three...'

She didn't say that having another child would mean such different things for the two of them. For him, an extra little person to play with in the garden and to tickle in the bath. An extra person to love him and ask for stories and to put on his shoulders when they went to the park. But for her, it was endless washing and tidying and cleaning up. Another couple of years of sleep so broken she didn't think she could survive it. She tried to picture herself with a daughter. Anna had never told Edward ... a name picked out for a girl. Eva. In both pregnancies, she'd held her breath at the twenty-week scan, wondering whether it might be Eva this time. But no. It wasn't enough, that hope. It wasn't enough to make her change her mind.

They spent most of the Tube journey in silence, and while they were walking back to the house, Anna tried to think of ways to fix it. Edward let them in and went through to the kitchen. Anna went to the living room to find the babysitter.

'They've been absolutely fine,' Keira said.

'Great,' Anna said.

'Did you have a nice night? Happy anniversary, by the way.'

Anna tried to smile. 'Yes,' she said. 'A lovely night, thank you. I'll just go and get some cash for you.'

'No need, your husband took my bank details. He said he'd transfer the money. I'll see you at nursery.'

As soon as Keira was gone, Anna searched for a CD and put it on. Edward came into the room when he heard the song she was playing. *'Something Changed'*.

'Dance with me?' she asked.

He shook his head a little, then smiled and held out his arms. He would get over it, Anna knew. This desire for another child. And then they would have everything. Their two boys, healthy and full of love. Each other. Yes, she'd made the right decision. She had. Edward spun her away from him and she ducked under his arm, laughing.

'Come here,' Edward said, his voice full of want. And she went to him, kissed him, pushed him back on the sofa.

13

NO

Monday 5 June 2006

Anna's phone rang when she was walking from the subway to the office. Nia.

'Hey.'

'Anna,' Nia said, her voice little more than a whisper.

Anna stopped walking, moved to the side of the street. 'What's happened? Are you okay?'

'Anna, everything is so fucked up, Jamie's gone and—'

'Jamie's gone?'

'We had this massive argument. You know I thought he was cheating?'

'No!'

'Oh, I thought I told you.'

I thought I told you. It was like a punch. If she'd been there, in London, Nia would have told her. They would have dissected it all a hundred times.

'Was he? Cheating? Is he?'

'I don't know. I don't think so. I went to see Magda.'

Anna was twenty-two again for a moment, drinking cheap wine in Nia's parents' kitchen, her mind on James. Jamie. How strange, Anna thought, that both of them had asked Magda for guidance regarding this same man. And Nia didn't know that.

'And?'

'She said she didn't think I had anything to worry about, but I couldn't believe it. He was coming home late, all those things.'

'Maybe he was working,' Anna said.

'That's what he said.'

'But you don't believe him?'

Nia was sobbing again. Anna waited, wishing she was there and could put her arms around her friend, look her in the eyes and try to make her laugh through her tears. It was never the same on the phone. They pretended it was, but it wasn't.

'Why wouldn't he cheat?' Nia burst out. 'Since I had Cara, I'm so different. I'm boring, I'm fat, I have nothing interesting to say...'

'Nia, none of those things are true.'

'You don't know, Anna. You're not here.'

Anna didn't know what to say. And then she did. 'Shall I come? If you need me, Nia, I'll come.'

Nia wailed. When she was upset, she couldn't cope with people being nice to her. Anna knew this. But still, she wasn't going to retract the offer. She meant it.

'Don't come,' Nia said through sobs. 'But thank you for offering to come. And stop being so nice to me, you bitch.'

Anna laughed, and it made her realise that she was close to tears herself. On that manic knifepoint where you're a second away from all the emotions.

'Nia, I'm sure it's a misunderstanding. Jamie adores you.'

'How do you know?'

How did she know? It was a feeling, more than anything.

She'd only seen them together on that trip back to London just after Cara was born, but it had just been so clear. That was what had made it easy to push the James fantasy to the back of her mind. Here he was, this man she thought might have been perfect for her, so clearly perfect for her best friend.

'I just know,' she said. 'I could tell when I was there, and I can tell when you talk about him. I mean, isn't this the first argument you've had?'

Nia was quiet. 'Pretty much.'

'Has he really left?' Anna said it quietly, scared to set Nia off again.

'He's gone to a friend's for a couple of nights. He said he needed some time.'

'Because you didn't trust him?'

'Yes.'

'And you went to see Magda?'

'He doesn't know about that. But he does know that I went through his phone.'

'Oh, Nia.'

Anna hated to think of her friend, worried and sad.

'I'm so fucking scared of losing him,' Nia said.

Anna wanted to reassure Nia that she wouldn't, but she bit the words back. She couldn't know, could she?

'Tell him that,' she said instead. 'I bet he needs to hear that.'

'Okay.'

'How's Cara?'

'Perfect. Sleeping. It'll be a different story in an hour.'

'Send me pictures, please.'

'I always think I send too many pictures, that everyone will think I have nothing else going on in my life. Which I don't.'

'Nia, why are you being so down on yourself? You've been a

mum for just over a year. It's a massive adjustment. Give yourself a break.'

'My world is just so small, Anna. I go to work some days, and other days I'm at home with Cara, and we go to baby groups or swimming lessons or for a walk to the bloody supermarket. Sometimes I find myself telling Jamie a story about buying baked beans and I sort of catch myself and wonder who the hell I am.'

Anna didn't say anything. She didn't know what to say. It wasn't hers, this life that Nia described. It might have been, but it wasn't. And she didn't know how to reassure her friend when she'd never been in that world.

'What about work? Are things okay there?'

'Well, Ellen's menopause is causing a fair few problems.'

Anna laughed, couldn't help it. 'Tell me more.'

'She won't stop going on about it. Calls it "the change". Says it in one of those stage whispers that are louder than her normal speaking voice. She has about five hundred hot flushes a day and every time she rushes out to the toilets for ten minutes, and I have to cover for her when the boss comes out of his office to poke around, which is basically every single time. I think he thinks she has some serious digestive issues.'

'I wonder who covers for her on the days you're not in.'

'God knows. Last week, she came back in from the toilet while he was standing by my desk. She was fanning herself with a leaflet for printer ink and when she saw him, she started mumbling all this stuff about her body going through some things. He went as red as that time I was throwing a tampon across the office to Ellen – before "the change", obviously – and he was walking past and it hit him in the chest. Scuttled off, didn't come out again for a good hour.'

Anna could hear the laughter in Nia's voice. It felt good, to hear it.

'Nia, I love you,' she said. 'I just want you to know. I'm not going anywhere. And I don't think Jamie is either. I know you feel a bit lost right now, but you won't always. And I know I'm far away, but I can come. Don't forget that.'

Nia was quiet for a moment, and when she spoke, Anna could tell that she was trying to hold her voice steady. 'Thank you, Anna. I just bloody miss you. When you've finished having the time of your life out there, come home, will you? There are people here waiting for you.'

They ended the call, and Anna finished the short walk to her office. Sometimes, when she spoke to Nia, it made her question what she was doing all these miles away from her life. And then she remembered that that was part of her life, and this was part of her life, too. This huge lobby. This shiny lift that carried her up twelve floors to the space where her cubicle was. Her plants, her stack of books, her mess of Post-it notes and to-do lists. Her job that she loved. She wasn't really concentrating as she got out of the lift and started to cross the floor to her desk. And then somehow she collided with a woman carrying a stack of photocopies.

'Shit, I'm sorry,' Anna said, bending down to pick them up.

The woman was tall with a mass of dark curls. Anna's age, more or less. She bent down too. 'No problem,' she said lightly.

Anna gathered most of the paper together and picked it up. 'Do they need sorting or is it all single pages?'

The woman winced. 'It's twenty sets of twenty pages. For an acquisitions meeting,' she said. 'But don't worry. I've got' – she looked at her watch – 'ten minutes.'

'I'll help you,' Anna said, ushering her into an empty meeting room. 'It's the least I can do.'

They worked side by side, standing in front of a big desk.

'I haven't seen you here before,' Anna said. 'Are you new?'

'First day,' the woman said. 'Got here early and asked if there was anything useful I could do. I'm Sarah, I'm on the publicity team.'

Anna had forgotten someone new was starting. The early morning conversation with Nia had thrown her off a bit. Her head was in London.

'Same team,' she said, smiling. 'Anna.'

'Ah, Anna. David talked about you. Sounded like you're his number one publicist.'

Anna felt her face redden. She didn't know what to say to that. She looked down at the paper they were sorting.

'Thank Christ the pages were numbered, right?' Anna said, and Sarah smiled.

There was a warmth about her, Anna thought. She liked it. She could imagine them becoming friends.

'Do you live in Manhattan?' she asked.

Sarah shook her head. 'Brooklyn.'

'Oh, me too.'

'But you're from...'

'London,' Anna said. 'Over here for a few years. Or forever, I don't know.'

'Are you married?' Sarah asked.

'No. I was, back home. But then it fell apart and that's when I came here. Are you?'

Anna loved this back and forth, this getting to know a new person. She was never sure how far to push it, what was okay to ask, so she was glad Sarah was asking just as many questions as she was.

'I've had a girlfriend for a while, but I don't think it's a forever thing. I'm not sure that's for me.'

'What about kids?' Anna asked.

Straight away, she wished she could take it back. She hated it when people asked her. Do you have kids? Do you want them? Everybody wanting to know the whens and wheres and hows.

'Sorry,' she said. 'I shouldn't have asked that. It's—'

'I don't mind,' Sarah said, shrugging. 'I don't have any. I don't think I will.'

'I don't have any either,' Anna said.

It felt good to say it to someone who you were sure wasn't going to judge you. Over the years, Anna had been asked and asked, and she'd never quite found the right way to say that it was none of the other person's business, or found a concise way of saying why she wasn't a mum.

The sorting was finished. Anna lifted the pile and handed it to Sarah.

'I really am sorry about that,' she said.

And Sarah waved her hand as if to say that it was nothing. When they were leaving the meeting room, Sarah turned to her.

'Listen, shall we get a drink one night after work?'

Anna smiled and nodded. 'That sounds good. Maybe next week?'

'Great.'

David was standing by Anna's desk. 'Oh good, you two have met. That saves me a job. Anyone need a coffee?'

14

YES

Tuesday 5 June 2007

Anna was starting to think about leaving the office when Ellie appeared in front of her desk, looking flustered.

'What's up?' Anna asked.

Anna liked Ellie. They got on well, had a similar sense of humour. She enjoyed having lunch with Ellie or chatting about books or films. But when it came to work, Anna found Ellie massively frustrating. She had a big blind spot when it came to organisation, and it grated on Anna because Ellie had been promoted twice while Anna had stayed in the same role they'd both started in.

'I've fucked up,' Ellie said.

Anna tilted her head, raised her eyebrows. 'What? What's happened?'

'You know I've been organising a bookshop tour for that reality star, Nina?'

'Yes...'

'I've somehow messed up the dates. She gave us a list of

dates when she's filming, and I thought it was the list of dates she was free, and I've booked all these slots in bookshops and sent her the schedule, and she's furious. Says she can't do any of them.'

Anna remembered the day Nina had come into the office. She was one of those celebrities who'd come from nothing but now believed she was owed everything. Anna had made her a cup of tea and she'd looked at it in disgust and said 'too weak', then stared until Anna had walked off and started again. When she'd left, Deborah had declared Nina was the worst star she'd ever had to work with, but she was hopefully going to make the company a lot of money. And now this.

'So what are you going to do? Does Deborah know?'

Ellie looked close to tears. 'I can't tell her. I sent some proofs out to people who'd already had them last month and Deborah was furious about the waste. She can't know about this.'

'So how have you left it, with Nina?'

'I said I'd sort it. I need to call the bookshops, see if we can shift things around. And I was hoping...'

Anna knew what Ellie was hoping. She was hoping that Anna would help her. And Anna would. And then later, she'd moan to Edward about how unfair it all was. About how she wouldn't have made the error in the first place, let alone dragged anyone else into the fixing of it.

'Let's split the list,' Anna said. 'But listen, show me the dates she can do and the dates she can't. I need to be really clear. We can't have any more mistakes.'

Ellie nodded. 'Thank you so much, Anna. I won't forget this.'

Anna went over to Ellie's desk and they sat together, heads close, checking and double-checking what Nina had said in her emails, which bookshops had been booked for when, and they came up with a plan.

Anna was on her fourth phone call when her mobile beeped and she saw a message from Edward.

'I'm picking up the boys tonight. Meet us at Phaedra's at seven.'

Anna read it a couple of times. Phaedra's was their favourite Greek restaurant. But why would Edward have booked them in there on a weeknight? And why was he getting the boys? He never left work early enough to pick them up. She started to type a message to him asking various questions, and then she deleted it, typed 'Okay...' instead, and carried on with her work. It was coming up for six. She had time to make a few more calls.

When she reached the end of her list, Anna went back to Ellie's desk. Ellie was just ending a call.

'Done,' Anna said. 'She'll have to double back on herself a bit at this point' – Anna pointed to where she'd had to swap around the order – 'but it's all within the same county.'

Ellie put a hand to her chest. 'I don't know how to thank you, seriously. I thought I was going to lose my job.'

'I need to go,' Anna said. 'Family dinner. See you tomorrow.'

Ellie stood up, came around her desk to the front. She was a little too close, and Anna wanted to step back.

'Thank you, really,' Ellie said, pulling Anna in for a hug. 'I couldn't have done it without you.'

* * *

Anna was out of the Tube and walking towards the restaurant when it hit her. It was their anniversary, hers and Edward's. They'd been married for... She thought about it for a minute. Eight years. She knew how lucky she was. Things felt like they were properly back on track after the time they'd spent apart, and their sons were healthy and happy and brilliant. She'd commented to Edward a few nights ago that it was finally letting up, becoming a bit easier. Thomas and Sam played together a bit sometimes, and she could imagine a future in which she had a bit of time to herself.

When she pushed open the restaurant door, she saw them immediately. They were in the booth where they always sat, in the back left corner. There was a highchair in place but Sam was sitting on Edward's knee. Thomas had coloured pencils and was drawing on the back of the kids' menu. She made her way over to them, kissed them all in turn.

'This is a nice surprise,' she said. 'Happy anniversary.'

Edward smiled at her. 'Happy anniversary.'

'Happy MummyDaddy day!' Sam shrieked.

'I was trying to explain what an anniversary is,' Edward said, laughing.

Anna slid into the booth next to Thomas, reached for the drink Edward had ordered for her. There was something so nice about a person knowing you well enough to do that. It was comforting.

'Hey you,' Anna said, her hand on Thomas's neck.

'Hey you,' he replied, without looking up.

The waiter came over, pad in hand, and they ordered what they always did. Chicken kebabs with very plain salads for the boys, moussaka for Edward, a chicken and spinach dish for Anna. She thought about the baklava she and the boys would eat afterwards, while Edward had a coffee. She pictured Sam with honey dripping from his fingers, his face a portrait of bliss.

'Thank you,' she said, her hand on Edward's arm. 'This was such a nice idea.'

Edward smiled. 'It was Sam's idea, wasn't it, buddy?'

'My idea,' Sam said, solemn.

Anna reached for him and Edward passed him over from his

lap to hers. She squeezed him the way she always did when she saw him at the end of the day, hard enough to let him know she'd missed him. Then she nuzzled into his warm neck and blew a raspberry. He giggled, trying to bat her away with chubby hands, even as she held him at the waist.

The food helped to relax her. It was always good, and because she always ordered the same thing, it was like a comfort blanket.

'I was thinking we should book a holiday,' Edward said.

Thomas's eyes went wide and Sam did a little cheer. Anna looked up. They'd been to Tenerife at Easter and when she'd asked him whether he thought they should have another holiday in the summer, he'd been non-committal. He did this, sometimes. Made decisions alone and let her know at the same time as the kids.

'Where?' she asked.

'I don't know. Spain, Turkey, Greece?'

'Turkey is an eating thing,' Sam said. 'Not a holiday.'

'Luke went to Greece last year, didn't he?' Thomas asked, looking at her.

Luke was Steve's son. Anna nodded her head. 'I think he did, yes.'

And just like that, Anna was trapped in a memory. She'd seen Steve a week or so after he'd returned from Greece. They'd gone for coffee, and he'd told her it was over with Theresa. They'd decided while they were away. No big argument, no drama. It just still wasn't working and they both knew it. Anna had watched his face carefully as he'd told her, looking for hurt. The skin on his arms was a little red and flaky and she'd wanted to reach out and touch him, to suggest he needed some aloe vera. He'd looked deflated, said something about letting Luke down. And Anna had told him he mustn't think like that. That

Luke had two parents who loved him and that was good enough. And Steve had smiled at her as if he didn't believe that was true, but he was grateful to her for trying. When she was preparing to leave, packing up the toys she'd got out for Sam to play with, Steve had taken her hand and his touch had felt like fire. Dangerous and hot. He'd looked at her then, really looked at her, and said that he knew she was trying to make her marriage work, but if it didn't, he would be there. And Anna had muttered something that didn't make any sense and lifted Sam into her arms and left.

'What do you think?' Edward asked.

Anna looked at him. 'About a holiday?'

'Greece,' he said. 'Food like this every day. Sunshine. Mountains. Reading by the pool. History.'

Anna smiled, imagining the sun on her face. 'Let's book it,' she said.

'Why don't we get baklava to go and have a look at some options at home?' Edward asked. 'The boys can help us choose.'

Edward carried Sam on his shoulders for the short walk back to their house. Anna held Thomas's hand.

'Can Luke come round after school soon?' he asked.

'Sure. I'll talk to Steve.'

Anna had chosen, and she didn't regret it. This life, this family life, it was what she wanted. She'd believed what she'd said to Steve, about it being okay that him and Theresa hadn't stayed together; she didn't think people should keep a marriage going for the children. But if you could, if you did, keep it going, then that was surely the best thing for everyone? Sometimes she wished Thomas and Luke weren't such good friends, though. Because it meant seeing Steve, and it was hard, when she saw him, to remember the decisions she'd made, the reasons behind them. It was hard not to think about the time he'd kissed her, the way that kiss had made her feel, the way it had felt as right as breathing, as straightforward. All those times, with him, that she had allowed herself to glimpse a different life, one that might be better.

But she wasn't looking for better. She had everything she needed, right here.

She squeezed Thomas's hand, listened to him talk about the story his teacher had told, about a fish that didn't look like all the other fish, didn't know where he fit in. And when they got home, and Edward opened the door, she stepped inside the warm house and told the boys to take off their shoes and took the baklava into the kitchen to put it in bowls, and she felt safe. Whole.

15

NO

'Want another?' Sarah asked, holding up her empty glass.

Anna nodded, and they both looked around for a waiter. At least every couple of weeks, they went out for cocktails straight from work. It was quieter than at the weekend, and it felt decadent. Sometimes they went for dinner afterwards, sometimes they saw a film, sometimes they just went home.

Sarah caught someone's eye and asked for another round, and meanwhile Anna's phone beeped, and she stole a quick look at the message before putting her phone back on the table.

'Who's that?'

'My mum.'

Sarah tilted her head slightly to the side. 'Do you need to call her?'

'No, she's just checking in. We're not... close.'

'How come?'

Anna loved that Sarah just asked the questions, never shying away from topics that were difficult or holding back with her thoughts or advice.

'We just never were. It was just me and her, when I was growing up, and we just sort of lived together but separately, once I was old enough to have a bit of independence. We both like our own company, and we just didn't do any of the typical mum and daughter things. Shopping trips, going for lunch, any of that. I don't really know why. And then I moved out to go to university and now we just see each other a few times a year – less now I'm out here – and I think we're both fine with that.'

Sarah was twisting one of her curls around a finger. 'That's kind of sad.'

'I know, it is. But it just doesn't feel it, somehow. I guess because I don't know any different.'

A few months before, on another night out like this one, Anna had leaned across a different sticky table and kissed Sarah, startling herself as much as anyone. And since that night, they'd settled into something. Not a relationship, not a partnership. Sometimes they kissed, sometimes they slept together. Sometimes they didn't. It was easy, fun. They'd never put a label on it, never talked about it being exclusive. Anna hadn't been on other dates because she hadn't really wanted to, but she knew that Sarah did sometimes. It was kind of confusing, Anna was finding, when you were friends first. When you asked the kind of questions that friends asked, did the kind of things friends did. When you were never sure whether Tuesday evening cocktails were going to lead to something or nothing.

Sarah was quiet.

'What?' Anna asked.

'Nothing. I just like trying to figure you out.'

Anna took a long sip of her drink, felt the sharpness of the cranberry mixed with the sweetness of the orange and the kick of the alcohol. Vodka? Gin? This was only their second and yet Anna already felt looser, warmer.

'So,' Sarah said, 'barely any family. Although Nia's sort of like family to you, isn't she?'

Anna nodded.

'And an ex-husband who wanted children. You didn't.'

Anna nodded again.

'Are you dating anyone?' Sarah asked. 'I mean, other than me? I can't work out what you want.'

There was no trace of jealousy in her voice. Anna believed that she was genuinely just curious. It was one of the things she liked about Sarah, how interested she was in people and what drove them.

'I'm looking for something,' she said after a pause. 'I used to talk to Nia about it, when we were younger, about how I didn't know what it was or what it looked like. I know I haven't found it yet. It's not about marriage or kids, I don't think. It's a feeling. I didn't have it with Edward. I haven't had it with anyone I've dated over here.'

Sarah looked thoughtful. 'Have you ever had it with anyone?'

Anna thought about James. Jamie. Could she tell Sarah? It would feel like a betrayal of Nia, in two senses. Because Nia was the one she usually told everything to, and because Jamie was her boyfriend.

'It's going to sound weird, but I had this date once, years ago. And I thought I felt it then. But I never saw him again.'

Sarah's eyes widened. 'What do you mean you never saw him again? Why not?'

Anna shrugged. 'He didn't call. I didn't have his number.'

'We should track him down!'

'Please don't tell me you're one of those Americans who think we all know each other in tiny old England.'

Sarah threw back her head and laughed, and Anna had a sudden urge to kiss her throat. She could put a stop to all this, suggest they go back to her place. She had to put a stop to it, because she wasn't planning to tell Sarah the bit about running into him again, in her best friend's flat. And if she wasn't careful, Sarah would be going online to try to find him.

'It's stupid,' Anna said. 'It just felt different to anything else. But I'm not about to go looking for him. It was about fifteen years ago. He could be living any kind of life.'

'Any kind of unfulfilled life! Not realising you're the one he needs to feel complete!'

'Sarah, leave it,' Anna said, a little sharply.

Sarah shrugged. She was good like that. When she was asked to leave something, she left it.

'What are your plans for the rest of the evening?' she asked.

Anna didn't have any. 'Do you fancy dinner?'

Sarah shook her head, her curls flying. 'Sorry, can't tonight. I've signed up for this yoga class at six in the morning and I know if we have dinner I'll have a late one and skip it.'

'Okay. Do you know any good Greek places? I used to go to one back in London and I've been having cravings for this spinach chicken thing I used to eat there.'

'Cravings for baklava, more like. Let me think. Greek. There's a good one in Tribeca, on Washington. And one on East Twelfth Street that I've heard is good, but I haven't been there. Are you going to go alone?'

'Yes.'

In London, Anna would never have gone out to eat alone, but in New York, she did it often. It came from necessity, she supposed. When she'd first moved here, she hadn't known anyone, and she'd wanted to try out some of the amazing restaurants more than she'd cared about being seen eating alone. And now it had become a habit. She wondered whether she'd do it in London when she moved back, now it didn't faze her.

They got up, walked to the door. The street was busy and Sarah pulled Anna around a corner onto a quieter road. She kissed her, the kind of kiss that made Anna want to beg her to change her mind about spending the evening together.

'I hope you find your spinach chicken dream,' she whispered in Anna's ear, and Anna laughed. 'See you tomorrow,' Sarah said, and walked away.

Anna was close enough to Tribeca to walk there, so she did, dodging the people walking towards her in big groups. She loved walking in New York, loved the way the tall buildings made it feel enclosed somehow, loved the way there were always people around, no matter what time of day or night it was. She didn't know exactly where in Tribeca Washington Street was, so she just wandered around, adding the street names she passed to her internal map. Manhattan was small enough to be manageable, to know. She was determined to know as much of it as possible in her time here. She imagined coming back, years in the future, possibly with a friend or lover, and being able to take them by the hand and say 'I know this great place to eat around this corner' or 'you have to see the view from over here.'

Anna found the restaurant before she saw that she was on the right street, and soon she was inside at a small, round table, drinking water. She glanced through the menu and saw that there was something very similar to the dish she'd been thinking about, and she was so excited to eat it after so long that she starting scanning for a waiter, trying to make eye contact so she could place her order. She'd been thinking a lot about London recently, which was probably what had brought on this yearning for a particular Greek dish she'd often eaten. The job in New York seemed to be open-ended. There'd been no talk of it ending, but something in her was starting to miss home. She'd only ever intended for this to be an adventure, not her life. There was no rush, and she could easily imagine herself staying for another few years, but she felt quite sure that she would settle back in London eventually. And it was nice, that knowing. It was comforting. Like being out at night, having fun, but knowing you have a home to go back to.

* * *

'Can I get you anything else?' the waiter asked, reaching for her plate.

'Do you have baklava?' she asked.

'Of course.'

'I'll have that, please. Could I take it with me?'

'I'll put it in a box for you.'

'Great, thanks. The bill too then, please.'

Ten minutes later, just as the sun was starting to go down, Anna was out on the street, a box of sticky dessert in her hand, heading for home. She passed a film crew, a cordoned off street, and scanned the faces for anyone she recognised. The first time this had happened, she'd stopped and watched for an hour or more, fascinated. But she'd soon learned it was something you got used to in this city. Waiting in the subway station, she saw a rat darting across the platform and shuddered, picturing the tiny mice she'd sometimes glimpsed on the tracks of the Underground in London. And then she spotted her boss, David. He was alone, hands clasped behind his back, one foot tapping the floor. He must have felt her eyes on him because he looked up then, and put up a hand in a small wave. Anna wasn't sure what to do. Should she go over? Would he come to her? Would they both stay where they were and carry on as if they hadn't seen one another? Before she could make a decision, it was taken out of her hands. He was walking over.

'Hey,' he said. 'Having a good evening?'

It was awkward, almost embarrassing, a little like seeing a teacher out of school as a child. She wasn't really sure why. Perhaps because she had never seen him out of the context of the office, had never socialised with him or run into him in a park or in a shop. She realised that he hadn't really existed, for her, outside that space they both worked in. He was a caricature, almost. The absurdly handsome manager. God, those lips.

Anna said something about drinks and dinner, wondered briefly whether he knew that she and Sarah were... whatever they were.

'You?' she asked.

'Nothing special,' he said.

She realised that he was drunk and wasn't sure why she hadn't noticed it before. Was it just because she'd been so thrown by seeing him at all? He was unsteady on his feet, rocking back and forth.

'Listen, Anna, do you want to get a drink?'

16

YES

Thursday 5 June 2008

Anna remembered it was their anniversary the moment she woke up. She had a card, written and waiting in her bedside drawer. They'd stopped giving each other presents at some point. She couldn't quite remember when. They still did birthdays and Christmases but they'd stopped buying presents for their anniversary and Valentine's. She didn't mind. She liked to mark the day with a card, though, because she thought it was important to look back over the years and assess. They'd been married for nine years, together for about thirteen. It was something, she felt. It meant something.

She went into the bathroom for a shower before Edward was awake, and when she emerged, the boys were fighting in her bed and Edward was shouting at them to go and get dressed.

'Morning,' she said, and Edward looked over at her, and she tried to guess whether he'd remembered or not.

'Mummy,' Sam said.

'Yes, baby?'

'You look beautiful.'

Anna laughed. She was wrapped in a towel, her hair dripping onto her shoulders, unbrushed. 'Thank you, my angel,' she said, leaning over the bed and kissing him on the top of his head.

'Happy anniversary,' Edward said, just as she'd started to believe he wouldn't.

When she turned her attention to him, he was holding out a thick white envelope. The card inside was simple, elegant. Two hearts, a plain white background. Inside, he'd written:

Thank you for everything, Anna. For loving me, for our boys, for our lives together. There's nothing else I want.

She felt close to tears, and he saw that when she looked at him and mouthed a thank you, and he got out of bed and put his arms around her, his warm body against her damp, towel-covered one. How long had it been since they'd held one another like this? There never seemed to be time, to just be still, and to comfort each other with their bodies. Anna resolved to start going to bed earlier, to start making more of an effort. There was always so much to be done, swimming badges to be sewn onto uniforms, shopping lists to be made, clean clothes to be folded and put away. But this, this closeness, it was important too.

Half an hour later, they were all dressed and Edward had gone, saying he would pick up breakfast on his way into the office. Anna and the boys were sitting at the table, eating Rice Krispies.

'When is it too?' Sam asked.

Anna looked at him. So often, he had questions she didn't understand. 'What do you mean?'

'I know when it's Monday and Tuesday but when is it too?'

Anna was at a loss. She looked at Thomas. Sometimes he understood his brother in a way that she couldn't. He shrugged his shoulders, and Anna could see that he was close to laughing.

If he laughed, Sam would cry. Anna knew this from bitter experience. He needed to feel taken seriously, listened to.

'Can you try to explain it a bit more?' Anna asked.

Sam burst into song. 'Monday, Tuesday, Wednesday, Thursday, Friday, Saturday, Sunday too.' He paused. 'We sing it at nursery. Is there a day called too?'

Anna smiled but didn't allow herself to laugh, but Thomas erupted into fits of giggles and Sam frowned at him, looked almost ready to tip over into tears of frustration.

'No, baby,' Anna said, tapping him on the nose. He had a Rice Krispie stuck to his cheek and she had no idea how he'd managed it, how he always managed it. There was milk spilled on his place mat. On Thomas's too. 'Too means as well. Like, I might say we were all going on a walk, me, you, Thomas and Daddy too.'

'Oh!' Sam looked delighted with his new nugget of knowledge. 'Daddy too!'

Anna knew he would use this word endlessly now. She glanced at her watch. They needed to leave in ten minutes.

'Can I take something in for show and tell?' Thomas asked, breaking into her thoughts.

'Yes, what do you want to take?'

'That dinosaur we made out of a milk bottle.'

Anna wanted to protest – she was terrible at craft and she was embarrassed for anyone to see the mess they'd made, but then she realised it was ridiculous. Thomas had loved making it, and he wanted to show it to his friends. Who was she to stand in his way just because she thought it looked more like a camel with a broken neck than a stegosaurus?

'Of course,' she said.

'And can I take something?' Sam asked.

'You're not going to nursery today,' Anna said. 'It's a mummy day.'

She waited for Thomas to protest that it wasn't fair, that he didn't get a day at home with her. She always explained, as patiently as she could, that he'd had his time with her before school, and now it was Sam's turn, but Thomas didn't say anything. Perhaps he was growing up. Perhaps he was beginning to understand things, to accept them. Or perhaps a day at home with her didn't have the same appeal as it once had. He picked up his bowl and put it down by the dishwasher without her having to ask. One day, she realised, they would both do this. One day not so far in the future, she wouldn't have to remind them to do things like brush their teeth and put their shoes on. She had longed for these things, but somehow, there was a sadness to realising they were getting there. That Thomas had less need of her.

When they'd dropped Thomas off at school, the dinosaur handed over to the teacher in a carrier bag, Anna took hold of Sam's hand. She could see Steve out of the corner of her eye, and she wanted him to call out to her, and she didn't, too. Sometimes, they chatted for a bit before going off in different directions. She didn't like to admit how much of a difference it made to her, the days they did that. She walked slowly, one hand in Sam's, hoping Steve would appear at her side.

'Do you want to go to playgroup?' she asked Sam.

Sam shrugged. 'Not really.'

He could be an easy child, at times. A handful at others. She'd heard friends say that second children just slotted in, which was exactly what Sam had done, but she'd also heard they could be more naughty, more adventurous, more to handle. Which was also true.

'Hey, Anna.'

Anna turned to see Steve dodging through the crowd to get to her.

'Hi,' she said when he reached her. She bent down and picked Sam up, and then she wasn't sure why she'd done that.

'How are things?' Steve asked.

'Not bad,' Anna said. 'Sam and I were just trying to decide whether to go to playgroup.'

'Not playgroup,' Sam said, and Steve laughed.

'Well, sounds like that decision's been made, then,' Anna said.

'Listen,' Steve said. 'Do you have time for a coffee?'

This was new. Since that time in the coffee shop when he'd made his feelings clear, things had changed between them. They had the odd five-minute chat at the school gate, yes, but they didn't go for coffee. Not any more.

'Sure. Do you want to come back to mine? Sam can play, then.'

Steve nodded, his jaw set. And Anna slid Sam down off her hip and they fell into step for the familiar walk home.

* * *

Anna had no intention of telling Steve what had happened the previous week, but as they sat there on the sofa, Sam colouring on the floor, she found the words tumbling out.

'I had a... a miscarriage,' she said quietly.

'Shit,' he whispered. 'I had no idea you were... I mean, I thought you'd said you weren't going to have another one.'

'It's complicated,' she said, and then she felt like a teenager. 'Edward wants more, at least one more. I don't. And then, I don't know, I fell pregnant by accident, back in April.'

Steve was nodding, leaning in. Both of them were talking in low voices, but Sam wasn't listening. He was in his own world, scribbling and making patterns with coloured pencils, trying to do the things he'd seen his brother do.

'I'm so sorry,' Steve said, even though it was clear that the story was far from over.

'About what? The pregnancy, or the miscarriage?' Anna asked. She laughed, and then it turned into a sob, and she was crying hard, and Steve was putting his arms around her.

'All of it,' he whispered into her hair.

They didn't say anything for a few moments, and Anna eventually stood and went through to the bathroom to sort herself out. When she returned, Steve was sitting a little closer to Sam, asking him questions about his picture. He looked up and gave Anna a smile that was easy to read, despite the message being complicated. The smile meant 'I'm sorry you're upset, and I wish I could comfort you, but I don't know quite where I stand'.

'Does anyone else know?' he asked, once she'd sat down again.

'Just Nia.'

'And are you talking to her much?'

'Yes, almost daily.'

'Good. I'm glad you have someone. And what about Edward?'

'He's just so disappointed. And I feel like we can't connect properly because he knows it wasn't really what I wanted. But we'll be okay. We'll get through it.'

She looked at Steve and he looked back at her, his eyes clear. She thought for a moment that he was going to lean in and kiss her, and she knew she would have to stop it, if he did. She knew, too, that it would be hard.

'Anyway,' she said. 'Was there something you wanted to talk about?'

Steve looked a little pained. 'I just wanted to let you know that we've decided to move Luke to a different school after the summer holidays.'

Anna wasn't expecting that. A different school. No more meetings at the gate. Would she run into him at all?

'Why?'

'Theresa's moving to Tooting. We couldn't afford the Clapham place any more and she's found somewhere she likes, but with both of us there, it just makes sense for him to go to a school nearby.'

Anna nodded. It did make sense.

'So...' Steve trailed off, and Anna wondered whether he hadn't been able to say what he wanted to, or whether he hadn't known what to say at all.

'All change,' Anna said.

There was a beat of silence before Steve spoke again.

'Do you ever wish that we'd met before?' he asked.

Anna took a deep breath. She looked at Sam's whorl of hair, at his scribbling fingers.

'I know, I know,' Steve said, before she could speak. 'It's impossible. We wouldn't have our boys. And you're still in your marriage. I shouldn't have asked; it isn't fair.'

Sam looked up, then. 'Mummy, can I have a drink?'

Anna went through to the kitchen to get a cup of squash, flicked the kettle on to make tea for her and Steve, and thought about what he'd said. There was something between her and

Steve that she'd never have with Edward. She'd come to accept that. He seemed to understand her in a way that Edward didn't, knew what she needed and when. If she let herself think about it, she imagined that would translate into a very good relationship. And if she'd met him first, like he'd said, things could be very different. But she hadn't. She'd met Edward, and he might not be perfect for her, but he was a good man. Suddenly, she hoped Steve wouldn't stay too much longer. She felt like she was on dangerous ground. She took the drinks through and tried to change the subject to something less loaded.

'How are things with Theresa?' She passed him a mug of tea, put Sam's squash on the coffee table.

Steve pulled a pained face. 'I mean, they're probably as good as they can be. We don't dislike each other. And we're united when it comes to Luke. You hear about people fighting over their kids but it just makes sense to us that we both want to be with him and we need to keep communicating to get it right.'

'So no animosity?' Anna asked. It hadn't been like that with Edward, when they'd had that time apart and it had seemed, for a while, like it might be over. It had been wall-to-wall animosity, until Edward realised that he was never going to win her back like that.

'Not really. She's met someone else, and he seems like a nice guy. He seems like a better fit for her than I was.'

'Is there no jealousy?' Anna was surprised. Even if you knew the relationship was dead, she felt sure it would be strange to see the person you'd married and had a child with start up with someone else, especially if you were still single.

'I mean, it's strange, don't get me wrong. Luke keeps asking when I'm going to move back in and why Mummy's friend is around all the time. And I wish we could have held it together, for him. I mean, we could have done. But neither of us was happy, and I think he would have started to sense that. But no jealousy, no. If he makes her happy, that's all right with me.'

Steve stood up and took the mugs back to the kitchen. She liked that he did little things like that, in her home.

'Thank you for trusting me enough to tell me, about the miscarriage,' he said. 'If you ever want to talk about it...'

'Thank you,' she said. Had it been a betrayal of Edward, talking to him about this? When she'd brought it up, it had felt as if she couldn't keep it in. But now, she thought perhaps she shouldn't have.

'I should go,' he said.

Anna nodded, relieved.

'Feel whatever you need to,' he said. 'Grief, rage, relief, it's all okay. It's all part of the process. Keep talking to Nia. And me, if you want to. I'd like to be there for you.'

Anna felt a single tear track down her cheek, because she knew he meant what he said, and she also knew she'd never take him up on it. Steve brushed the tear away with his thumb. And that touch, it was exactly what she needed.

'Will you be okay?' he asked.

'Yes.' She believed that. She would be okay, in time. 'Thank you,' she said again.

Steve shook his head. He bent down to ruffle Sam's hair. 'See you soon, Sam.'

Sam barely looked up. He was in the world of his drawings, which looked like scribbles to Anna, but which she knew from previous conversations contained monsters and castles and dragons.

In the hallway, Anna opened the door and saw that it was raining lightly.

'Do you have an umbrella?' she asked.

'No. But I'll be fine.'

She thought of a thing Edward always said when she asked if he had an umbrella. He always said he'd rather get wet and be able to see the sky. And maybe that was what it all came down to. Compromise. Having one thing but losing another.

'Bye, Steve,' she said.

And he kissed her cheek and was gone. It felt like an ending.

17

NO

Thursday 5 June 2008

At five o'clock on the dot, Sarah came and stood over Anna at her desk.

'Time to go,' she said in a sing-song voice.

Anna had been messing about with a spreadsheet for an hour; she gladly closed it down. She looked up at Sarah and grinned. 'Road trip!'

'Have a good time, you two.'

Anna looked up and saw David standing a few feet away from her desk. It was hard to read his tone. He knew about the trip, had approved the time off for both of them, and the previous night, he'd asked Anna not to go. Asked her to spend the time with him, instead. Wasn't this what she wanted? Days on end spent together like a proper couple? But no, not quite. Their relationship – whatever it was – was still a secret and that always made her feel slightly grubby. Still, she'd been tempted to cancel. David was like a drug to her. But this was Sarah, one of the most important people in her life, and Anna knew she'd feel like shit if she lied to her and let her down. She was pretty sure Sarah would be in her life long after David had left it. She looked him in the eye, gave him a stiff smile and turned back to Sarah.

They'd been planning this break for weeks. They were going straight from the office to a car-hire place and then driving to Boston, because Sarah couldn't believe Anna had never been there when it was only three hours from New York. They'd taken a couple of days off so they could make it a proper trip. Anna was excited. She'd explored New York pretty thoroughly in her time there but hadn't made many trips to other places in the States. When she thought of Boston, she thought about the Cheers bar and the marathon, but Sarah had told her they were going to go to Chinatown for food, laze in the parks with their books and walk The Freedom Trail for a bit of history. Anna was more than happy to let her lead. Anna was the designated driver, because she missed it, and Sarah was the tour guide.

An hour later, they were on their way. Anna welcomed the sense of freedom she always felt when she got behind the wheel. She'd started out slow but was gradually gaining the confidence to go a little bit faster.

'How long since you were in Boston?' she asked.

'Years,' Sarah said. 'We used to go there when I was a kid, sometimes. And I've been with girlfriends but not for a long time.'

Sarah reached across and put her hand on Anna's thigh, and Anna tensed involuntarily. She didn't know how to say it to Sarah, who she so enjoyed spending time with, but she wanted them to go back to just being friends. At least, she thought they should go back to that, because of her feelings for David. She loved him, and although she was sure he wasn't faithful to her, she felt uncomfortable sleeping with anyone else.

'You okay?' Sarah asked.

Anna nodded.

'What are you thinking about?' Sarah asked.

'The future,' Anna said. It was true. She worried about the future in a way Sarah never seemed to.

'In terms of...'

'I don't know, everything. You and me. Love. Where I'll end up living. Babies.'

'Babies? I thought you'd decided babies were off the table.'

Anna sighed. She had decided that, hadn't she? And yet, sometimes she saw a woman with a baby strapped to her front and felt a pang and couldn't settle to anything all day. Was that just biology? Or societal expectation?

'I think I have. I'm just, sometimes, not sure. Have you always known?'

'What, that I don't want to have kids? I think so. Actually no, that's not quite true. When I was about twenty-five, I was broody as hell for about a year. I was single at the time, and I even started looking into adoption and sperm donation, and then I met someone and it just sort of... went away. I always assumed it was biological.'

'Maybe,' Anna said.

'As for the rest, I'm not sure it's love, for us. I'm not sure it's ever heading that way.'

Anna nodded. She did love Sarah, but she wasn't in love with her. 'I know that,' she said. 'Don't worry, I know that. I just get so confused sometimes, and feel like I'm treading water.'

'I know, you're still looking for it, that thing, that feeling.'

The truth was, Anna thought she'd found it. When she was

with David, she felt happier and more secure than she ever had. But it was all still a secret, and she knew the power dynamic made it complicated, and she felt like a fool.

'Let's talk about something else,' Anna said.

'Okay, how's your friend Nia doing?'

Anna changed lanes and looked at a sign as they passed it. She was stalling, trying to gather her thoughts. She and Nia weren't as close as they'd once been. It was inevitable, she supposed, with the physical distance between them, but the gap had definitely been widened by Nia's journey into motherhood.

'I think she's okay. We Skype and email. She tells me funny things Cara has done, sends me photos. She doesn't talk much about herself, about how she feels about things.'

'I guess there just isn't as much time to reflect on that, once you're a mom.'

'Yes.'

They were silent for a little while, and then they were getting into Boston and Sarah was directing Anna to the hotel she'd booked for them. It was a nice place, compact and family run. They had a small room on the third floor, and the décor was a little tired but there was a vase of fresh flowers on the windowsill, and that made Anna smile. She was exhausted, she realised, after a day at work and the long drive.

'Shall we order room service?' Sarah asked. 'The guy at the desk said they could do sandwiches.'

'I love room service!'

When they were eating, and Sarah was telling a story that made her snort with laughter, Anna felt less tense. Sarah leaned across the bed and kissed her, and Anna opened her mouth and closed her eyes. When David came into her mind, she pushed him into a corner. This was where she was, she told herself. This was what she had.

* * *

They woke to a clear, bright sky and wandered around for hours. Anna liked to get to know a place by getting lost in it, so Sarah let her lead them, and they discovered corners of the small city that Sarah had never seen before. When they were eating lunch, greasy burgers in the small garden of a restaurant, Anna asked a question that often came up for her.

'Do you ever wish we hadn't done this? That I hadn't kissed you that day and we'd just stayed friends?'

Sarah's expression didn't change. 'No. Why, do you?'

'No, I don't think so. But I worry that I will.'

'What do you mean?'

'Well, you're my best friend over here, and I thought we'd always stay in touch, even if I go back to London, but now it's more complicated than that, isn't it? When we decide to put a stop to this, do you think we'll be able to be friends?'

Sarah appeared to think this over. 'I think so. I hope so. The way I see it, this works while it makes both of us happy. If it stops making you happy, just tell me. And I'll do the same.'

'Would it bother you, if I was seeing someone else?' Anna asked.

'No,' Sarah replied without a pause. 'You know it wouldn't. Are you?'

Anna wanted to tell her. She wanted to say that sometimes when she stayed late at work, she and David were waiting for everyone to leave so they could have sex in his office with the door locked. She wanted to say that what had started out with hotels she could never afford to stay in had taken its inevitable tumble and landed with hasty kisses in the lift that left her wanting. She wanted to say that she had got into something that had promised to be fun and light and had ended up being terrifying.

That she loved David in a way she'd never loved anyone, and she wasn't sure he loved her at all.

'No,' she said instead. 'There's this guy I met, he asked me out. That's all.'

'Do you want to tell me about him?'

'No.'

There was a pause, and when Sarah spoke again she said something Anna would never have expected.

'Why do I feel like you're going to tell me you're moving home?'

In her saddest moments, when David had left her feeling abandoned and worthless, Anna thought about going back to London. Pretending it had never happened. Letting herself heal in a city that was too far away for him to persuade her to change her mind.

'I don't know,' she said. 'I don't have any plans to leave at the moment.'

Sarah smiled, but looked like she wasn't quite convinced. 'Let's get the check.'

Anna stood up to leave, and then she heard someone call her name, and when she turned, she saw James. Jamie. Nia's boyfriend, Jamie.

'Hey,' he called, moving between tables to reach her. 'What are the chances? I told Nia she should tell you I was coming to the States, but she said you never leave New York.'

Anna was confused. It was like being in a dream, where you see someone in a place where they shouldn't be. Jamie, with his London accent, in a restaurant in the middle of Boston, on her first ever trip there. She realised she hadn't said anything, and that Sarah was looking at her a little strangely, waiting for her to introduce them.

'God, sorry,' she said, coming back to life. 'What are you doing here?'

'I'm here for work.'

Sarah cleared her throat and Anna realised she'd been standing there, too shocked to speak, for a long moment. She gathered herself.

'This is my friend, Sarah. Sarah, this is Nia's boyfriend, Jamie.'

Jamie grinned. 'Hi, Sarah.'

'So, work trip,' Anna said.

'Yes, just having lunch with clients. I'd better get back to them, actually. But do you fancy grabbing dinner later?' He pulled a business card from his pocket and handed it to her. 'No problem if you want it to be just girls. Just text me and let me know, okay? I know Nia would love it if I came home with all your news.'

And then he was gone, and Anna and Sarah were making their way out into the bright sunshine, and Sarah was giving Anna a funny look.

'That was weird, right?' Anna asked.

'So weird.' There was something in Sarah's voice that Anna hadn't heard before. Something sharp and jagged. It was something Anna didn't want to look too closely into.

Sarah pulled a map from her bag and began to direct them. They were heading for the Freedom Trail. Other than discussing their route, they didn't talk. It was over an hour before Sarah brought Jamie up again.

'So this Jamie, how well do you know him? I mean, he's your best friend's guy, right, but didn't they get together after you moved out here?'

'Yes,' Anna said. 'I've only met him properly twice, on visits home. First when Cara was born, and then last Christmas. But I stayed with them both of those times, so when I say I've only met him twice, it's kind of more than that.'

'There's something between you,' Sarah said.

It was a statement, not a question. Anna stopped walking. She felt a flush spreading up from her neck. And she was angry, too. 'What the hell do you mean?'

Sarah had stopped walking too. 'I don't mean anything has happened. But there's something. It's like electricity.'

Anna felt like turning around and disappearing into a crowd. Like hiding away.

'Nothing's happened,' she said instead. 'Of course nothing's happened. What kind of person do you think I am?'

Sarah reached out and put her hands at the top of Anna's arms, which were folded across her chest. 'I didn't mean you'd done anything wrong, or that you ever would. I know what kind of friend you are. I just felt it, between you.'

Anna thought about what Sarah was saying. For all those years, she'd thought about James, hoped to see him again. And when she had, when she'd realised that he was Nia's, she'd had to make a big adjustment. But she thought she'd done okay. So what was this that Sarah could sense between them? Another thought crept in. Perhaps, if there was anything real between her and David, Sarah would have been able to sense that too.

'Do you remember me telling you about that date I went on with that guy, years ago?'

'The one who never called?'

'Yes.'

Anna waited for Sarah to put the pieces together, knowing she would.

'That was him?' Sarah asked. 'And by the time you realised, him and Nia had a baby together?'

Anna nodded.

'God, Anna, why didn't you say something? Are you okay?'

They were standing near a bench, and Sarah gestured for Anna to sit down. She sat heavily, relieved that this piece of information was finally out in the open. That one other person knew. It had been heavy to carry alone.

'I'm fine,' she said, in the end. 'I just, I put too much expectation on it. It was just a date. And years have passed and he's with Nia, and that's that.'

'I get it,' Sarah said, 'but that's a hard thing to deal with.'

Again, Anna wanted to tell Sarah everything about David. To let it out and ease some of the tension she felt in her body. But she could only deal with one thing at a time.

'I have to go for dinner with him,' Anna said. 'I'd hate for him to go home and tell Nia he ran into me and then I blanked him.'

'Do you want me to come with you?' Sarah asked.

'No, I need to do it on my own. Is that okay?'

'Of course,' Sarah said. She put an arm around Anna and pulled her closer, and they sat there like that for a few minutes, Sarah's chin resting on Anna's head.

* * *

A few hours later, Anna was sitting across from Jamie with an untouched rice dish in front of her. She couldn't help but compare it to the last time they'd eaten together, all those years before. Jamie had had pizza, she remembered. She'd had salmon.

'Look,' Jamie said, after they'd caught up on all the basics. 'This is weird, but I feel like I have to bring it up and I'm never going to get a better chance.'

Anna felt her stomach twist.

'After your last visit, Nia talked about you, about this thing you have going on with Sarah, about your ex-husband. And she talked about this guy you went out with once, how you always hold him up as the one you should be with. And it seemed like...'

'It's stupid,' Anna said, feeling her cheeks burn.

'No, it's not stupid,' Jamie said. 'I just, I didn't realise I meant something to you, not like that. I didn't know it was something you'd held on to. And of course, Nia doesn't know. So she was talking about how we should launch some big campaign to find this guy. She wanted to get that friend she has in radio involved...'

Anna burst out laughing. What else could she do? Jamie laughed too then, and it took some of the embarrassment away.

'What did you tell her?' Anna asked.

'I said that maybe we should leave your love life to you. She was in a mood about it for days.'

'I'm not in love with you,' Anna said.

It was true. She had been, once. Or at least, she'd been in love with the idea of him. But now there was David, and he was real and solid and when he touched her, she felt entirely alive, and also like she might die.

'I know,' Jamie said, and there was a genuine kindness in his voice. 'I know you're not, Anna. But I just wanted to apologise, again, for not calling, for being twenty-two and a bit of a shit.'

'You said you lost my number!'

Jamie reddened slightly. 'I did, I did lose your number. But even if I hadn't, and I'd called, I would have ended up being a shit at some point. We were so young.'

It was the first time he'd suggested the idea of anything more happening between them, and it made Anna a little uncomfortable.

'It's all right,' she said. 'Look, you're with Nia, and she's happy, and you have Cara. I'm so pleased about all of that. Honestly, you don't need to apologise.'

'Well, I think I did. But thanks for being so good about it.' He pushed his plate to one side, finished. 'Now, I hear you like dessert?'

18

YES

Friday 5 June 2009

'I think I'll hear today, about the job,' Anna said.

Edward looked up from his toast. 'Let me know,' he said.

Ellie, who'd started as a publicist alongside Anna almost a decade ago, had moved to another publisher, and Anna had applied for her role. It was a bit of a stretch, given that Ellie had been promoted a couple of times while Anna had stayed where she was, but she knew she could do it. Both boys were at school now, and she felt like it was time to give her career a much-needed boost.

Anna was distracted as she walked Thomas and Sam to school for breakfast club; she was distracted as she caught the Tube to the office – she couldn't settle to the paperback in her bag or the *Metro*. When she'd booted up her computer and got herself a coffee, she sat down at her desk and settled in for a long day of waiting. But as it turned out, she didn't have to wait at all. Deborah walked past her desk and asked her to come in at exactly five past nine, and Anna followed her, hoping this was going to be a day that she'd look back on, as one on which her life had changed for the better.

Deborah ushered Anna into a small meeting room, the same room where the interview had been held. She waited for Anna to sit down, and then she started to speak.

'Thanks, Anna. I'm always keen to promote from within, so I've thought about this appointment long and hard. But I'm sorry to say that, on this occasion, we've gone with someone from outside the company.'

Anna felt as if she'd been punched. The interview had gone well, she'd thought, with none of those moments you look back on later and feel annoyed about. And she could do the job, she knew she could. All she needed was to be given a chance.

'We really appreciate your role in the team,' Deborah was saying, 'and we hope you'll be with us for many years...'

'Is it because I'm older?' Anna asked.

Deborah looked taken aback. It was as if she'd had this speech planned, and hadn't anticipated any interruptions.

'I can assure you, age doesn't come into it,' she stammered.

'Or because I have children?' Anna pressed.

Deborah didn't have children. She was in her fifties and single. She liked to say that she was married to her job. The publicists she hired never had children either. Like Anna hadn't, when Deborah had hired her.

'Absolutely not,' Deborah said firmly. 'Look, I know this is a disappointment and I'm sorry to be the bearer of bad news, but I won't stand for accusations like that.'

'How old is the person you're hiring?' Anna asked. She knew she should stop, should say thank you and walk out meekly and get back to the job she still had, but something was pushing her onwards, making her ask the questions that she would normally keep inside.

'I don't see why that is relevant,' Deborah asked.

'I'm going to leave,' Anna said, standing.

'Good idea, why don't you take the day?'

'No, I don't think you understand. I'm going to leave. I resign. I'll write a proper letter and serve my notice but I'm done here.'

She left the room before Deborah could say anything else. She gathered up her things and walked out of the building before she could change her mind.

She felt furious and sad about the job, but it was all mixed with an odd sense of freedom. She was in the middle of London, without Edward, without the kids, without work. And it was barely half nine. She could go anywhere, couldn't she? She could pretend to be anyone. She could pretend she wasn't a mum in her late thirties with no job. She sent a message to Nia.

> Can we please have lunch? Any time that suits.

She didn't have to wait long. She never did, with Nia.

> Sure. The Dog at one?

So now she had something to anchor her, and she'd be able to eat a greasy sausage sandwich and tell her best friend all about the unfairness of being passed over for the job, and they would imagine the person who'd been hired instead, a pretty blonde, twenty-three years old, with no commitments. But there were over three hours to fill before that. Anna headed for the National Portrait Gallery, which she'd passed hundreds of times, promising herself she would go one day, on her lunch break. The day had finally come.

As Anna walked around the gallery, seeing people standing back and taking in the art, as if they had all the time in the world, she felt a shift in herself. She was always rushing, always trying to be a better mum or a better worker or a better wife. Always balancing, juggling. She never had a moment to just be. So that was what she did for the next couple of hours. She just walked around that building, up and down stairs, looking at familiar and unfamiliar faces, really studying them.

By the time she went to meet Nia, she felt much more at ease. So it took her by surprise, at first, when Nia exploded in rage. And she'd only told her about not getting the job at that point. She'd said nothing about walking out.

'What the hell? You are perfect for that job and they should know that. All those years you've been sitting behind that desk, wasted.'

'Wasted?' Anna asked, starting to laugh.

'I don't mean wasted, like, drunk. Unless you've been keeping that very quiet. I mean you're wasted in that job. You can do so much more.'

Anna appreciated the fact that Nia was her loudest cheer-leader. But most of all, she felt tired. Had she done the wrong thing, storming out like that? Was she wasting her time trying to reach for something more? It was enough, wasn't it, to look after two children and keep a house going, all those things that needed to be remembered? Birthday presents and dentist appointments and the pile of washing that never went down. Wasn't it enough to do all of that and have a job, to bring some money in to help pay the mortgage? Did you have to be constantly stretching yourself at work, too? Did you have to always be living up to your full potential? Couldn't she just have a nap? Often, Anna noticed the gap that had existed between her and Nia since she'd had children, and just then, it yawned wider.

'It's just, it's like a kick,' Anna said. 'Like you say, I'm sure I can do that job, and they all rely on me so much but they don't think of me wanting to step up because of the kids. Sometimes I have to leave early or take a day off because they're ill and all that, and it's just easier for them to hire a bright young thing who won't care what they pay her and doesn't have any other commitments. It's just... annoying.'

'It's more than annoying,' Nia said. 'It's just plain wrong.'

'Well, then you might be happy to know that I've left.'

'Left?'

'Resigned, quit, walked out.'

A smile spread over Nia's face. 'Have you, really?'

'I really, really have.'

Anna hoped Nia wouldn't ask her what she was going to do next. And Nia didn't. Instead, she went to the bar and came back with two glasses of fizz.

'Champagne?' Anna asked.

'Well, cava. Kev doesn't get a lot of requests for champagne, especially at lunchtime.'

They lifted their glasses, chinked them together and drank.

'Do you know it's my tenth wedding anniversary today?' Anna asked. 'Does it feel like a decade to you?'

Nia shook her head. 'Wow, ten years. It's probably time for me to admit to you that I threw up in the bushes outside the reception venue.'

Anna laughed. 'I've always known that. The barman told me.'

'Wow, so we really haven't had any secrets from each other. So what are you doing to celebrate, you and Edward? Want me to look after the boys?'

Occasionally, Nia looked after the boys, and when Anna and Edward returned, they were always high on sugar and doing something borderline dangerous, like playing a game where you couldn't touch the floor and had to go from sofa to coffee table to armchair by any means possible. They loved Nia, because she never said no to them and she never had to deal with the consequences.

Anna shrugged. 'No plans,' she said. 'I don't even know whether he's remembered.'

'Well,' Nia said, raising her glass. 'Here's to you.'

After a beat of silence, she pulled a face.

'Did I tell you that Ellen and the boss are a thing now?'

'No!'

'Yes, after all those formal warnings and what have you. I try not to think about whether they incorporate office roleplay into their bedroom activities. I only found out a couple of weeks ago but I think it's been going on for a while.'

'Do they know that you know?'

'Yes, it's common knowledge now. Sometimes he gives her a bit of a grope when he passes her at the photocopier. And then he has a quick look around to see if anyone's noticed, and I bury my head in my keyboard and wish I was dead. Anyway, she's floating around the place now and I think I preferred it when she hated men and was furious all the time. The other day I came out of one of the toilet cubicles and she was there in front of the mirror, redoing her lipstick. I don't even want to think about why. And she turned to me and asked me if I'd noticed the colour in the sky that morning, the pink clouds. I didn't know what to say. You know what I'm like in the morning, I barely open my eyes before I've had three coffees. I just washed my hands a bit hastily and rushed out of there.'

'Love,' Anna said. 'Who'd have thought it? I'd have put money on you being the one most likely to meet someone in your office.'

'Well, that's just it, isn't it? You never can tell.'

When Nia went back to her office, Anna headed home. She let herself in and revelled in the quietness of the house. She had a long bath, reading a book that was nothing to do with work, and then she moisturised her body from head to toe. It was the kind of thing she never had time to do. When it was time for school to finish, she thought, briefly, that she could have cancelled after-school club and picked up the boys, but it was so rare for her to have a day to herself that she tried not to feel guilty about taking it. Soon enough, it was time to collect the boys and hear about their days and then Edward was home and all four of them were in the bathroom, chatting as the boys took it in turns to shower and clean their teeth.

'Reuben's tooth fell out in assembly,' Sam said.

Anna looked at him. 'That's exciting,' she said. 'Did he keep hold of it?'

Sam shrugged. Some days, he came home with endless stories and other days, this sort of minor detail was as much as she got out of him.

'Did you know that half the parents don't know what digraphs and trigraphs are and they're going to invite you all in to learn about them?' Thomas asked.

Edward and Anna shared a look. Hers said 'you're going to that' and his said 'no, you're going', and it made her laugh, the way they could have a conversation without words.

After stories and kisses, they left the boys to go to sleep.

'You go through to the living room and sit down,' Edward said. 'I'm doing dinner tonight.'

It felt nice, being cared for like that. She turned on the TV and watched something mindless about a family who were trying to lose weight. Sam came into the living room after about twenty minutes, sucking on his snuggly and holding his bear beneath his arm.

'I think there's something in my room,' he said sadly.

'What kind of something?' Anna asked, standing up.

'Something a bit scary.'

'It's probably sleep,' Anna said, steering him back up the stairs.

Sam looked up at her, puzzled. They were in the doorway to his bedroom. Anna could hear soft snores coming from Thomas's room, next door.

'At night, sleep comes into your room. It's dark and it's mostly invisible, and then when you're ready, it gobbles you up for the night. Didn't you know that?'

Sam shook his head, and Anna lifted him into her arms and kissed his forehead.

'Just let it come,' she said. 'If we fight it, that's when things get difficult. We need sleep to be able to play and go to school and do all the things we like to do the next day.'

She laid him down in his bed and he turned on his side and pulled the cover up to his chin.

'Night night, baby.'

When she reached the bottom of the stairs, Edward called out that dinner was ready, and she saw that he'd set the table and bought a nice bottle of wine and there was a small, square box next to her wine glass.

'What's this?' she asked.

He was serving up pasta into two bowls.

'Happy anniversary,' he said, handing one of them to her and leaning forward to kiss her lips.

'I thought you'd forgotten,' she said.

He pretended to be wounded and then laughed. 'Ten years,' he said, and they were both quiet as they sat down. Anna was thinking about what a length of time that was, and how they'd spent it, and she wondered whether Edward was doing the same. Whether he had regrets, or thought about a different kind of life.

Anna reached for the box and flipped it open. Inside, there was a ring. Not an eternity ring, to be worn with her engagement and wedding rings. It was a delicate band with a tiny knot that looked a little bit like a heart. She looked up and saw that Edward was watching her.

'I just saw it and thought you might like it,' he said, and there was something almost timid in his tone, and Anna thought how funny it was, that after more than a decade with someone, you could still see a side you didn't expect.

'I do,' she said. 'Thank you.' She slipped it onto the ring finger on her right hand and held her hand up to admire it. It was lovely. Elegant. Perhaps more the woman she'd like to be than the woman she was.

'I have to tell you something,' she said. 'I didn't get the job. And I walked out.'

Edward put a hand to his forehead. 'I forgot to ask, I'm sorry. Wait, you walked out?'

Was he annoyed? The money he earned was more than enough for them to live on. And hadn't he always wanted her to give up work?

'Yes. I'm just fed up of being relied on but not valued. I work hard for them and I'm good, and it's not enough.'

Edward smiled. 'Good for you.'

Anna was pleased that he didn't ask her whether she had a plan, what she was going to do next.

'I'll find something else,' she said.

'You don't have to,' he said. 'But if you want to, I know you will.'

He held up his glass then, and Anna picked up hers. 'Here's to the next ten years,' he said.

19

NO

Friday 5 June 2009

Anna made sure she was the last in the office, and hated herself for doing so. When Sarah asked if she fancied a drink, she shook her head and said she had something to finish off. She tidied up a couple of spreadsheets and replied to some emails that had been hanging around for days, knowing David would emerge from his office eventually. When he did, she didn't look up.

'Anna,' he said. 'I didn't realise you were still here. Don't you have a home to go to?'

It was a lame joke and she didn't laugh.

'Have you spoken to Deborah yet?' she asked.

David ran a finger along the gap between his lower lip and his chin, and Anna thought about the last time they'd kissed.

'Come into my office,' he said, jerking his head in that direction as if she might not know where his office was.

She followed him, saying nothing. Anna sat in a chair and he sat on his desk, facing her. Too close.

'I haven't spoken to Deborah yet because I wanted to be sure you were making the right decision. But if you're absolutely sure, I'll call her. I know she'll have you back in a heartbeat. Someone just went on maternity over there and...'

'Yes,' Anna said. 'Please. Call her. I want to know where I stand, whether I should give notice on my apartment.'

David nodded his head slowly. 'I'm sorry it's turned out like this, Anna,' he said.

She didn't know what to say to that. If she'd known, that night she'd seen him on the subway platform, that they'd end up here, would she have declined his offer of a drink? No, probably not. She thought it had probably been worth it, because their time together had made her feel alive in a way she'd never felt before. And now she was paying for it.

'I'm just not the settling down type, Anna.'

'Don't,' Anna said. 'Please. I can't hear it again.'

A few times, she'd let herself entertain the idea of them being properly together. Living together on the Upper East Side, taking walks in Central Park hand in hand, no longer having to hide. Had he ever meant the promises he'd made to her in dark rooms, his lips tickling her ear? Once, he'd said he wanted them to have children together, and Anna had known that she would do it. That she would do anything, to keep him. And then, just a few weeks later, it had all been over.

Anna wanted to curl up in a ball and lie in bed forever. But the next best thing was to go home. To give her life a reset, to set herself up in a place where there would never be the risk of turning up on his doorstep late at night, banging on the door and bawling. Where if he called and said he wanted her back, she wouldn't be able to go to him.

'We'll miss you,' David said.

He meant the team. He meant the office. He didn't mean him.

'I'll miss it here, too,' she said.

She lifted her chin and looked at him, and his face was full of apologies and she saw him, then, for what he was. A man who swore he loved you but never quite enough to tell the people in his life that you existed. A man who let you cry into his chest in his office after hours but didn't offer to make sure you got home okay, or message you to check that you had. Why hadn't she been able to see it before? She'd been blinded by hope, she supposed. She'd wanted to believe.

Back at her apartment, she called Nia.

'It's over with David,' she said.

Nia was quiet.

'Please don't say I told you so.'

'I wouldn't, Anna. I'm sorry.'

'And I'm coming home.'

'To London? For a holiday or for good?'

'For good.'

Nia let out a scream that made Anna laugh, and then she heard Cara in the background, muttering questions.

The line went a bit muffled, then Nia's voice came back, clear. 'No, baby, Mummy is fine. I didn't mean to scare you. I'm just happy. I'm getting my best friend back.'

Anna made another couple of calls after she finished talking to Nia. And within the hour, she was sitting at a sticky table in her favourite bar with Lee and Sarah.

'What exactly do you mean by leaving?' Lee asked, sucking on a tiny straw.

Anna had bought them cocktails to soften the blow.

'Going back to London,' Anna said. 'I don't know when yet, but I've asked David for a transfer.'

Sarah put a hand to her chest, near her heart, and made an

agonised face. 'You bitch,' she said. 'Just when I thought we really had you for good.'

Things were pretty good with Sarah. It had been a while since anything romantic or sexual had happened between them. It had just sort of fizzled out without either of them having to say anything, and they'd managed the transition from lovers back to friends better than she'd dared to hope. For the past few weeks, Sarah had been seeing a woman called Alex, and whenever she talked about her, her voice changed slightly and Anna knew she was falling in love.

'You'll be fine,' Anna said now. 'You have each other.'

What if that was my role, here, when it came to friendship? Anna thought. Befriending Lee and then Sarah so that they could go on to befriend each other. They got on like a house on fire, always had. And sometimes, when they saw one another without Anna there, she felt oddly jealous. She imagined herself back in London, in a flat somewhere south of the river, Skyping Sarah and seeing Lee in her apartment in the background. She imagined them waving and making sad faces and then going back to their lives.

'I mean, Sarah's okay,' Lee said, cutting into Anna's thoughts, 'but damn, we'll miss you.'

'Well, like I said, it could be months. These are not my leaving drinks. These are just my breaking the news drinks.'

'Can we have your leaving drinks here?' Sarah asked. 'Just the three of us? I don't really like anyone else.'

Lee laughed. 'Other people are overrated.'

Anna thought about all the leaving dos she'd been to, in chain restaurants and bars around the corner from the office. How the management would pay for the first round of drinks as long as you chose a cheap beer or the house wine. How someone would drink too much too early and start spilling secrets. How some young thing from sales and someone old enough to know better from legal would sneak out together hand in hand, thinking no one had noticed. How the person leaving would cry. She'd never really thought about the day it would be her.

After they'd drunk three cocktails and it was getting on for eleven, a small corner of the bar became a sort of makeshift dance floor, and Lee pulled Anna and Sarah onto it, holding their hands and shaking his slim hips. Anna felt free and light, and wondered whether her mind had been working away on this decision without her realising it. She closed her eyes and spun around, feeling a little dizzy, a little drunk.

'I have to go. I have a date,' Lee said.

'At half eleven?' Anna asked.

Lee shrugged. 'I mean sex, okay? I'm going to a man's apartment for sex.'

Anna hugged him, turned to Sarah. 'Shall we make a move?'

They left the bar together and Lee hurried off to somewhere uptown.

'Want to walk back to Brooklyn?' Sarah asked.

It was late, and Anna knew she would regret it in the morning, but it was a warm evening and she wasn't quite ready for the night to end. She took Sarah's arm and they headed in the direction of the Williamsburg Bridge. Sarah was quiet for a few minutes, and Anna wondered what she was thinking about, but she knew better than to ask. When Sarah was ready, she would say what she needed to. They'd walked almost ten blocks by the time Sarah spoke.

'I know about you and David, you know,' she said.

Anna hadn't expected that.

'How long have you known?'

'Oh, ages.'

'Does Lee know?'

'I doubt it. He once told me he thinks David's gay and doesn't know it yet.'

Anna laughed. 'Why did you never say anything?'

'Because you never told me. I was waiting for you to tell me.'

'I'm sorry, it was complicated. I loved him, and I thought for a while that he loved me, but then...'

Sarah stopped walking, rolled her eyes. 'He screwed you over. How unsurprising.'

Anna wished she was on a subway, then. She admired Sarah's directness, the way she never let anyone get away with anything, but she was so bruised, so broken. Couldn't Sarah sense that, and be gentle with her?

'Is he the reason you're leaving?' Sarah asked.

They were walking again, and Anna couldn't look across at Sarah. 'Maybe. I don't know. Sometimes it's just time to go home, you know?'

They'd reached the bridge. Anna thought about how her relationship with David had taken place solely in Manhattan. He'd never once come over to Brooklyn for her. He was one of those people for whom Manhattan was the whole of New York. He didn't like things to have edges, for anything to be messy or difficult.

'I thought he loved me,' she said. 'But he didn't. And I can't go into work and see him every day and pretend I'm okay with that. I need to remove myself, while I still have a bit of dignity.'

'I'll miss you,' Sarah said.

And when Anna looked at her, there were tears in Sarah's eyes. Anna reached for her hand and squeezed it. 'I'll miss you too.'

'Have you thought about what it's going to be like seeing Jamie all the time?' Sarah asked.

Anna hadn't thought about that. She'd been focused on getting away from David, on being closer to Nia, on enjoying the things about London that she'd missed. But since David, Jamie had faded. He was someone she could have imagined herself being with, who she *had* imagined herself being with, for all those years. But she wasn't going to yearn for him while he was making a life with her best friend.

'It'll be fine,' she said. 'The only bit of it that's hard is that we've lied to Nia.'

Sarah nodded. 'Yes, I see that. But you did it for good reasons. I think she would have done the same.'

They stepped off the bridge and Anna realised that they were close to the crossroads where she would go one way and Sarah would go another.

'You have a good heart, Anna,' Sarah said. 'Be careful with it.'

Anna intended to. No more falling for the wrong men, no more letting herself be pulled into things that weren't right for her. Perhaps, she thought, that thing people looked for, that forever love, perhaps it wasn't for everyone. She could still close her eyes and imagine the way she was striving to feel, the thing she'd tried to explain to Nia all those times. But perhaps there was another way to find it. Perhaps you could get there through having friends who you loved and who loved you, through doing a job you loved. Perhaps she'd been looking for it in all the wrong places.

'Well,' Sarah said.

They were at the end of Sarah's street. She pulled Anna close to her body and Anna let herself be held. Sarah's body was familiar, comfortable, warm. Once, she would have pulled on Sarah's hand and led her to her apartment, gone upstairs, removed her clothes. But she was happier with what they had now. It felt firmer, more solid.

'Thank you,' Anna said. 'You've been the very best of friends.'

'Can we fit in another road trip before you go?' Sarah asked.

'I hope so.'

Anna pulled away from the embrace, though it was hard. She gave Sarah a wave and walked the last couple of blocks to her apartment. She tried to take in the sights and sounds of the streets she'd come to know so well. But in her heart, she was already gone.

20

YES

Saturday 5 June 2010

While Anna was getting ready, Edward stomped around. She knew he didn't want to go to the party, although he hadn't said. Edward liked parties on his terms – the ones where he knew everyone and could move from group to group, feeling relaxed and comfortable. At Nia's party, he would only know her and Nia. While she straightened her hair and did her makeup, she watched him in the mirror. He had slate-grey trousers on, slim fitting, and a black shirt. Over the past few years, his hair had turned from jet black to salt and pepper, and she liked it. He looked distinguished, handsome.

The door opened and Sam came in. 'Why are you wearing that?' he asked, pointing to Anna's dress.

'I told you, me and Daddy are going out tonight. It was Nia's birthday last week. She's having a party.'

'Will there be ice cream?'

'I don't think so.'

'Will there be soft play?'

'Definitely not.'

Sam looked at her as if he didn't understand why she would be going to such a dull party, but then Edward crossed the room and picked Sam up.

'I thought you guys were watching *Transformers*?'

'We were but there was a scaredy bit and Thomas wouldn't make it go faster.'

Sam got most of his words right now but he still said 'scaredy' when he meant 'scary' and Anna hoped he wouldn't stop. She wanted to cling on to the last reminders of babyhood. Sometimes, when he cuddled her, she felt his plump cheek against hers and thought about the way Thomas's cheeks had slimmed down as he'd got older. It was so intense while you were in it, that baby and toddler phase, but it was heartbreaking to realise it was coming to an end, too. She listened to Edward and Sam leaving the bedroom and going downstairs. The babysitter would be arriving any minute.

She looked at herself in the mirror. She had turned forty a month before, and she tried to see whether it showed on her face. Some days, she thought she still looked young. And then someone would reference something, at work or in a shop, and she would realise that people thought of her as a middle-aged woman. Mumsy. Boring. Done. It wasn't often that she made an effort these days, but she thought she was looking pretty good. She'd bought a new dress that skimmed over the tummy she'd gained with her pregnancies and never quite managed to lose. It was short, and it showed off her legs, which Nia always said were her best asset. She smiled at herself as she applied eyeliner and a bold red lipstick. She felt a little daring. Remembered how it had felt when she'd gone out in her twenties, the way men had looked at her. The way Edward had looked at her, the night they met. Could you still be looked at that way, at forty? She hoped so.

When they arrived at the bar Nia had booked, Anna thought about her own fortieth. She hadn't wanted a big party like this. Instead, she had gone away for a spa weekend with Nia and had a child-friendly dinner with Edward and the boys on the night itself. It had been nice, but now she was wondering if maybe she'd sold herself short. Nia had gone all out, and the room she'd hired was filled with gold and black helium balloons and elegantly dressed people. On a table in the corner, there was an enormous cake. Nia had said she might as well treat it as if it was her wedding, and she'd laughed, but there was an edge to it. Anna knew that, at times, Nia was tired of being the fun single one.

Edward put his hand on the small of Anna's back and steered her into the room. Nia screamed when she saw them, as if she hadn't seen Anna about four hours earlier to discuss last-minute arrangements.

'Wow, she's in full Nia mode,' Edward whispered into Anna's ear. 'I'm going to the bar. Gin and tonic?'

Anna nodded. She hated it when Edward said anything vaguely negative about Nia. She hoped it wouldn't be like that all evening.

'Hello, gorgeous,' Anna said, stepping into Nia's embrace.

'Everyone came!' Nia said, holding Anna at arm's length as if she'd forgotten what she looked like. She was wearing a dress that looked grey in some lights and silver in others, and her long hair was scooped up messily and somehow pinned to the back of her head. Her silver heels were five inches high.

'Of course they came,' Anna said. 'Why wouldn't they?'

'Oh, you know how it is when it's your party. You always think no one will turn up. I'm just so relieved.'

Edward reappeared at Anna's side and handed her a tall glass. 'Happy birthday, Nia,' he said, leaning forward to kiss her cheek.

'Don't you look gorgeous?' Nia asked, and Edward broke into a smile.

'Don't you?' he countered.

* * *

An hour later, Edward and Anna were standing in a corner, trying to have a conversation over the pounding music.

'Did I tell you I'm seeing Sam's teacher next week?'

Edward looked a bit pained. 'Again?'

'Well, it's not getting resolved, is it?'

'It's just kids' stuff. They can't all like each other.'

Anna tried to fight down the fury that was rising up in her chest. 'It isn't just kids' stuff. Thomas hasn't had anything like this. He mentions it nearly every day.'

'Did you ever go through something like that at school?' Edward asked.

Anna thought about it. 'Nothing physical, but some name-calling. Clare Walsh in my year three class was an absolute bitch. Used to decide each day who she was going to make life miserable for, and she had this little gang of followers.'

Anna reflected for a moment on Clare Walsh. Where did people like her end up? Surely they didn't just carry on writing bitchy notes about people's hairstyles and who fancied Sean Davies in their adult lives?

'Did your mum go into school?'

'What? Oh, no, I don't think so. Things were different then, weren't they?'

Edward made a noise that could have been a snort. She knew

that noise. He made it when she said she was going to stop eating so many biscuits and when she said she was meeting Nia for one drink. But this was different. They were talking about their son, about his welfare. Anna dug her nails into the palms of her hands.

'What?' she asked.

'I just think you're smothering him. He's not always going to get on with everyone, is he? Are you going to go into his office when he's twenty-five and having problems with his boss? It'll be good for him, this kind of thing. It'll toughen him up.'

Anna couldn't say anything for a minute or two. Her mouth hung open. 'Do you really think those things? Or are they just things you say?'

'What do you mean?'

'All that man up bullshit?'

'Well, he's quite different to Thomas, isn't he? He's softer, gentler. It's lovely, but I think it's hard for a man to go through life being like that.'

'I can't listen to this,' Anna said.

Nia danced over to them and then stopped, sensing the tension that sat between them like a black cloud. 'Did I interrupt something?' she asked, a little drunkenly. 'Should I go?'

'No, Nia, you're fine. I'm going,' Edward said.

He walked off and Anna watched him leave the bar without looking back, without checking how she would get home. She finished her drink and immediately wanted another. It didn't happen often, but sometimes she felt she and Edward were so misaligned that she couldn't believe they'd chosen to live their lives together, to raise children together.

'What was that?' Nia asked.

Anna shook her head. 'A fucking shitshow.'

'Want me to ask if any of the waiters have J names?' Nia asked.

Anna laughed and shook her head. Nia linked her arm through Anna's and they went over to the bar to order more drinks.

It was while they were waiting at the bar that Anna saw Steve out of the corner of her eye. She turned her head quickly, and Nia noticed, and followed her gaze. She hadn't seen Steve for a couple of years, and it was like a punch to the heart. What was he doing at Nia's party?

'Who are you looking at?' Nia asked.

'The guy with the sandy hair and the beard.'

'Oh yes. He's hot, right? He's going out with Chloe from work. I think his name's Steve.'

'It is,' Anna said, and Nia gave her a quizzical look.

Chloe. Anna was running through her mental rolodex of Nia's friends. She thought she might have met Chloe once or twice, at some other birthday drinks. If it was the woman she was thinking of, then Chloe was one of those fun, pretty girls who always gave the impression they'd made zero effort and didn't know what it was like to feel awkward.

'We were friends,' Anna said. 'When the kids were little.'

'Wait, that's that Steve? Your Steve?'

'He's not my Steve!' Anna's voice came out too high, almost like a squeak.

'You know what I mean. The one you kissed?'

Anna felt herself flush, even though she knew Edward had gone and Steve was too far away to hear.

'Yes.'

'You never told me he...'

'What?'

'Well, that he looked like that.'

Anna stole another glance at Steve and felt like she was standing on the edge of a cliff, looking down.

'Yes,' she said. 'He looks like that.'

Anna went to the toilet. She locked herself in a cubicle and thought about what she would say to Steve when they inevitably ran into each other. She remembered what Nia had said. He was there with Chloe. He was seeing someone. Of course he was. It had been a while since his divorce and, as Nia had pointed out, he looked 'like that'. And he was kind, too. Attentive. Funny. Not the kind of person who would stay single for long. Anna wondered whether this woman he was seeing had met his son, whether things were serious.

Back out in the noisy bar, Anna looked for Nia. She was on the dance floor and she beckoned for Anna to join her. And for the next half an hour, she danced with her best friend, her arms in the air and her worries half forgotten. A couple of times, she wondered whether Steve had seen her. And then she chastised herself and tried to get lost in the music. She and Nia had done a lot of this in their twenties and not nearly enough in their thirties. Anna vowed to do it more in their forties. Once a month, at least.

When Steve approached her, Anna had almost stopped thinking about him. She was the perfect level of drunk, bolder than usual but not yet sloppy and slurring. Nia had gone to the bar and Anna was standing at the edge of the dance floor, waiting for her.

'Hey,' Steve said.

'Hi.' Anna flashed a bright smile.

But inside, she felt a little like she was falling. Whatever it was she'd felt for him, she still felt it.

'Can I get you a drink?' he asked.

'Nia's getting me one.'

'So my girlfriend Chloe works with Nia, and you and Nia are best friends. Right?'

'Right. So how long have you and Chloe been together?'

'About six months.'

It hurt more than it should have done. It was ridiculous. She had taken Edward back, told Steve nothing could happen. It was all her. She'd known he would move on. It would have been ridiculously selfish to hope he wouldn't. But she hadn't known how it would feel when he did.

'How's Luke?'

'He's great. I just miss him so much when he's with Theresa. What about your two?'

'All good, thanks. Thomas is learning to play the recorder, so that's a delight. And Sam is just... well, you know Sam.'

'I do.' Steve nodded and then tilted his head. 'Where's Edward?'

Anna thought about making up an excuse and then decided against it.

'He was here but then we had an argument about Sam being bullied and he stormed off.'

'Oh.'

She'd made him uncomfortable. He was just so easy to talk to. She wondered whether other people found that, whether he was always having to listen to everyone's secrets and difficult truths, or whether it was something particular to her, to them.

'Sorry.'

Steve shrugged. 'Don't be sorry. What's going on with Sam?'

'Are you sure you want to hear about that? At a party?'

He shrugged again. 'Sure. If you want to tell me?'

'What would you do if Luke was crying every night about a boy in his class pushing him and saying he was smelly or stupid or whatever?'

'I'd talk to his teacher, or the head, or whoever.'

'And what if you did that, and it just kept going on?'

'I'd keep trying.'

Anna nodded. He'd keep trying. She felt suddenly close to tears, and wasn't sure if it was the gin she'd been drinking all evening or the fact that this man seemed to be more closely aligned with her on the parenting of her sons than her husband.

And then she decided to say something, knowing that it was dangerous.

'It could have been us, here at this party together, if I hadn't pushed you away, couldn't it?'

Steve looked at her with an expression that was all kindness. Was it pity? She'd said too much. She wouldn't have said it if she hadn't been drinking.

'Anna...' he said.

But she couldn't wait to hear what he was going to say. There was no answer that would help her. She turned and fled. Left the party without picking up her jacket or saying goodbye to Nia. Just walked away and kept on walking.

21

NO

Saturday 5 June 2010

'Do you feel like you've settled back in?' Sarah asked.

Anna thought about that. It was a Saturday afternoon and she was walking on Tooting Common, coffee in one hand and phone in the other.

'I do, yes. It took a while. You know it took me ages to find a flat and that things were different at work, but I'm there, I think.'

'Good.'

'How are things in the office there?'

It was the closest she could get to asking about David. Sarah would know, she thought, that that was what she meant.

'Busy. The person David hired to replace you ended up being hopeless, so she's gone and we're a woman down.'

Anna was quiet. She didn't know what to say.

'Are you over him? David?'

'No.'

'You will be. Give it time. What are you working on?'

'This book we're calling the modern-day *Pride and Prejudice*. I don't think it's sold over there yet but it will. I'm not a massive fan because the hero is this whiny guy she meets on the Tube and it's hardly Darcy in the lake, but it's going to be huge.'

'Huh. Remember when you made me watch the whole BBC adaptation of *Pride and Prejudice* in a single day?'

'I do.'

While Anna was so happy to be back living close to Nia, she missed Sarah acutely. Nia was a mum now, so she didn't have time at weekends to lounge around talking about Colin Firth coming out of the lake.

'I miss you,' Sarah said.

'I miss you, too.'

And then Anna stopped walking, because she felt like she'd seen a ghost.

'Sorry, Sarah, I have to go.'

'Me too, actually. Alex just got here.'

'Have a good morning.'

'Have a good afternoon.'

Anna put the phone in her pocket and took a sip of her coffee. It was definitely him. Edward. He was looking in the other direction, entirely oblivious to his past life standing metres away from him. He was dressed in jeans and a T-shirt she had never particularly liked but had probably washed and folded fifty times. And he was pushing a buggy.

Before she could change her mind, she walked over to him, said his name out loud. Edward turned, took her in. His eyes widened. They'd exchanged emails for a while, while everything was sorted out. But then she'd moved away and there had been nothing left to tie them, and the emails had dried up. And this was the first time they'd run into one another in the street. It had been years, Anna thought. About six years.

'Anna,' he said.

She wanted to save him. It was clear that he didn't know what to say to her, and she thought for a moment that she hadn't done the right thing after all, but then he spoke again.

'Anna, God, it's so nice to see you!'

Anna's face relaxed into a smile. 'You too,' she said.

She looked at his face and tried to be objective. He was handsome. He'd always been handsome. If she met him now, for the first time, she would be attracted to him. She wondered whether he was making the same kind of assessment of her.

'How are you? How was your time in the States?'

Anna thought. How did you sum up an experience like that? She'd gone for a year and ended up staying for seven. Living in Brooklyn, working in Manhattan, walking past those buildings that were so iconic you felt like you were on a film set. All the adventures she'd had, and all the days she'd sat in her apartment alone, missing London.

'It was incredible,' she said. 'It was wonderful.'

He smiled, and she saw that he was genuinely pleased for her, that there were no hard feelings. Or that if there were hard feelings, they were pushed down, far below the surface, and they wouldn't come out during this chance meeting. It was time to address the elephant in the room, Anna thought. There was no reason not to do it.

'So, a baby?' she asked, and then she thought that that might have been the most stupid thing she'd ever said. She gestured towards the buggy, as if he might not know which baby she meant.

'A baby,' he said, his face all light. 'Ella. She's six months.'

Anna peered into the buggy. Ella was sleeping, her arms up by the side of her face.

'Did you get married again?' Anna asked. And then she wasn't sure why she'd asked it. What did it matter? Perhaps he had, and if he had, that was fine, wasn't it? And if not, and he'd had a baby without going through all that again, well, that was fine too.

'Engaged,' Edward said. 'And you?'

'I'm single,' Anna said.

She felt the familiar urge to make an excuse for that, to say that she hadn't been back from New York for long or that she was busy with work, but she resisted it. And she was proud of herself for doing so. It was okay, to be single. It was fine.

'What's she like, your fiancée?' she asked.

Anna wanted to know everything. Was she one of those girls you saw on the Tube who looked up at their boyfriends adoringly through false eyelashes, or the kind of woman who went to the gym every day and lived on fresh air and smoothies, or was she someone Anna would like, that she would have as a friend?

'She's great. I met her through work and we just hit it off.'

Was he asking her to give up her career, or was it a given that her career was important, because she was in the same field as him? Why were all the questions she wanted to know the answers to the sort you couldn't ask?

'That's great. I'm glad it worked out for you.'

'Thanks, and...' He broke off, looked down at his feet. 'I'm sure it will work out for you too.'

Anna realised that he felt sorry for her, and was embarrassed. There was no easy way to show an ex you'd met on the street that you were happy enough as you were, that you were fulfilled. Pushing a buggy was like a trump card, and he'd played it.

'It's good to see you, Edward,' she said, turning to walk away.

He reached out a hand, touched her wrist. 'Do you have time for a coffee?' he asked. He gestured in the direction of the little café in the middle of the common.

Anna thought about that. She did have time. She was going home to an empty flat, to rustle through her cupboards looking for something she could turn into dinner. But would it help? Would it help him, or her, to spend an hour going over things? Going over the past, or the present?

'Sorry,' she said, 'I need to get going.' And she held up the coffee cup she was holding, as a sort of excuse.

He looked a little crestfallen and Anna almost changed her mind. But then she reminded herself that he was part of a family, that he had someone to go home to. She didn't need to feel bad for him. He had Ella. Sleeping and perfect, a whole new life ready to uncurl. Anna rummaged in her bag, pulled out an old press release and a pen, scribbled down her number.

'Another time?' she asked, handing it over to him.

He nodded, folded the paper up and stashed it in the basket of the buggy. 'Another time.'

And then, before she could say or do anything else, Anna held up her hand in a little wave and turned away, heading back in the direction of her flat.

She could be a mother, she thought. She could have stayed with Edward and built a family. That baby in that buggy could be hers. Or another baby, with another man. She felt a kind of ache at the thought of it. It wasn't about Edward, she was pretty sure. Turning forty had felt like a full stop on any questioning about motherhood. She knew that people still did it after forty, but she felt sure she wouldn't. Suddenly, she wasn't sure if it had all been a terrible mistake. Had she put her career ahead of her happiness? And if she had, had it been worth it? She stood at the edge of the common, her hands on her hips, finding it hard to breathe.

Before she really knew what she was doing, Anna found herself heading for the Tube, into the station, going to Clapham.

It wasn't really a decision she made; it was all instinct. Was she going back to the flat she'd shared with Edward, pretending it was a different time? No, she was going to Nia's. That was what she did when anything big happened. She went to Nia and they raked over it, looked at it from every angle, until they'd made sense of it. She hadn't done it much since she'd been back, but Nia had. A handful of times she'd turned up on Anna's doorstep, needing to talk about an argument with Jamie or something about Cara that had made her worry. Anna had been pleased, that she still held that position in Nia's life, after the years apart.

It was Jamie who came to the door. He welcomed her warmly, as he always did. 'Anna, come in. Nia's in the shower but she won't be long.'

He led her out to the flat's patio garden, where Cara was running around in her pants, chasing the bubbles he was blowing.

'Hey, Cara,' Anna said, and Cara gave her a shy little wave. Not for the first time, Anna wondered about the relationship they might have had, if she'd been in Cara's life from day one.

'Can I get you a drink?' Jamie asked.

Anna shook her head. 'I'm fine.'

They sat down opposite one another at the little table for two that sat in one corner of the small garden.

'Did Nia know you were coming?' he asked.

'No, I just... I ran into my ex-husband and I needed to talk to someone about it.'

'Oh. Well, when she's out of the shower I'll put this one to bed and you two can hash it out over a glass of wine.' Cara ran towards him and launched herself at his body, and he caught her and then pretended not to let her go while she struggled against his grip.

Had she been a fool to say no to this life? Sitting there, the early evening sun slipping down the sky, Anna felt like she might have made the biggest mistake, choosing to live alone while everyone was settling down in these little groups of three or four. But then she reminded herself that it wasn't Nia's family she'd turned down. It was Edward. And things hadn't been right between them. She knew that was true.

When Nia appeared, her hair damp on her shoulders, she grinned at Anna. 'What a nice surprise!'

Jamie stood up. 'I'm sorting Cara out. Anna needs a glass of wine and an ear.' He lifted Cara over his shoulder and she giggled. 'Say goodnight to Mummy and Anna!'

'Goodnight, Mummy! Goodnight, Anna!'

Nia smiled as they retreated, then turned to Anna with a worried look. 'What's happened?'

Anna felt the breathlessness returning. She'd been able to cover it while she was talking to Jamie, had been able to pretend she was fine.

'Have I made a huge mistake, not having children?' she asked.

Nia's eyes widened. 'Where has this come from?'

'I just saw Edward. On the common. With a baby.'

'His baby?'

'Yes. It's not about him, I know that. I just... It's like I suddenly realised that I'm forty and I've closed the door on something for good and I don't know whether it was the right thing to do.'

'Wine?' Nia asked, and Anna nodded.

Anna took a long drink when Nia handed her a glass.

Just then, Jamie put his head around the door. 'Sorry, N, she wants you to say goodnight to her again.'

Nia smiled an apology at Anna and disappeared inside, and

Jamie took her place at the table for a minute, even had a few sips of Nia's wine.

'Are you okay?' he asked Anna.

'I'm fine.'

'Must be rough, seeing him like that, out of the blue.'

Anna wondered what exactly Jamie knew about her relationship with Edward. What would Nia have seen fit to divulge? It wasn't as if there was anything shocking or terrible. It hadn't been a bad marriage. It just hadn't been right.

'He had a baby,' Anna said.

'Ouch.'

'I mean, it's not like... I knew that's what he wanted. He wanted us to have one and I just wasn't ready and...'

'You know, I grew up without a dad. I think you did too, if I remember correctly. And it really messed me up in terms of becoming a parent. I was terrified I wouldn't know how to be a dad, because I didn't have one. If it hadn't been for Nia getting pregnant unexpectedly, I'm not sure I would have done it. I wonder if you have the same fear, but the opposite way around. A fear of being left to bring up a baby on your own, like your mum was.'

Anna didn't know what to say. It was like he'd reached inside her and got to the very heart of things. She wasn't sure it was entirely accurate but it was more the fact that he'd thought about her childhood and how it might impact her as an adult, as a mum.

'Sorry,' Jamie said, 'I interrupted you. You said you weren't ready then. What about now?'

'Now I'm forty and I live alone and come and interrupt your family evening when I have a crisis,' Anna said, laughing to show him she wasn't feeling too upset.

'We wouldn't have it any other way,' he said, getting up again and switching places with Nia without another word.

'Tell me again what it's really like, being a mum,' Anna asked.

'It's the best and the worst thing I've ever done,' Nia said. 'It's exhausting, it's boring, it's thrilling, it's wonderful. Mostly exhausting. I feel like, if it wasn't for the sleep deprivation – which isn't only a baby thing, don't be fooled about that – I would love it. But I'm so tired all the time.'

Anna wanted to ask if Nia thought she would have another one. She'd never said, and Anna had never quite felt like it was okay to ask. What if they'd tried, or were trying? She would tell Anna, wouldn't she, if she wanted her to know? She recalled what Magda had said about Nia, that night so long ago. One big love, one child.

'Am I missing out?' she asked instead.

'Yes,' Nia said, and Anna wished she hadn't asked. 'In that you're missing something, but you'll never know what it feels like if you don't do it, so it's hardly like missing anything at all. And you're gaining other things, like freedom and peace and space to think. Don't do this, Anna. Don't agonise. You have a good life.'

She did, Anna thought. There were days like this, when it hurt to be alone. But there were so many other days that she felt grateful for the life she'd chosen. For the travelling she could do, the long hours she was able to put in at work, when she needed to, without making arrangements and phone calls. For the way her weekends were hers alone, to do with as she pleased. For the time and space she had to think and to just be, with no one pushing at her boundaries and closing her in. Did it all make up for the feel of a soft cheek against yours and the weight of a small person in your arms? She hoped it did.

22

YES

Sunday 5 June 2011

Anna laid her open book down on her chest and closed her eyes. The combination of the quietness and the feeling of the sun on her skin was bliss. It felt like her first holiday in years. And it was, in a way. She and Edward had taken the boys away at least once a year, but holidays with them weren't really holidays at all. They were fun, but they were full-on, with very little time for relaxing. At the end of the week, she always found herself back at home with a mountain of washing to do and feeling more tired than she had when she'd left. When Nia had suggested this, a week away, just the two of them, Anna had tried to imagine what Edward might say. But then she'd mentioned it, and he'd been all in favour. Each night just before the boys went to bed, she called them for a chat, and they seemed to be getting on fine. It was only a week, she reminded herself. She wasn't indispensable.

'Do you want a drink?' she asked Nia, sitting up.

Nia was lounging on the next sunbed in a red bikini. 'Yes please,' she said. 'Something... fruity.'

Anna walked to the pool bar in her bare feet. She loved the feel of the warm tiles on the soles of her feet. She was wearing a bikini for the first time since before her pregnancies, but she threw on a coverup whenever she went anywhere. It was a small step forward. She ordered two pineapple-flavoured cocktails and watched while the barman made them. At home, she would pull out her phone or try to make a mental shopping list or just do something whenever she was waiting to be served. It was nice to be lazy. To just stand there, warmed by the sun. Taking stock.

The barman turned and put the two drinks down on the bar with a flourish.

'Can I put them on my tab? It's room 224.'

'Of course.' He leaned forward, a little closer. 'I've seen you around. You and your friend.'

Anna smiled. Was he interested in Nia? He looked like he couldn't be much older than twenty-five.

'Nia,' she said.

'What?'

'My friend. Her name is Nia.'

'And what's your name?'

Anna's heart sped up a little. Was it her he was interested in? Was he flirting with her?

'Anna.'

'Nice to meet you, Anna.' He slid a piece of paper across the bar for her to sign. 'Maybe we could have a drink one night, after I finish?'

Anna laughed. 'How old are you?'

He shrugged. He was tall and lean, tanned. Was he Spanish? His English was flawless. 'I'm twenty-seven. How old are you?'

She thought about lying. But what would be the point? She

wasn't going to act on this, was she? 'I'm forty-one,' she said. 'I'm married. I have children.'

He shrugged again. 'If you change your mind...'

Anna picked up the drinks and walked back to the loungers. She didn't tell Nia about what had happened, because she knew that she would make it a joke and Nia would laugh. There was a part of her that wasn't ready to treat it that way just yet. It had been a long time since someone had looked at her that way. A long time since she had felt wanted. She wondered whether he did this all the time, a different older woman every week. Whether he laughed with his friends about how grateful they were, how easy. And then she stopped herself. It didn't matter. It had been nice to feel like a woman. To feel desired.

She thought back to Nia's party the year before, the text Steve had sent her afterwards. *It's always been you.* It had been so tempting to act on it, but then she hadn't, and by the time a week had gone by, it seemed ridiculous to reply. She'd lost herself again in the day-to-day of her life.

'Do you miss the boys?' Nia asked, taking the drink Anna was holding out to her.

'Yes,' Anna said. 'But it's not quite as simple as missing them. I feel like they're a part of me, so it's strange when we're not together. But it's so wonderful to have time to myself, to not have to make anyone dinner or wash anyone's football kit.'

It was day five of the holiday and Anna felt settled into it. The weather had been mid-twenties and sunshine all week, and her stress was falling away.

'I don't miss anything,' Nia said, taking a long drink. 'Is that bad? Does that mean there's something wrong with my life?'

'I don't think so,' Anna said. 'But at the same time, I bet you'd miss stuff if you were here for longer than a week. A week's nothing.'

'What would I miss? My tiny flat and my boring job?'

Nia laughed to show that she was joking, but Anna felt uneasy. Was Nia unhappy? And if she was, why didn't Anna know about it? Over the years, she'd talked about her lack of a family, about how it wasn't really a choice she'd made but a set of circumstances that had come to be, but Anna didn't think it was something that plagued her. She loved Anna's boys and spoiled them every birthday and Christmas with extravagant presents Anna and Edward would never have chosen, and Anna had thought she was mostly content in that role, in her life.

'Your flat is lovely and you really like your job, you can't fool me.'

'I do like my job,' Nia said. 'But I could do without the drama sometimes. Did I tell you Ellen and the boss have split up?'

'No!'

'Last month. It's horrendous. You can tell he's just hoping she'll leave but there's no way she will. She's been there longer than I have. They're being super polite to each other and then making faces behind each other's backs when they think no one's looking. It's like I'm invisible to them or something. And when he goes into his office, she starts talking about things I really don't want to hear, like how he does yoga DVDs in his pants. Can you imagine? I had to stop her the other day because I just knew she was going to talk about his sex face and there's only so much I can take. Anyway, now she has a new man, apparently, and she's made her screensaver a massive picture of his face to make a point. It's really off-putting when you have to go to her desk for anything. She's always minimising everything on the screen so you have to look at it, almost daring you not to say anything.'

'What does he look like? The new guy?'

'He looks like the boss, that's the thing. At first I thought it was him, thought she'd gone absolutely mad. But then I saw he had this awful teardrop tattoo by his eye...'

'Isn't that supposed to mean you've killed someone?'

Nia's eyebrows shot up and Anna knew her eyes, behind her sunglasses, would be wide. 'Does it? Why don't I know that?'

'I don't know. Not enough true crime documentaries.'

'Fuck me. I wonder whether she knows that! Okay, now I sort of can't wait to get back. Thanks, Anna. Anyway, how's work going for you?'

Anna had been working part-time at the boys' school library for a few months. It made a lot of sense, in that the work was term-time only and the hours matched school hours. It was a job share, between her and a pleasant woman in her fifties called Sandra, who was always happy to swap days if required, like for this holiday. And she loved helping the kids find books they would enjoy. But a lot of what she did was mindless and she still looked longingly at job sites for publishing roles at least once a week.

'It's fine, just dull.' She drained her drink.

'Another?' Nia asked.

'Not for me. I'm going to read for a while.'

Nia shrugged. 'Just me then.'

Anna picked her book up again. It was one her old company had published, and it was being billed as the big romance hit of the summer, but she couldn't quite get into it. It was clear that the two main characters were going to end up together and Anna just didn't like the man very much. If she'd worked on it, she'd have called it *Pride and Prejudice* meets *Before Sunrise*.

A shadow came over her book and Anna saw that Nia was back.

'You didn't tell me the barman was hot,' she said, sitting back down and putting her drink on the floor next to her. 'Not a J though, before you ask.'

'Did he try it on with you?' Anna asked, ready to tell her story.

'He did. And we're going to go for a drink tonight when he finishes.'

'Are you sure about that?' Anna asked. 'He's so young.'

Nia sighed. 'God, so what? I'm not planning to marry him. But it's a long time since I slept with a twenty-seven-year-old and I wouldn't mind reminding myself what that's like.'

Anna was quiet. It wasn't up to her what Nia did. But over the years, their job had been to protect one another, to give advice. Shouldn't she let Nia know that this guy was sleazy, that he hit on every woman who went to order drinks? Or didn't it matter? She decided to say nothing. And she allowed herself to feel quietly hurt that his interest in her had been nothing to do with her, after all.

That night, Anna phoned home before bedtime, like always. The Wi-Fi in their hotel room wasn't strong enough for a video connection and it was strange to hear her boys' voices without being able to see their faces. After telling her a bit about their days, they disappeared to watch TV and it was just her and Edward.

'I think Nia's about to start a fling with the barman,' she said.

Edward laughed. 'Of course she is. That's so Nia.'

He trusted her completely, she thought. There wasn't a flicker of worry in his voice. It wouldn't cross his mind that she might sleep with the barman, or anyone else.

'We miss you,' he said, after a pause.

Anna felt tears prick her eyes. He hadn't said that before. Had she? She'd said it to the boys, but not to him. But she did miss him, she realised. She missed him more than she'd expected to.

'I miss you, too.'

There was a silence, and she wondered whether they'd been cut off. But then she heard Edward's voice again. 'Sam made me show him where you are on the globe, and then he said it looked so close that maybe you could come home to give him a kiss at bedtime. So that kickstarted a discussion about how big the world is and how far away countries are from each other.'

'Are they okay, the boys? School and everything?'

'Did Sam tell you he lost a tooth?'

Anna felt a pang. The first time he'd lost a tooth, she'd sat on her bed after he'd gone to sleep, holding it in her hand and silently weeping. It was a rite of passage she struggled with, parts of her children's bodies falling out and being replaced. She wished she was there to hold him, take in the clean scent of his warm neck, to be the one to sneak into his room in the middle of the night to replace his tooth with a coin.

'You won't forget to do the tooth fairy thing, will you?'

'I won't. We're fine, Anna. But we're ready for you to come home.'

Anna nodded, although she knew he couldn't see her. She was ready to go home too, she thought. It had taken five days of doing exactly what she wanted to realise that she quite liked what she already had.

'I'll see you soon,' she said.

'See you soon. Oh, and Anna?'

'Yes?'

'Happy anniversary.'

23

NO

Sunday 5 June 2011

Anna looked at her watch, even though she knew what time it was. It was a good twenty minutes after the time she'd asked Marco to meet her.

'Maybe he went to a different Pizza Express?' Nia suggested.

'I mean,' Jamie added, 'there is one on practically every corner in central London.'

'Maybe he isn't coming,' Cara said, and both her parents gave her a stern look.

Anna sent him a quick message, confirming which Pizza Express they were in, and saying that if he wasn't there in ten minutes, they were going to have to leave without him. While she was looking down at her phone, she felt safe, but she knew that when she looked up and saw the pity in Nia's eyes, she might feel like crying.

She'd met Marco at work a few months earlier – he'd burst into her team meeting and sat down, all flustered, and then realised that everyone had gone silent, and that he was in the wrong room, and had been incredibly charming and apologetic. A week after that, she'd stood behind him in the queue for coffee and noticed the way his shoulders filled out his shirt and when he'd turned, unexpectedly, she'd found herself blushing slightly, and he'd said, 'Oh, it's you, the meeting room woman.' There'd been a coffee, and then a drink after work, and they'd been seeing each other for about four months. Nia had met him, had declared him 'ludicrously hot', and he'd started to spend two or three nights a week at her flat. He was a little younger than Anna, a little more junior in his sales role, and he lived in a houseshare that he wasn't keen to take Anna back to.

It was going pretty well, she thought. When Nia had suggested this particular outing, she hadn't been sure. She and Nia were taking Cara to see a matinee of *The Lion King* while the men were going to go for some drinks. But Marco had seemed keen when she'd brought it up, so she'd said yes. And now, she was watching her friends finish their dessert and feeling increasingly like she'd been stood up.

'We have a while yet, Anna,' Nia said, reaching across to rub her arm. 'Do you want to finish my cheesecake?'

Anna nodded and Nia pushed the dish towards her.

'I don't know why you can never finish a dessert,' Jamie said, laughing.

'I could finish it. I just know how much Anna likes dessert.'

'So it's a pity half cheesecake, is it?' Anna asked, managing to smile.

'Look, if he doesn't come, nothing's lost,' Jamie said. 'I can just head home, it's no big deal.'

And Anna was about to answer, but then the door opened and he was there, scanning the restaurant for them. Anna put up a hand, waved him over. She knew she should be annoyed with him but she couldn't really be bothered with it. She was just so relieved that he'd come.

'I'm so sorry,' Marco said, leaning across the table to kiss Anna, then pulling a chair over from a vacant table nearby.

Anna waited a beat for him to offer an explanation before realising he wasn't going to, that he didn't have one.

'Why were you late?' Cara asked.

Anna loved this little girl for her ability to just say what everyone else was thinking, but she could see that Nia was poised to tell her off.

Marco looked flustered. 'Trouble with the Tube,' he said, clearly unused to having to explain himself to a six-year-old girl.

Nia disappeared to pay the bill and they got ready to leave. In the confusion of picking up bags and jackets, Marco took Anna's hand in his and whispered in her ear. 'I really am sorry. I'll make it up to you later.'

Anna felt her insides turn to liquid. Marco did things to her, without even touching her, that no other man had. Just his voice, that hint of an Italian accent, turned her on. She went up on tiptoes and kissed his full lips. It was little more than a peck, pretty chaste, but there was a part of her that was ready to give up on the whole afternoon and take him back to her flat. She closed her eyes for a moment, imagined pushing him inside the door to her room and up against the wall, how he would press himself into her body and then very slowly start to remove her clothes. She snapped back to the present, chastised herself for letting her sex thoughts in on this family day out.

'Anna,' Cara said as they bustled out of the door and into the street, 'you've gone red.'

Anna laughed and made eye contact with Marco, whose expression told her he knew exactly what she'd been thinking about.

'So Marco,' Jamie said, clapping him on the back. 'Are you a football guy?'

'Of course. I mean, you know I'm Italian, right?'

Anna watched as they got into an animated conversation about football. She'd worried that they might have nothing in common, but she needn't have done. Nia had predicted that sport would be their common ground. Nia was holding Cara's hand and Anna noticed that Cara was holding out her other hand for Anna to take. The street was crowded but she took it anyway, letting the men go on ahead, dodging the crowds.

'Is there a real lion in the play?' Cara asked.

'No, just people dressed up as lions and other animals,' Nia said.

Cara looked disappointed.

'And is there singing?' she asked.

'Yes, lots of singing.'

'Have you seen it before?'

Nia nodded. 'Twice, I think.'

'Have you, Anna?'

'No. It's my first time.'

'If you are scared of the animals, you can hold my hand. But remember that they're only people,' she said, a very serious expression on her face.

At the theatre door, they parted ways.

'Do you know where you're going to be?' Nia asked. 'We can come and find you, after.'

'Not sure yet,' Jamie said. 'We'll message you. Have fun, girls!'

Anna looked at Marco and Jamie standing side by side, trying to work out whether he might be a permanent fixture in her life. She didn't love him, not yet, but she loved the way he touched her, and she loved the fact that she didn't think about David when she was with him.

Inside the theatre, they went straight to their seats. Everyone had been too polite to say, but Marco's lateness had meant they were only just on time. Anna noticed Cara's jaw drop open when they stepped into the darkness of the theatre and she saw the stage, and she tried to remember what it had been like to see things for the first time, to be so impressed by the everyday. She couldn't, of course. She was too far from her own childhood to recapture it. Perhaps that was one of the reasons why people had children, she surmised. To regain that sense of wonder. To see it through their eyes.

They had good seats, near the front of the circle, and they sat with Cara between them and waited for the curtain to go up.

'What do you think was going on with Marco?' Nia asked in a whisper. 'Just late?'

Anna shrugged. 'He's always late,' she said. 'Drives me crazy.'

She thought of Edward, how he'd always been early, but how that had been a tiny thing when compared to everything that was wrong between the two of them.

'Is everything okay with you two?' Nia asked.

If they'd been in a bar, without Nia's child sitting between them, she would have said that she was having the best sex of her life, and it made up for a host of other things. That she was ignoring the fact that Marco was younger than her and a little unsettled, that he sometimes talked about moving back to Italy. That she was really trying to just focus on the present and the way he made her feel when they were together. But they weren't, and Cara was watching them avidly, her eyes swivelling from her mum to Anna to make sure she didn't miss a whispered word.

'I don't think it's forever,' Anna said. 'But things are fine.'

Nia pulled a face that Anna knew meant 'let's talk about this another time' and then the curtain started to come up and Cara did a huge gasp and the people sitting around them smiled and laughed a little. And Anna turned away from her friend and towards the stage and allowed herself to be swept up in the magic of it all.

Halfway through the final rendition of '*Circle of Life*', Anna heard a shriek and turned to see that Cara had a hand clasped to her mouth. There was blood on her fingers. Nia was rooting in her handbag for a tissue.

'Are you okay?' Anna asked.

Cara shook her head.

'Her tooth's come out,' Nia whispered. 'Just looking for something to wrap it in to keep it safe.'

An older woman in front of them turned around and gave them a stern look, and it made Anna want to laugh. She tried to remember what it was like to lose a tooth, but she couldn't. She put out a hand for Cara to hold and Cara took it, slowly pulling her other hand down from her mouth. It was one of the big front ones, Anna saw, and she had a brief flashback to one of her own school photos. Her gappy smile. Cara's hand was warm in hers, and Anna gave it a squeeze. But when Nia had finished wrapping the tooth in a tissue and stashed it away somewhere, she pulled Cara towards her and she dropped Anna's hand. And for a second, Anna felt like she'd lost something precious. And then she turned her attention back to the stage and tried to forget.

When they met Jamie and Marco after the show, the men had obviously had a few drinks and were laughing and agreeing with each other about everything.

'Friends for life,' Nia whispered to Anna.

Marco stood up and put his arms around Anna. 'How was the show?'

'The daddy lion died!' Cara announced.

'He did, yes, but we got over that and enjoyed the rest of the show, didn't we?' Nia asked.

'And look, I lost a tooth!' Cara grinned and Jamie inspected her, gave her a high five.

They all hugged, and then Nia and her family left, Cara between her parents, holding both of their hands.

'Let's go home,' Anna said.

They set off for the Tube.

'Was it okay, with Jamie?' she asked.

They were standing on the platform, waiting for a train to arrive. It was busy and hot, and Marco had pulled her in close to him.

'It was good, he's a nice guy.'

'What did you talk about?'

'Oh, you know, football, work, family. Do you want all that?'

'All what?'

'You know, kids. I want that, one day.'

Anna felt a lurch inside her. He'd never said anything like this to her before, and anyway, wasn't it too soon? But then she went over his words again and realised he hadn't actually said he wanted those things with her. Was this just a general opening up about the future? Or was he just drunk? And did he know that she was forty-one and had probably missed her chance?

'I don't think I do,' she said.

Marco seemed unfazed by her response. 'You should think about it,' he said. 'We should think about it.' And then he leaned in and kissed her and Anna forgot about everything other than the dizzy feeling that kissing him gave her.

24

YES

Tuesday 5 June 2012

While Miss Bright matched up the children with their adults, Anna held Sam's hand, ready to pass him to the friend who'd offered to wait with him while Anna talked to his teacher.

It was the third meeting this school year. Last year, she'd been in four times. She felt like she was probably one of those mothers the teachers talked about, rolling their eyes. And Edward had made it clear, several times, that he thought she was overreacting. She didn't care. She was the one who Sam came to, achingly sad. She was the one he asked why people didn't like him. Who asked what was wrong with him.

'Right, sorry about that, come in.' Miss Bright ushered her into the brightly decorated classroom. 'What did you want to see me about?'

Anna smiled tightly. 'It's about the bullying. It's no better.'

Miss Bright sat down behind her desk on the only full-sized chair in the room. Anna was left with the option of sitting on one of the tiny kids' chairs and feeling stupid, or standing. She stood. 'We try to be very careful about how we label these kinds of incidents,' Miss Bright said. 'It's only bullying if it's sustained...'

'And it is,' Anna interrupted. 'It is sustained. It's been going on for months. Years, even.'

Before she'd had children, Anna had never been an angry person. And she still wasn't, on the whole. But a ball of rage had formed in her stomach along with swollen feet and fingers and milk-filled breasts. It could sit there, still and unnoticed, for months, but it could also flare up in a second if anyone hurt either of her babies.

Miss Bright held up a hand, as if Anna was being unreasonable and she was trying to get her to calm down.

'I keep an eye on it,' she said. 'I make sure I catch up with Sam once a week on his own, but he usually says things are okay.'

'They're not,' Anna said, feeling close to tears, willing her voice to hold firm. 'They're not okay. I don't know why he says that. But at least two or three nights a week, at bedtime, he's in tears. You can't play that down. That's not okay.'

There was a clutching pain in Anna's chest. She felt it when Sam nuzzled into her shoulder and his hot tears slid onto her skin. She felt it when Edward dismissed it, said that all boys went through this kind of thing and Sam just needed to toughen up a bit. She felt it now, when this woman, who was tasked with taking care of her son for thirty hours a week, didn't seem to grasp how serious it was.

'Is it the same boys as last time?' Miss Bright asked, her voice softer.

'Yes,' Anna said. 'Jack, Billy and Harry are the names that he mentions most. Look, I know he's not your typical boy, playing football and running around. He likes My Little Pony and having his toenails painted. He mostly plays with girls, as you know. And I love all that about him; I encourage it. But I also know it leaves him wide open for this kind of treatment. My husband thinks we should, I don't know, encourage him to be more of a boy's boy.'

Miss Bright frowned. 'I've seen children picked on for all kinds of things. Wearing glasses, being overweight, even not watching the right programmes on TV.' She put her hands up to make air quotes around the word 'right'. 'And yes, not conforming to gender norms is a big one, but we have to stand up to it. Getting Sam to change isn't the answer.'

In that moment, Anna's rage retreated. 'Thank you,' she said. 'That's what I always say to him. This is who he is, and I think we should celebrate it.'

'I completely agree. I'm sorry the measures we've put in place so far aren't working, and I want you to know how seriously I take this. How seriously we, as a school, take this. I'll talk to Sam again, tell him he needs to be honest with me for this to work. And I'll talk to the boys involved, too. We'll do some work as a class, about celebrating difference and being kind. We'll get it sorted, I promise.'

'Thanks,' Anna said. She meant it. She stood up to leave, brushing away tears.

On the walk home, Sam was quiet and she left him to his thoughts. They were nearly home when he spoke.

'Ella is having her birthday party at that trampoline place.'

'Are you invited?' Anna asked, silently praying that he was.

'Yes! And not everyone is. Only ten people.'

'What shall we buy for her?'

'A game with a horse. She likes horses.'

Anna added that to the mental shopping list that was never

finished. She was pleased he was invited, pleased he had something to be excited about.

'How was school today, Sam?'

His hand tightened in hers. He knew she meant the bullying.

'Harry says girls are stupid and I'm like a girl.'

And just like that, the ball of rage fired up again. Anna let it burn, but was determined not to let Sam see it.

'You know what? Even when I was at school people said things like that. That girls are better, or boys are. It's just nonsense. You know that, right? Everyone is different, and has good points and bad points, things they're good at, things they need more help with. You can't take a group as big as boys or girls and say that they are like this or like that.'

Sam was looking up at her, his eyes wide. There had been a time when he'd believed everything she said, no question. But lately, he often countered things she told him with 'But Miss Bright said...' Where would he stand on this?

'I think Harry is stupid and girls are brilliant,' Sam said.

Anna squeezed his hand a little tighter. It pained her to have to correct him. 'We don't call anyone stupid, baby. But most people are brilliant, when you get to know them.'

Not Harry, she thought.

Sam shrugged, and then they were at their house and Anna was fishing the door key out of her pocket. Once they were inside, Sam went straight up to his room. Anna checked the time. Thomas would be home from football in half an hour. She stood with her back to the kitchen counter, thinking about how Miss Bright might make some progress with Sam's bullies but it wasn't long until the summer holidays, and in the new school year Anna would have to start all over again with a new teacher. It was exhausting. Why Sam? Why her funny, brilliant and loving son?

When Thomas arrived home, he was monosyllabic. He slunk off upstairs and Anna was making a start on dinner when she heard a thud and some shouting. She ran up the stairs and found the boys in Sam's room. They were caught in a tussle that looked like the playfighting they'd always done but that Anna knew, in an instant, was something different. She shouted Thomas's name and he turned to look at her, and Sam used his distraction as an opportunity to get the upper hand. He pulled back his fist and slammed it into his brother's cheek, and Anna was so shocked she just stood there, watching.

After a moment, it was like she came back to life. Thomas was lying on the floor, clutching the side of his face and crying, and Sam was standing over him, looking a mixture of scared and triumphant.

'Sam! What did you do?'

Anna fell to her knees beside her eldest son, gently prised his hand away so she could see if there was any damage. There was no blood. There would be bruising, she was sure, but for now, he looked okay. Still, she could see that he was hurt and it made her ache.

'It was him!' Sam shouted. 'I hate him! He's worse than the boys at school!'

Thomas sat up and Anna could see that he was checking his teeth with his tongue.

'Are you okay?' she asked him, and when he nodded, 'What did you say to him?'

'What the hell?' Thomas asked, standing up. 'He punches me in the face and you're still on his side? Are you joking?'

He left the room, slamming the door behind him. Anna made eye contact with Sam, who looked sad and sorry.

'What happened?' she asked.

'He said I'm weird because I don't like football,' Sam said quietly.

Anna nodded. She wanted to pull him towards her for a hug.

'I'll talk to him,' she said. 'I'll tell him he needs to be kind. But you cannot punch people, or hurt people at all, Sam. You know that.'

Sam's shoulders sagged. 'You don't know what it's like. Those boys are so horrible to me at school and I can't wait to get home, and then...'

'I know,' she said. 'I know.'

And when he came to her, she wrapped him in her arms and let him cry.

When they were little, Thomas three and Sam a baby, Thomas had sung Sam to sleep, held him with a look of complete wonder, and Anna had felt like this was the best bit of all of it. Not creating these two people, but enabling this relationship to exist. It was so pure, so full of love. She remembered Sam at two or three, saying he wanted to marry his brother, Thomas agreeing, her having to gently explain that you couldn't marry someone in your family. Thomas saying he would marry the neighbour's dog instead, then. It all seemed like so long ago.

Anna knocked on Thomas's door. He was lying on his bed, staring at the ceiling.

'You always take his side,' he said.

'I don't mean to.'

'Well, you do.'

Anna sat down by his feet. 'The truth is, I worry about him more than you. He's always found things more difficult, making friends and that kind of thing.'

'That's not my fault.'

'No, of course it isn't. But is there anyone in your class who gets picked on all the time?'

Thomas turned on his side, looked at her. 'Kind of.'

Please let him not be involved in that, she thought. Having a child who was bullied was awful, but she suspected having a child who was a bully would feel worse.

'Well, that's what school is like for Sam. Every day. And when he gets home, he needs to feel safe and loved. I know you love him, Thomas...'

Thomas snorted.

'You're cross with him right now, and rightly so. But I know you wouldn't want him to be sad.'

'Sometimes it feels like he's your favourite,' Thomas said, and there were tears in his eyes.

Anna reached out a hand, pulled him up to sitting, and hugged him tight. There weren't as many opportunities to do this these days, and she relished it. She thought of the times when it had just been her and Thomas, before Sam was born. How she'd fallen in love with him, how he'd shown her how to be a mum.

'I couldn't love either of you any more than I do,' she said.

Thomas didn't say anything. But he didn't let her go for a long time.

* * *

Edward arrived home just as she was tucking Sam into bed. Thomas was reading a Harry Potter book to himself. Anna told him she'd come back to turn off his light in half an hour and kissed his forehead.

'All okay?' Edward asked when she went into the kitchen.

'Tough day,' she said.

'At work?'

'No, here. I went to see Miss Bright about Sam and the bullying...'

Edward raised his eyebrows. 'Again?'

'Yes, again, because that's what you do when a problem isn't getting solved,' she said, trying to keep her voice level. 'Anyway, I went to talk to Miss Bright about it, and she seems to get it, to be taking it seriously. So we'll see.'

Anna's 'unlike you' was unspoken but she knew it was clear.

'Okay,' Edward said.

'And then the boys had a fight. Sam punched Thomas in the face.'

Edward looked shocked. 'Is he all right? Thomas?'

'Yes, he's fine. But I just feel pulled apart. Both of them hurt, you know?'

They were standing at either side of the kitchen counter and Edward shook his head slightly. 'They're okay, Anna. They're both okay.'

She wanted to scream. Perhaps this was why he had always felt he had the capacity to have another one, and she didn't. The small things that happened to them, that made up their childhood days, didn't seem to affect him the way they affected her. She went to the fridge and opened it, more for something to do than anything else, but when she saw a half-full bottle of wine in the door, she pulled it out.

'Wine?' she asked, reaching up for glasses.

'Why not? It's a celebration, after all.'

Anna didn't turn back to face him. She poured the wine slowly, trying to work out what he meant. And then the song he'd put on started, those familiar notes that took her back in time, and she realised that it was their anniversary, and she counted the years. Thirteen.

'I haven't got you a card,' she said. 'I'm sorry, it's just...'

'It's fine,' he said. 'I haven't got one either. But we should acknowledge it, right?' He took a glass from her and held it up, and she chinked hers against it and looked in his eyes.

'Dance?'

She shook her head, feeling strangely self-conscious. Edward looked slightly hurt, so she stepped towards him, went up on tiptoes to kiss him.

'To us,' he said. 'To the future.'

'To the future,' she repeated.

She wondered, as she did sometimes, who they would be when this long, hard job of parenting was over. She could imagine how they would age, the way their hair would grey and they would put on some weight. But she wasn't as sure of what would be left of them. It felt like all their conversations these days were about the boys. And there were so many years of parenting ahead, she knew. But at the end of it all, when the boys were grown and gone, what then?

25

NO

Tuesday 5 June 2012

Anna had been mentally preparing herself for David's visit to the London office since Sarah's phone call to warn her. But it was impossible to know how she'd feel when she saw him. Or perhaps it was impossible to admit to herself how she would feel when she saw him. She was at her desk, absorbed in emails, when she heard his voice. She looked up. He wasn't speaking to her, but he was close. Had he thought about how it would be to see her? She doubted it. He was about ten feet away, sideways on to her. Did he look different, older? Not noticeably. Her body was desperate to betray her. To shout out his name or to get up and run away or to just keep staring at him until he asked her to stop. She forced herself to look back at her screen. It was going to be a tough week.

He didn't speak to her until mid-afternoon, when she'd pretty much stopped expecting it. But at some point between three and four, when Anna was feeling like she needed coffee but shouldn't drink one if she wanted any chance of sleeping later, he turned up at her desk. She sensed him there, looked up.

'Hey, Anna,' he said.

'Hey.'

'I'm over for the week, and I was wondering whether you had some time to...'

He trailed off, leaving her unsure whether he was asking her to have a meeting with him, which could be strictly professional, or whether he was asking her to go to dinner with him, or for drinks, or just back to his hotel room. She maintained eye contact, raised her eyebrows. She was going to make him say it, make him be clear about what he was asking.

'Um,' David said, 'you know, time to catch up?'

'Sure, how about tomorrow afternoon?' she suggested.

'No, I mean, yes, that would be great, it would be good to hear what you're working on, but I actually meant outside of the office. Dinner or something.'

Anna made him wait. Made him stand there until it was verging on uncomfortable. She thought about what Sarah had said, how she'd made Anna promise that no matter what happened, she would not agree to be alone with him outside the office. How they'd both probably known that Anna's promise was a lie.

'Okay,' she said. 'But I can't do Thursday.'

She was seeing Nia, but even if she hadn't been, she would have said there was a day she couldn't do. She didn't want him to think she had no social life.

'Can you do tonight?' he asked, his eyes sparkling with humour as if he already knew she would say yes.

'Yes.'

Anna's relationship with Marco had ended about three months before. He'd wanted different things to her. At times, it had seemed he'd wanted different things to himself. He'd started to talk more and more about settling down and having children, and Anna had known she would have to let him go. But then Nia had seen him with another woman and Anna had stopped agonising and just thrown him out. She'd cursed herself for letting him move in when his landlord gave him notice. It was never a good idea to move in together before you were ready because of rental circumstances. She'd known it even as she'd suggested it, as he pushed her back on the bed and said she wouldn't regret it.

She wasn't heartbroken. It had never been much more than great sex and company. She hadn't had the feeling she was looking for, and she still believed she might find that. She was over it. And since he'd left, she hadn't been on any dates. She hadn't felt like it. So now, this dinner or whatever it was with David, it felt like something she didn't quite know how to do any more. It felt like something alien. She messaged Nia about it, knowing that if she messaged Sarah she would try to convince her to cancel. Sarah had seen the havoc David had wrought, the mess he'd left Anna in. Nia only knew bits and pieces of it.

> I've agreed to go out with David from New York tonight.

Nia replied almost instantly.

> Is that wise?

Anna laughed to herself. It was such a Nia thing to say.

> Probably not.

As the day drew to a close, Anna was frustrated. David

hadn't suggested a time, and he'd been in one meeting after another for the past couple of hours. She didn't want to seem like she was just waiting around for him, despite the fact that that was exactly what she was doing. She went to the toilets, sprayed on some perfume and fixed her makeup, and all the time, she hated herself for it. He wouldn't be making any effort for her, she was sure. But part of her had to go through with this. Had to know. Would he just want to catch up, because they'd been friends and colleagues once, as well as lovers? Or would he ask her to go back to his hotel room? And if he did, would she go? She thought she knew the answer but she wasn't 100 per cent sure.

At six, he came to her desk and she didn't look up straight away. When she did, she tried to conjure up an air of *Oh yes, I'd forgotten all about meeting you.*

'Meetings,' he said. 'But I'm ready to go whenever you are. I'd kill for a good martini. Do you know somewhere?'

Anna did, and she led him there, past pubs with people spilling out onto the pavement. David lit a cigarette and offered her one. She shook her head. Did he remember she didn't smoke? Was it just a reflex, offering her one? Or was he confusing her with someone else he'd been sleeping with?

* * *

At the bar she'd chosen, he held the door open for her. He put a hand on the small of her back and Anna felt she might come undone, there in the doorway of a cocktail bar in Soho. The warmth of him, the memory of him. She forced herself to stay upright, to go to the bar and order drinks. To find a table. To pretend this was any other day.

They drank three cocktails while chatting about work, and

just when Anna had stopped expecting it, David asked her something personal.

'Did you leave New York because of me?'

'Yes.' Anna had had just enough to drink (combined with nothing to eat) to be honest.

David put his head in his hands. What was that supposed to mean?

'And how are you faring, back in London? Are you happy?'

Always the question about being happy. No one was happy all the time, were they? How did you gauge how much happiness was enough?

'I think so.'

'Are you seeing anyone?'

'No.'

A few years ago, she would have qualified that, said that she'd not long come out of a relationship. But now, she didn't feel the need to.

'I'm sorry to hear that.'

'Why sorry? I'm fine.'

'Look, I think about you – about us – all the time. So I wondered...'

'What? Whether we could have a fling while you're over?'

David smiled and shook his head.

'It isn't like that, Anna. You and me, we were good together.'

They had been good together, in various ways. They'd made each other laugh, and they'd always found it easy to talk to each other. And she had loved him.

'I need to go to the toilet,' she said, pushing back her chair.

She stood in front of the mirror, and then before she could change her mind, she messaged Sarah.

I'm drinking cocktails with David.

Sarah's response was quick, and Anna was grateful.

Go home.

Anna had known what Sarah would say, and yet seeing it there on her phone screen was reassuring, somehow.

I don't know whether I can.

You can. Go home, and then call me.

Anna went back to the table, saw that David had bought another round while she'd been gone. She was feeling a little soft around the edges. Not yet drunk, but not entirely sober. She knew another drink would lead her down the path she was so desperately trying to avoid. She sat down, took a sip, and then she remembered the weeks after David had left her. The way she'd shut herself in her apartment, failed to get dressed for days, and stopped eating proper meals. The ache of it all.

'I need to go home,' she said.

David wasn't the type to plead. He put his hands up in a gesture of surrender.

'Will you finish your drink?' he asked.

'No, I don't think so.'

How many women had there been? How many women had he talked to the way he'd talked to her? It was hard to accept but she knew she was one of many. That it hadn't been love, for him. That it hadn't ruined him. She stood up again. And he stood up too.

'Let me walk you...'

'No,' she said, a little sharply.

A woman at a nearby table looked round, and Anna knew she was assessing the situation, trying to determine whether

Anna was in danger, the way women did. She smiled at her, hoping to convey that she wasn't. Not that sort of danger, anyway.

'I just... need to go,' she said.

He nodded, and they shared a look, and she thought that he was sorry for what he'd done to her, not just that day but back in New York. She hoped he was. That he knew. That he understood.

On the Tube home, Anna sat next to a young girl with massive headphones, her music turned up loud. The sound was tinny, but Anna recognised the song immediately. It was her song, hers and Edward's. The one about meeting someone, about all the small things that could stop you from meeting them. She considered how different her life would be if she'd never met David. If she'd never met Edward. Or if she had met Edward, and she hadn't left. What would that be like?

As soon as she'd let herself into her flat, she messaged Sarah to tell her she was home. Sarah said she loved her, told her to call if she needed to. She felt protected, safe. Like she'd avoided something toxic. And she had, undoubtedly. She imagined David, back at the bar, finishing off both their drinks and then looking around for someone else to pick up, to take back to his hotel. It wasn't about her, she could see that now. It was about him, and his ego, and his need for attention.

When he messaged her, pleading with her to come back, she could see it for what it was. Pathetic. He must have failed, she thought, failed to find someone else. She typed out several replies, from the polite to the blisteringly rude. And then she decided that the best response would be no response at all, and she went to bed.

26

YES

Wednesday 5 June 2013

Anna took the Tube into town and headed for The Dog, where she was meeting Nia for lunch. They hadn't been able to do this while she was working at the school, and when she'd left, they'd agreed they would do it every other month. When she got there, Nia was already sitting at their usual table with two drinks in front of her and she held one up to Anna, to show that she didn't need to stop off at the bar.

'Sausage sandwiches ordered,' Nia said, by way of greeting.

'You're very efficient today,' Anna said, leaning over and giving her friend a hug before sitting down.

Nia shrugged. 'I'm starving. So what's new? How's the new business?'

'It's going well,' Anna said. 'But Edward isn't being very supportive, so that's annoying.'

'Why not?'

Why wasn't he? It wasn't about money, she didn't think. He

earned enough to keep everything running and she'd hardly been earning a lot at the school library.

'I don't know,' she said. 'I don't get it. I want him to be happy and fulfilled and have the things he wants. But I'm not sure he feels the same way. Sometimes I think he's still angry with me that we never had a third child. He never stopped wanting another one.'

Nia sipped her drink through a straw and kept her eyes on Anna, giving her permission to carry on.

'You know, I was entirely consumed by motherhood for such a long time. I can't even explain what it's like, but I didn't have the headspace for anything else. And now I've emerged from that, the boys are a bit older and a bit more self-sufficient, and I feel like it's my time. Thomas is about to go to secondary school and it won't be long before Sam is there, too. But it takes a while to build anything up and at the moment I'm barely even covering the cost of the childcare – before and after school clubs, holiday clubs, all that. And every now and then, my brain turns on me and I feel like maybe Edward was right all along. Maybe I should have just stopped work when I became a mother. Maybe I've been doing all this juggling for all these years for nothing.'

Nia held up both her hands. 'That's a lot,' she said.

'I'm sorry.'

'Don't be sorry. I just mean, let me process that for a minute.'

Kev came over just then with their sandwiches, and Nia grinned at him and took both plates from his outstretched hands.

'Got everything you need, ladies?' he asked.

'Yes thanks,' they chorused.

'So,' Nia said once she'd taken a big bite out of her sausage sandwich, 'let me get this straight. You feel like Edward doesn't really value your work, even though the freelance publicity stuff you're doing now feels like it's the right thing for you. And sometimes you struggle to value it too, because of that.'

Anna thought about that. 'Yes. Do you remember when we were at school and I was always in competition with Max Ashwood over our marks in English? Do you know what he's doing now? He's a reporter for the *Guardian*.'

'How do you know that?'

'Facebook.'

'Ah, yes.'

'I mean, they don't tell you, do they, that you can do as well as you like at school, and you can go on to university, but if you want to have a family, which most people do, then you're completely fucked? You have to either take years out of your career, or wait until you're more established to have your kids, by which point you might not be able to have them. And all of that is assuming you meet the person you want to have children with at the right time in your life.'

'Anna, I agree with you, but you look like you might have a heart attack. Calm down.'

Anna took a deep breath and burst into tears.

'Oh, Anna! I'm sorry, come here.' Nia pulled her friend into her body, and Anna let herself be held. Sometimes, she thought, that was all she needed. It was a shame Edward never seemed to realise that.

'I feel like I don't know who I am,' she muttered into Nia's chest.

'I know who you are,' Nia whispered. 'You're my fierce and funny best friend. You're someone who manages to juggle motherhood with a career...'

Anna snorted on this last word.

'Oi, don't be so hard on yourself. You're starting your own business, and that's tough! And like you said, it will take time to build. You show your boys, every day, that it's possible for women to work and be mothers and wives and have ambition and be compassionate, all at the same time. That's an important lesson.'

'Thank you,' Anna said. She lifted her head and smiled a little. 'You always say the right thing.'

'I admire you, Anna, I really do. Sometimes I find it hard to manage my own life and you have everything on your plate that I have plus these two people who you made and who rely on you for everything. It's pretty incredible, if you ask me.'

Anna shook her head. 'It's something millions of women do.'

'And I think they're all amazing, but we're talking about you, Anna, not them. Brilliant, wonderful you.'

Anna felt tears start to prick at her eyes again. 'Let's talk about something else,' she said.

'Any change with your mum?' Nia asked.

Anna shook her head. Her mum had lung cancer. Stage four. She'd been diagnosed a month before and Anna was struggling with it. They'd never been close, and her mum had never made much of an effort with her boys, but she was Anna's mum, and she was dying.

'I went up for the weekend, a couple of weeks ago. Just me, because we weren't sure how she'd be feeling and whether seeing all of us would be too much. She hasn't started chemo yet so she feels okay, but I just thought there might have been a change in her, that it might have got her thinking about her life and who she loves and whether she regrets anything. But she was just the same. Barely asked about the boys. I asked if she wanted to talk about it, about dying, but she just shook her head, said she'd made her arrangements and that she'd send me an email with her funeral wishes in a few months. It was so hard, being there. I wanted to scream. And I wanted to comfort her too, you know, but she wouldn't let me. I guess why would she let me now? She's still the same person.'

Nia shook her head. 'I just don't understand her.'

Nia had grown up in a busy, happy family. She had two parents and three siblings. They fought and made up, but they were never cold. Anna had been on holiday with them a couple of times when they were teenagers, and it had been like peering into a different world.

'Enough misery,' Anna said. 'Tell me about Aidan.'

Nia's face lit up at the mention of his name, and Anna couldn't help smiling. Almost a year before, Anna and Nia had gone out for a night of drinking and dancing at a kitsch bar in Shoreditch, a proper chance to catch up, and Nia had met someone, met Aidan, almost as soon as they'd got there. Anna had spent several hours with Aidan's friend, Ben, talking about their children and their marriages (his was over) and watching Nia and Aidan move closer and closer to one another at the other end of the sofa.

'I think this is it,' Nia said. 'At long last. I think he's the one.'

'One big love, one child,' Anna said softly.

'What?'

'It's what Magda predicted for you. Remember?'

'Oh yes. Well, I might be a bit late for the child part. Back then, I thought it wasn't much, what she said I'd have, but now, well, I think I'd settle for the love.'

'Tell me about it?' Anna asked. 'The love, I mean.'

Nia smiled, lit up like a torch. 'I want to be with him all the time. I miss him when I'm at work, or when he goes back to his flat for a night. He's going to move in; we decided last week. And I can't wait. When I leave the office, I spend the journey home thinking about the fact that I'll get to spend the evening with him. That we'll cook together, or watch a film, and he'll tell me about his day and I'll tell him about mine. It's so simple, but I think I've been really lonely for a long time, and I only realised it when I wasn't any more.'

It was Anna's turn to offer a hug. And Nia took it, but Anna could see that she wasn't sad about the way things had been, she was just delighted at the way they'd turned around.

'I'm sorry if I didn't see it,' Anna said. 'If I didn't try to include you when you were on your own.'

Nia waved a hand to dismiss this. 'You always included me. The thing is, there's nothing anyone can really do when you're on your own like that, for a long time. Don't get me wrong, I loved joining you guys for Sunday lunches and coming with you on day trips, but sometimes it just reinforced what I didn't have. I'd get home and mope about because I knew you were all still there, being a family, and I was back on my own. And I didn't want to be jealous of you, but it was hard, sometimes.'

Anna thought hard before asking her next question. She didn't want Nia to think that she thought marriage and children were the only ways to have a happy, fulfilled life. But of course Nia knew she didn't think that. Nia was well aware of the gaps in Anna's life.

'So what do you think the future holds for the two of you?' Anna asked. 'Beyond moving in, I mean.'

Nia's eyes were bright, and Anna wondered for a moment whether she was close to tears or whether it was just happiness, making her sparkle.

'I don't know,' she said. She held her hands up, as if to show that she had nothing in them. 'He wants to get married and have children, all of that. But I don't know whether we're too old. I'm forty-three. It's okay for him, he could father a child in twenty years if he wanted to, but I might have missed my chance.'

Anna didn't say anything. What was there to say? It seemed

cruel that Nia might not get to experience all the wonder and torture of motherhood.

'I think we'll get married,' Nia went on. 'I think we'll definitely do that.'

Anna smiled. 'I'm so glad,' she said. 'I'm so pleased you found him. That we went out that night. But I'm sorry about the children thing. I'm sorry you might not get to have that.'

Nia nodded. 'I know you are. It really sucks to be a woman sometimes, doesn't it?'

'It does.'

'You know,' Nia said. 'You can tell me if I'm crossing a line. But I sometimes think about that feeling you always said you were looking for, when we were younger. That feeling you had on the date with James. I'm not convinced you've ever had that, with Edward.'

Anna was taken aback. 'We were just kids, Nia. What did I know about life?'

'Well, yes, I get that. But what I have with Aidan, I've never had that before. It took me forty-three years to find it. So...'

'So maybe I settled too soon?'

Nia grimaced. 'I don't know what I'm saying, Anna. Just that you don't always seem that happy. And you don't have to stick with something just because you made a promise a million years ago.'

'Fourteen.'

'What?'

'Fourteen years ago. It's our anniversary.'

Nia's hands flew up to her mouth. 'I'm sorry. Ignore me. I'm talking rubbish.'

Anna put a hand on Nia's shoulder, to show that she wasn't angry.

They'd both finished eating, and it was almost time to get

back to work. They took their plates up to the bar, as they always did. Paid the bill. Kev thanked them and gave them a wink, said he'd see them again soon. It was nice, Anna thought, to have a place in the middle of London where you could go and be known and welcomed like this, even if it was a fairly grotty pub.

'We'll be back soon,' Nia said. 'Best sausage sandwiches in London.'

27

NO

Wednesday 5 June 2013

'Look, everyone knows what he's done, so I don't think we should pretend it hasn't happened,' Anna said.

The comment was met with silence from everyone in the meeting room, and Anna felt put out. Was she invisible? It was an emergency meeting, called by Deborah after the news had broken that a fairly major celebrity whose autobiography they were publishing had been caught shoplifting. The book was due out in a month and the publicity for it was in full swing on both sides of the Atlantic. Anna had never seen Deborah so stressed.

'We can't pull it altogether,' Deborah said. 'That isn't an option.'

Suddenly, David's voice was loud in the room. Anna jumped; she hadn't known he was on the call. 'You're right, we can't pull it. But we could try to work the scandal to our advantage rather than trying to play it down.'

There were mumbles of agreement.

Someone from sales spoke up. 'Yes, that's good. I mean, it's not like he hurt anyone. It's not the kind of crime people feel strongly about.'

Anna couldn't believe what she was hearing. David had literally repeated the thing she'd said, the thing everyone had completely ignored, said it in a slightly different way, and now he was the hero of the hour? She looked at Deborah for some kind of confirmation that she was right to be outraged, but Deborah was still acting antsy, her eyes never resting on anyone or anything for more than a few seconds.

'I said that,' she found herself saying.

'What?' David asked. 'Anna, is that you? Can you speak up a bit?'

Anna imagined she was in the same room as him. She imagined picking up the coffee pot from the middle of the table and throwing the burning liquid in his face.

'I just said that there's no point in trying to pretend it hasn't happened. That we might as well make the best of it.'

'I don't remember hearing that,' David said.

'Deborah?' Anna asked, hating herself for the pleading tone of her voice.

'Sorry, Anna, I must have missed it, too.'

'Let's move on, shall we?' David said.

And that was that.

Anna fumed about it all afternoon. She was still angry when Deborah asked her to come to her office before she left for the day.

'I'm sorry about that, earlier,' Deborah said.

'The thing with David?' Anna asked.

'Yes. I missed what you said, but I know what it's like to be treated like that. You know, you hit forty and you become invisible, in all kinds of spaces. In some ways it's a relief – I've never missed the catcalls from van windows – but at work it's bloody infuriating. So I'm sorry.'

Anna wasn't sure what to say.

'Anyway, that's not what I wanted to talk to you about. I'm retiring, at the end of the year. I wanted to encourage you to apply for my job when I go.'

Anna was taken aback. Her brain hadn't quite made the shift from one thing to the other.

'Retiring?'

Deborah nodded. 'It's a little early. But that's not important. I'd like to see you take over from me. Between you and me, you're the best person for the job. I hope you'll give it a shot.'

'I will,' Anna said. 'Thank you.'

'Good.'

Anna stood and made to leave, but she could tell Deborah had something else to say.

'I know it's none of my business,' Deborah said, 'but what was it that brought you back to London?'

Anna had never told anyone in the London office about her relationship with David. Had thought it was inappropriate. That she would be judged over it. But Deborah was leaving, and Anna was starting to realise that she wasn't the sort of woman who judged other women for their mistakes.

'I had my heart broken,' she said. 'I needed to get away from him.'

'David?' Deborah asked, and part of Anna was shocked that she'd guessed, and part of her wasn't.

'Yes.'

'I'm sorry that happened. He should have known better.'

'Yes, he should,' Anna said. 'But so should I.'

'From a selfish point of view, it's been great, having you back.'

'Thank you.'

When Anna left the office that afternoon, she was thinking about what Deborah had said and she almost didn't notice the person who was standing outside waiting for her. She didn't see him, in fact, until he called her name. Edward. When she turned back and saw him, leaning against the outside wall of her office building, she couldn't quite put the pieces together. He was part of another life, but even when she'd been in that life, she'd never seen him here.

'What are you doing here?' she asked.

'I wanted to see you. Do you have time for a coffee or something?'

Anna met his eyes for the first time. He looked a bit bewildered, like he didn't know what he was doing or where he should be. And that wasn't the Edward she knew. It was enough to stop her from saying no, which was her initial impulse.

'Okay,' she said. 'There's a place just around this corner.' She gestured and began to walk, and he followed her.

In the café, the barista smiled at Anna and asked if she wanted her usual. She called in there most mornings on her way into the office. 'And for you?' The handsome young man looked up at Edward, who asked for an Americano. 'Sit down, I'll bring them over.'

Anna chose a table, making bets with herself about what he was going to say. It couldn't be to do with the divorce, with the sharing of their assets, could it? All of that was done and dusted so long ago. But what else? His new partner, his child? How could any of that have anything to do with Anna? She took a seat and waited for him to speak.

'It's good to see you,' he said.

Anna didn't say anything. What was there to say? Was it good to see him? She wasn't sure.

'Listen, I know this is a shock, seeing me like this. I've just... I've been thinking about you a lot lately. And especially today...'

He trailed off, and Anna tried to think what he might mean by that. And then it hit her. It was their anniversary. Or would have been. She did a quick calculation in her head. If she and Edward had stayed together, this would have been their fourteenth anniversary. What would her life be like? Would she be doing the job she was doing? Would they have children? Would she feel fulfilled, like she was on the right track?

'I don't know what to say,' Anna said, because she felt she had to say something.

'No, I know. I'm not explaining myself. Did you know it's exactly three years ago that we met on the common?'

Anna thought about that. Could it be true? She had no idea when it had happened, only that it had been early summer. So perhaps, she thought. And he seemed so sure.

'No, I...'

'I went home that day, my head full of you. You looked incredible, and seeing you was like revisiting an old life. A happier one. And I realised, when I got home, that it was our anniversary. It felt like fate. But I convinced myself it was nothing, carried on with my new life with Ella and Jen, but I just knew it was all a lie, and every time Jen talked about the wedding, I put her off. I just couldn't face it. Plus I lost my mum, and I was a mess. In the end, she confronted me, and I admitted it. I was having doubts. And she left me.'

Anna fixated on the news of him having lost his mum for a moment. They'd never been close, Anna and her mother-in-law, but it was strange to have known nothing of her death. She had a memory from the wedding, her mother and Edward's, both in slightly old-fashioned dresses and jackets, laughing together. And now, one was dead, the other dying. She'd been living with the knowledge that her mum had terminal cancer for a while now, and it didn't get any easier, no matter how patchy their relationship had been.

She snapped back to the present, to the news Edward had just revealed. 'She left you?'

'Yes. It was the right thing, I don't blame her. My heart wasn't in it. When we met, she wanted to have a child and I was so raw from you not wanting to, and so we jumped into it, and then Ella came along and she was just wonderful, it was everything I'd thought it would be, but it wasn't with the right person. It wasn't with you.'

Anna felt herself go hot across her neck and chest. Was that what this was? Was this an attempt to get her back? Just then, the barista brought over their drinks and Anna reminded herself of where she was, and when. She hadn't gone back in time. She was still forty-three. Edward was still her ex.

'I missed you, Anna. I missed you so much for the first couple of years and I was terrible to be with. But by the time I met Jen, I really thought I'd moved on. It was only seeing you that made me realise I hadn't. What a mess. I mean, I love Ella so much and I want to be the best dad I can to her, but Jen and I can't be together. Not with the way I feel about you.'

Anna knew that she was going to have to say something eventually. But what? That day she'd seen Edward with Ella, she'd felt shaken. She'd gone straight to Nia's, she remembered. But that was as far as it had gone. A week later, it had been gone from her mind. Just one of those things that happened, when old lives and new lives collided. Seeing Edward hadn't been painful, or wrenching, or anything like that.

'Edward, I...'

'Look, I know this is probably a shock. Me just appearing like this, with no warning. Perhaps I should have tried to get hold of your email address or contacted you on social media or something, but it felt right, to come here on this date.'

Anna reflected on this. It would have taken him less than a minute of online searching to find her email address. He was right, he should have done that. Should have approached her in a less confrontational way, given her some time and space to decide how she wanted to respond.

'Edward, I'm with someone.'

'Oh.' He looked shocked, as if he hadn't realised this was a possibility. As if the fact that she'd been single when they'd last met, three years ago, meant that she always would be.

'How long?' he asked.

'Almost a year.' She thought of Ben, of the way he made her laugh every day. How they'd met by chance on a work night out that had ended in a kitsch bar in Shoreditch, how Anna had very nearly said no when he'd asked for her number. How, after he'd put his number into her phone, she'd called him so he would have hers, and he'd answered and said, into the phone while looking her in the eyes, 'I'm so glad you called, I wasn't sure you would.' How she'd stopped looking for that feeling she'd always been chasing, because she thought she might have found it.

'Is he a good guy?' Edward asked.

Anna didn't want to answer. She wanted to make a point of it being none of Edward's business, the state of her current relationship. But it was easier, simpler, to go along with it.

'Yes,' she said. 'He's a good guy. I wouldn't be with him if he wasn't.'

Edward raised both of his hands up to show that he was backing off. 'I shouldn't have come. I'm sorry.'

Anna blew on her coffee, took a sip. Her instinct was to say that it was fine, but she stopped herself. He was right. He shouldn't have come. It hadn't done either of them any good.

'I think I'm going to go,' she said, standing. 'I'm sorry it didn't work out for you, with her. And I'm sorry about your mum.'

Edward pushed his chair back to stand. She saw that there were tears in his eyes. 'Thank you. How's yours?'

'She's dying, actually. Lung cancer. It's taking its time, but we all know how it's going to end.'

Edward put a hand on her arm. 'Jesus, I'm sorry.'

There was a moment of silence as they both considered the years that had passed since they'd been together. The bits of one another's lives that they had missed.

'Thanks for hearing me out,' Edward said.

So he left first, in the end. But Anna left a minute later, as soon as she was sure he'd be gone and they wouldn't end up walking down the street together. She thought about getting home, to Ben, about telling him this story. About how he would listen, and ask questions, and take it seriously without being jealous. She imagined telling him that she was so pleased she was with him now, and kissing him. And it all fell away, the tension and the worry of seeing Edward. And that was how she knew, that she was exactly where she should be.

28

YES

Thursday 5 June 2014

It took Anna a long time to come round and realise that her phone was ringing. By the time she was fully awake, Edward was sitting up, rubbing his eyes.

'Answer it,' he said.

She paused before doing so. Her mother had died a few weeks before but she was still terrified of phone calls that came in the middle of the night.

'Hello?'

'Anna.' It was Nia. 'I'm sorry to call you in the middle of the night. I'm...'

Her voice turned muffled and then disappeared, but Anna thought she heard a groan.

'It's okay, Nia. What's happening? Is it the baby?'

Anna felt cold, suddenly. She pulled the duvet over her knees. She was sitting up and she knew Edward was looking at her, waiting to hear what it was. She did a quick calculation. Nia was seven months pregnant. Aidan was away with work.

'It's coming,' Nia said. 'The baby's coming, and it's too early and Aidan isn't here. Will you come with me, Anna?'

'Of course. I'll come and get you. I'll be there in five minutes.' She was already up and out of bed.

'The baby?' Edward asked when she ended the call.

'Yes.'

'It will be okay,' he said.

'It might not. It's too early.' Anna pulled jeans out of a drawer, rummaged around for a top. 'I can't think straight. What do I need to take?'

Edward shook his head. 'It all feels so long ago. She'll have everything she needs. Just take some money for food and parking.'

'Will you and the boys be all right? Will you get Sam to school? Make sure Thomas gets up in time?'

'Yes, don't worry about us. Go.' He stood and kissed her on the forehead. 'And give Nia my love. It will be okay, Anna. I know it.'

Nothing much had changed in the years since Anna had given birth. She didn't know what she'd expected. On the drive to the hospital, Nia had been almost silent. She'd said she was just concentrating on getting through the contractions, but Anna could feel the fear coming off her in waves. They'd got lucky, Nia and Aidan, conceiving within the space of a couple of months, and Nia had said all along that she didn't trust it. That she was waiting for something to go wrong. But the twelve-week scan had gone without a hitch, and then the twenty-week one, and it had seemed like they were out of the woods. And now this.

When they'd arrived at the maternity unit of the same hospital where Anna had had her boys, a friendly midwife had bustled them in and examined Nia in a side room and found her to be in active labour. Since then, it had been quite relaxed, with Nia puffing away on the gas and air and handling the contractions much better than Anna remembered handling them herself. In between, she was classic Nia, telling stories and asking for snacks. They'd been assigned a room and a midwife called Eleanor who'd mostly left them to their own devices.

'How are you doing?' Eleanor asked, putting her head around the door.

Nia smiled a little weakly. 'I'm okay, thanks. Anna's looking after me.'

'Any word on your partner's arrival?'

'He's on his way. He should be here in a couple of hours. He won't miss it, will he?'

'I shouldn't think so.'

'Look...' Nia said, and Anna could tell from the tone of her voice that she was about to say something she found difficult. 'I know I'm really old to be a first-time mum, and the baby is coming too early, and I don't know whether people are saying everything will be okay because they don't want to tell me the truth, or...'

Eleanor came to the side of the bed and put a hand on Nia's shoulder. 'I've delivered a lot of babies, Nia. We never know for sure how it's going to go, what's going to happen, that everyone is going to be all right. We just do our best. And that's what we're going to do with you. There's a cot ready in special care, and the best obstetrician in this hospital is on duty, and I'm here. That's the best we can do.'

Anna was so grateful for Eleanor. She tried to remember the midwives who had helped her through her labours, but she couldn't. It was so long ago. All she could remember was that it was the worst pain she'd ever known. Eleanor had a calming presence, and Anna wondered whether it was that that had led her to this job, or whether the years in the job had taught her to be calm.

'Okay,' Nia said.

And then another contraction came, and Anna stepped forward to take Nia's hand, and she felt utterly helpless as her friend writhed and moaned her way through it.

'Tell me about your births,' Nia said when it was over.

'Didn't I tell you at the time?' Anna asked.

'No, don't you remember? I said I'd once googled the word episiotomy and the images had made my eyes water and I would thank you not to fill me in any further on the whole process.'

Anna laughed. 'Oh yes, I remember now.'

'What do you have?' Eleanor asked. 'How many?'

'Two boys,' Anna said, 'twelve and nine. And you?'

'I have one girl,' Eleanor said. 'She's six next week.' She turned to Nia. 'Do you know what you're having?'

Nia shook her head. 'We wanted it to be a surprise, and now it's decided to come two months early and when Aidan's not around and I think that's surprise enough.'

She put her head in her hands, and then another contraction came, and Anna remembered so clearly the feeling of hopelessness that had taken over her, both times, when she was birthing her sons.

'I'm here,' Anna said, 'and I know it's not the same, but let me assure you, one birthing partner is just as useless as another. It's all down to you, I'm afraid. But if you need anything, I'm here.'

When Aidan turned up, in the early afternoon, Anna felt as if a weight had physically been lifted from her shoulders. She was no longer responsible. She saw the relief in Nia's eyes, too, and she saw the way Eleanor smiled. All was as it should be. And it was then that Anna realised that Nia was part of a family now, and a little less part of her. It shouldn't have come as a surprise, or have winded her, especially since she had a family of her own at home, but it did, a little.

Aidan put his hand on Anna's shoulder, after he'd kissed Nia. 'Thanks for being here. I know it will have meant the world to her to have you with her.'

Anna shrugged. 'It was nothing.'

It was what you did for a friend. Anna turned to Nia. 'I'll go home now, and wait for news.' She reached for her friend's hand. 'You're doing brilliantly.'

Nia smiled up at her and Anna knew that she wasn't really there, not fully. She was exhausted and scared, and she would be until her baby arrived, and then for all the years afterwards. She was a mother.

Anna let herself into the house and stood in the kitchen, boiling the kettle. It felt so empty after the bustle of the hospital. She called Edward at work.

'Hey. Did she have the baby already?'

'No, but Aidan arrived so I came away.'

'Is everything okay?'

'Hard to say. It should be, I think.'

'You sound shattered. Why don't you lie down for a bit? You've got a couple of hours before school finishes.'

'I think I will,' she said.

She wanted to say something else, about how seeing Nia on the verge of becoming a mother had made her feel rootless, somehow. How seeing Nia and Aidan acting as a team for this ultimate act of partnership had made her feel as if she'd floated far away from him, her own partner. But she didn't know how to say any of it, so she just said she would see him later and ended the call.

Edward had been right about her being exhausted, but once

she was lying in bed with the curtains closed, she felt wide awake again. She thought about Nia, wondered how she was getting on, whether it was close to being over yet. It was strange to imagine Nia just entering this world she'd been a part of for more than a decade. She thought back to her early days as a mother and mostly remembered crying and feeling like she was getting it all wrong. She remembered Thomas thrashing in her arms, refusing to nap, refusing to feed. The way she'd wondered whether it had been the right thing to do, whether she'd made a dreadful mistake. She hoped Nia wouldn't feel like that.

And of course, those thoughts led her back to her own mother, as so often happened. At her mother's funeral, Edward had stood beside her with his hand on the small of her back, and she had hated herself for questioning her whole life, including her marriage to him, while he was trying to be there for her. Her mum had led a lonely, closed-up sort of life, and now it was over, and only a handful of people had come to say their goodbyes. Was her life so different? She hoped that her style of mothering was more generous and open. She knew, at heart, that it was. But what about everything else? Had she made much of a difference to anyone? Had she done the things she desperately wanted to? The things that scared her? She pictured Steve, that kiss they'd shared in the kitchen, how it had felt like coming home. You couldn't always live for the moment, could you? Yes, she had been drawn to Steve and she had felt like perhaps she loved him, but she had built her life with Edward. Wasn't it the right thing – the responsible thing – to stay true to that?

When she thought of Steve, she couldn't help but imagine the life the two of them might have lived together, if things had been different. If she'd turned her back on her marriage and given it a go with him. She would never know how it might have turned out. Whether it would have been a dream or a nightmare. She didn't know Steve's habits, his faults. That was the way things were. You took the chance, or you didn't. You went one way or another.

Anna's phone beeped and there was a message from Aidan. 'He's here! Everyone's doing well.' There was a photo of Nia holding their baby, her face clear and her eyes bright. She looked tired but somehow transformed.

'One big love,' Anna whispered to herself, 'and one baby.'

29

NO

Thursday 5 June 2014

Anna stood at the kitchen counter making cups of tea while Ben and his daughters ate chocolate biscuits at the kitchen table. He'd just picked them up from school, and they were staying for three nights.

'Stella, no more until Anna has had some,' Ben said.

Stella shrugged and walked over to the fruit bowl. She picked up two apples and a satsuma and juggled with them for a few seconds, before dropping them all on the floor, picking them up and taking a big bite out of one of the apples. She didn't look at Anna. She rarely looked at Anna.

Anna took the drinks over to the table and sat down opposite Tess.

'You okay?' she asked her.

'Why aren't you at work?' Tess asked.

'Your dad and I both took the week off,' Anna said.

'You know that,' Ben said, giving Tess's arm a playful tap. 'We just got back from Paris.'

Ben reached across the table and put his hand on Anna's wrist, and she knew he was trying to reassure her. He told her, often, that she didn't need to try so hard with the girls, that she should just be there, and let them learn to trust her. Ben had had one other girlfriend since the end of his marriage, and he'd told Anna that he'd introduced her to the girls too soon, and they'd been disconcerted when the relationship ended, as if they were now to expect a series of breakups, one after another. Anna wished for a moment that they were back in Paris, wandering the streets hand in hand, drinking wine in little squares in the afternoon and going back to the hotel to have sex and sleep before a late dinner. While they'd been there, it had been as if their real lives didn't exist.

'What shall we do?' Ben asked. 'Does anyone fancy Monopoly?'

Anna hated Monopoly. She willed the girls to say no.

'Can't we go out?' Stella asked.

'Out where?'

'Bowling and pizza?' Tess suggested.

Her voice was hopeful, and Anna saw the little girl in her. So often, she was trying to be more like Stella, to care about how she looked and what she was wearing, but when she was caught off-guard, it was clear that she didn't care about any of that stuff, not really. She was ten, her front teeth still a bit too big for her face. She had reddish hair and freckles, and she looked nothing like Ben, but not a great deal like the photos Anna had seen of the girls' mother, either. Stella was twelve and much more like her dad. Tall and wiry, her hair dark and a little unruly in a way that Anna thought would be the bane of her adolescence but which she'd learn to use to her advantage as an adult. Because of her similarity to Ben, Anna could see Stella as an adult, but she couldn't do the same with Tess. She was still a while away from puberty, still sometimes came into their room in the night when she'd had a bad dream. Still a girl.

'What do you think?' Ben asked Anna.

'Let's do it,' she said.

Anna knew that Ben struggled with getting the balance right, when it came to part-time parenting. They'd talked about it late into the night, several times. He didn't want to always be treating the girls, for them to see their mother as the tough parent and him as the fun one, but he wanted to make them happy, too. Anna had been careful about what she'd said. It wasn't her place to offer advice on parenting, she thought, but she firmly believed that Ben's daughters were good people, and that Ben didn't need to worry quite as much as he did. It seemed impossible to avoid, though, the worrying. Even Anna had started worrying about them in the quiet hours between three and five in the morning when she sometimes lay awake. What if one of them was being bullied and they had no idea? What if they were exposed to some kind of predator online? It was the worrying that alerted her to the fact that her feelings for them were deepening.

Tess put her arm in the air and pulled her fist down in triumph, and Anna thought she saw Stella grinning between bites of her second apple.

A couple of hours later, they were sharing pizzas. Anna was glad the bowling was over, but the kids seemed to have enjoyed it. Ben, too. She liked seeing him in dad mode. It was like opening up another facet of him. She loved how kind he was with the girls, how endlessly patient. Now, he turned to her, his expression a little worried.

'Stella's been gone a while, hasn't she?' he asked.

Stella had been a bit sullen, but she often was. She'd gone to the toilet a few minutes before.

'Shall I go and check on her?' Tess asked.

Ben nodded and she trotted off.

'What are you worried about?' Anna asked. 'Maybe she has an upset stomach or something.'

'I don't know. It's probably nothing.'

It was a whole new world, Anna thought. Knowing when to step in and when to stay back. And it must have been hard for Ben, with girls, who might have secrets they weren't prepared to divulge to a man, even if that man was their loving father.

Tess was back. 'She wants you,' she said, looking at Anna.

'Me?'

'Will you go?' Ben asked.

'Of course, I mean...' Anna didn't finish her sentence. She picked up her bag and went into the toilets.

There was no one standing by the sinks, and only one of the three cubicles was occupied.

'Stella?' Anna asked.

There was silence for a minute, and Anna thought about saying her name again, but it seemed pointless. They were the only two people in there, and she knew Stella could hear her. She waited.

'I've got my period,' Stella said eventually. 'And I don't have anything with me.'

Anna could hear tears in her voice and she felt this urge to pull Stella towards her, and it was the closest she'd come to feeling like a mother. She almost laughed, not because it was funny, but because her own periods were becoming irregular and she thought it was probably the beginning of the end. She couldn't quite imagine being back there, where Stella was, right at the start of it all. She'd been having periods for over thirty years, and for what? All those cramps, those clots, those days of feeling full of rage and desperate for comfort food, and no babies to show for it.

'Is it the first time?' she asked.

'No, I've had a few, but they're not regular. I just didn't think...'

Anna set her bag down by the sinks and started rooting through it. In a zipped pocket, she found two tampons. And then she realised Stella might not have started using tampons. The murkily lit toilets of a pizza place were not the place to learn.

'Don't worry,' Anna said. 'Pad or tampon?'

'Pad, if you have one,' Stella said.

Anna didn't, but she looked around the room and saw there was a machine on the wall. She found the right change in her purse, and then she handed the wrapped package over the top of the cubicle.

'Thank you so much.'

'Of course. Is there any blood on your clothes?'

'Just my knickers. It's fine.'

Anna didn't know whether she should wait for Stella to come out or go back to the table. Would Stella be embarrassed by this? Probably. Being a pre-teen girl hadn't changed that much since she was one. She waited, leaning back against the sink in a way she hoped looked casual.

'Thanks,' Stella said again, when she emerged. She was flushed, and she didn't look Anna in the eye.

'Stella, it's nothing, really. I'm glad I could help.'

'I don't know what to say to Dad.'

Anna thought about that. She remembered being around this age and feeling embarrassed about everything. She hadn't had a dad, but if she had, she was pretty sure she wouldn't have felt able to talk to him about what was going on with her body or her mind.

'We could say the lock was stuck?'

Stella was washing her hands. She laughed, and the sound of it brought Anna a wave of joy.

'Can we?'

'Of course we can.'

They walked back to the table, Anna in front and Stella just behind, and Anna knew that something had shifted between them. She wasn't naïve enough to think Stella would never again be grumpy with her, or angry, or try to shut her out, but they'd taken a step forward and that was enough.

* * *

Later, in bed, Ben asked about the incident in the pizza place.

'Was it her period?'

He was propped up on one elbow, gazing intently at Anna. Would it be a betrayal of Stella, to tell him? She decided it wouldn't be, as long as Stella didn't know.

'Yes, but please don't talk to her about it. She's embarrassed.'

Ben nodded. 'God, I wasn't ready for this. I mean, I know she's twelve, but she's still so young in my head. When she's with her mum, and I think of her, I picture her at about four.'

Anna tried to imagine how that would be. How it would feel to have known someone since their birth, to have loved them and lived with them all that time, and for them to be changing from a child to an adult in front of you.

'I'm glad she asked for your help, though,' Ben added.

'Me too.'

'I know it's not always easy, with them. I know you must feel pushed away sometimes.'

Anna felt tears prick at her eyes. It was hard, knowing where the lines were, when it was okay to step in and when she should stay out of it. Early on, Stella had been pretty horrible to her a couple of times, said that she would never like her or accept her relationship with Ben, and Anna had taken it hard, despite knowing that she, Stella, was going through something tough too.

'I want them to trust me,' she said. 'I want to be part of their lives. But you can't just create something out of nothing. It has to be built.'

'And it will be,' he said. 'It is being built. And I'm so grateful to you for wanting all of that.'

Anna lay on her back, letting the tears fall. They slipped down to her cheeks and fell off the sides of her face, and she just let them. After a few minutes, she sensed that Ben was asleep. His breathing had deepened, and his body was still. Early on in their relationship, they'd talked about children, about whether she felt she'd missed out, whether she wanted to try. Ben was happy as he was, with his girls, but he made sure she knew that he would go through it all again with her, if that was what she wanted. And if they were able to. Anna had said no. It had passed her by; it was too late. She still felt, at least 90 per cent of the time, that it had been the right decision. Perhaps if she'd met Ben earlier, it would have been different.

She'd been thinking more about it, since her mother had died. She'd always been scared that she wouldn't be a good mother because she hadn't had a good mother, that her relationship with any potential children would be deeply flawed or, worse, almost non-existent. She'd felt untethered since the news, since the funeral. She'd seen her mother so rarely that the weeks since her death could just have been weeks in which they didn't visit one another or speak. And yet, there was something about knowing that she was no longer in the world that had winded Anna a bit. Ben had been brilliant, but she knew he didn't quite understand the nature of her grief. His parents were both alive

and well, and he was close to them. They loved him uncompli-
catedly, loved the girls the same way, and they seemed to be
starting to love Anna, too. In all kinds of ways, she was part of a
family in a way she'd never been before. And yet, she had no
biological family left at all.

When they'd got back to the house that evening, Anna had
slipped out again, bought Stella a pack of pads. She'd debated
buying new underwear too, but she would have had to guess
Stella's size and she wasn't at all sure of her tastes. Plain black
pants from Marks seemed safe enough, but what if Stella
thought she was crossing a line, going too far? No. She was
bound to have brought spare knickers in her weekend case.
Anna had knocked on the door of the room the girls shared
when she got back, handed the pads to Stella discreetly. Tess was
sitting on her bed with her legs crossed, a book in her hand. She
was miles away.

'Thanks,' Stella had said.

And just as Anna was backing out of the room, she'd spoken
again.

'Thanks for everything, Anna.'

30

YES

Friday 5 June 2015

'I'm not going,' Thomas said. He was sitting on his bed.

Anna stood in his doorway. His room was a state; it always was. She knew he didn't like her going in there and she hated to think what he had hidden away under his bed or in his wardrobe. She hated that there was a room in her home that stank and was filthy. But now wasn't the time. She put her hands on her hips.

'I told Nia we'd be there,' she said, keeping her voice calm. Pleading with him was more likely to work than getting cross.

'But you didn't ask me,' he said, 'and I have plans.'

'What plans? Playing with Connor on the Xbox?'

Thomas looked hurt and Anna wondered whether he really did have plans. Whether he was doing something that he was nervous about, something that was important to him. She wondered whether he was seeing someone, whether there was a girl or a boy he liked. He kept his cards pretty close to his chest on that kind of thing, always had. She'd been delighted once, when he'd asked her to help him choose a Valentine's card for a girl in his class. But that had been a few years ago, when he was no more than ten, and he hadn't confided in her about his love life since.

'Mum, when you go out drinking with Nia, I don't take the piss out of that. My plans are my plans.'

So it was Connor and the Xbox, she surmised. She blew her hair out of her face and tried one more thing.

'You know your brother won't want to come if you're not coming.'

Thomas shrugged. 'That really isn't my problem, Mum.'

'Thomas, look at me. Please, I'm asking you to do this for me.'

Anna didn't wait for an answer. She went next door, to Sam's room.

'Why does Thomas get to do his own thing and I have to come to a baby's birthday party?' Sam asked.

He wasn't angry, just making sure she knew that it was unfair. He was too sweet-natured to be angry, this one.

'Because he's thirteen,' Anna said. 'And I can't make him do things he doesn't want to do any more.'

'But you still can with me?'

'Just about.'

Sam smiled, and she smiled back, and she thought of him at six, his front teeth missing. The way he'd held her so tight when they'd cuddled, and she'd almost been winded by it.

'Do you think there'll be good cake?'

'There is bound to be an excellent cake,' Anna said. 'Nia throws really good parties. We're leaving in about fifteen minutes, okay?'

Ten minutes later, while Anna was writing Theo's birthday card, Thomas appeared and took his shoes out of the chest by the front door. Anna made eye contact with him and smiled, and Thomas shrugged.

'Thank you,' she said.

When they arrived at Nia's flat, she ushered them inside and made a face at Anna. 'Everything okay?' she mouthed.

Anna gave a little groan. The boys had gone in ahead of her and were already out of earshot. 'Just one of those days,' she said. 'Got any wine?' She followed Nia through to the kitchen, where her friend poured her a large glass of red and handed it over.

'I hope it wasn't about the party,' Nia said.

Anna shook her head. 'Teenage stuff,' she said.

'Is work okay?'

'Work is good, really picking up. If anything, I have too much of it.'

'That's brilliant. Oh, and I have a book for you. Here' – she picked it up off the kitchen counter and held it out – 'it's about a decades-long friendship, like ours, and I loved it. I thought you might too.'

Anna looked at the book, saw that it was published by her old company. 'Thanks,' she said, wondering who had worked on it. Mostly, she didn't miss her old job, but when she saw that familiar logo, it always took her back.

Aidan came into the kitchen then, with Theo in his arms. 'Anna!' he exclaimed, swooping down to kiss her cheek.

'Hello, birthday boy,' Anna said, taking hold of one of Theo's chubby hands.

He grinned and pulled his hand away, did a couple of claps. He was wearing skinny jeans and a blue shirt covered with little embroidered cars.

'God, he's adorable,' Anna said. 'Were my two ever like that?'

She knew they had been, but it was hard to remember.

Thomas was tall and clumsy, his hands and feet enormous and his skin greasy. And Sam was caught in that in-between stage, not quite a little boy but not yet a teenager, and his teeth were a little goofy. He needed a brace. Anna looked at Theo, all cheeks and eyes, fluffy hair and wobbly steps, and she remembered when she'd thought it wouldn't get any harder.

Anna realised she was still holding Theo's present. She gave it to Aidan and he handed Theo to her so he could open it, and she enjoyed the warmth of his body, the way he put his hands on her, trusting.

'Thank you,' Nia said.

'It's just clothes,' Anna said.

'Perfect. He doesn't need any more toys and he's growing like a weed.'

All through the afternoon, Anna felt aware of Thomas sulking. He stayed in the corner of the living room, his phone in his hand, barely looking up. Sam mostly stayed with Anna, and she could tell he was bored, but he didn't complain about it. There were a few other kids around his age there, and he played with them a bit, and he jokingly joined in the games of pass the parcel and musical statues.

Edward arrived a little after six, looking hot and bothered from a day at work and the Tube journey home. He joined Thomas, leaning against the wall, looking at his phone, and Anna thought how alike they could be.

'Right, let's eat,' called Nia, gesturing over to the kitchen counter, where she'd laid out cold meats and cheeses and bread. Anna looked over to Edward, tried to catch his eye. He was typing. A work email or a tweet? Out of nowhere, she thought that perhaps he was having an affair. Perhaps he was standing in the corner of her best friend's son's first birthday party sending a message to his lover. And she was consumed with fury, as if she knew for a fact that it was true. She went over there.

'What are you doing?' she asked.

'What do you mean?' He looked up, slipped his phone into his pocket.

'I mean you've just arrived and you're playing on your phone. It's rude. Thomas is doing it, and he's thirteen. It's what thirteen-year-olds do.'

Edward rolled his eyes. 'Come on, Anna. I couldn't get here any quicker. I was at work! I've given up my Friday night to come to a first birthday party and now I'm not allowed to check what's going on in the world while we're here? Did I miss something important during pass the parcel?'

Anna bit her tongue, hard. She hated it when he acted like this, the way he sometimes twisted anything she criticised him for to make her feel small and petty.

'I don't know why you came,' she said, 'if you're going to be like this.'

'I didn't know it was optional,' he said.

She walked away. Picked up a plate and helped herself to some food. Had another glass of wine. In the kitchen, Nia was standing by the fridge with Aidan right beside her, and they were holding Theo between them and he had a hand on each of their faces. And they looked so happy, Anna felt herself starting to cry. She put her glass and her plate down and went off to the toilet, looking down to avoid meeting anyone's eye on the way, and when she heard Nia calling her name, she pretended she hadn't.

There was only one toilet in the flat, and Anna knew that she couldn't feasibly spend more than a couple of minutes in there. She stood in front of the mirror, watching the tears form and pool in her eyes. And then when she thought a minute had passed, she got some toilet roll and dabbed at her eyes carefully, trying to repair the damage.

Was she unhappy? Right now, she was. But what about when they were all watching a film together, pizza boxes on the coffee table and Sam snuggled into her? Or when she and Edward were alone, and he was making her laugh and touching her like it was the first time, after all these years? There was less and less of that, she thought. And it wasn't so much the sex she missed but the connection. They were drifting in opposite directions, Anna thought, and she needed to do something about it. She needed to do everything she could to reverse it, or at least to halt it. Because in a few years, the boys would be gone and it would just be the two of them, and what if they'd drifted too far, by then? What if they could no longer see one another?

When she unlocked the door, Anna hoped there wouldn't be a queue of people outside. And there wasn't. There was just Thomas.

'Hey,' he said.

'Are you waiting to use the loo?'

'No. I saw you come past. You looked upset.'

Anna met her son's eye. He was several inches taller than her, more man than boy.

'Are you all right?' he asked. He looked uncomfortable asking, but she was grateful that he had.

'I'm okay,' she said.

'I'm sorry if I...'

Anna waited, in case he picked the sentence up again, but he didn't.

'It's not you,' she said.

'Okay. I wasn't sure.'

'I'm sorry I made you come here,' Anna said.

'It's all right. The food's good.'

Anna laughed then, and she wanted to pull him in for a hug but she couldn't remember the last time he'd let her hold him, and she didn't want to spoil the moment.

'Did you eat anything?' Thomas asked.

Anna shook her head. 'I left my plate in the kitchen. I'll get it.'

He nodded, and they moved in the direction of the kitchen together. Anna wished he was young enough that she could squeeze his hand. Moments like this, she felt like her life had been worth something real. She'd brought up this boy who would soon be a man and be out in the world. And she'd done it well. Without her, he wouldn't have existed. There were gaps inside her, there were things she ached for, and sometimes she thought they'd been caused by motherhood, and sometimes she felt like motherhood filled and soothed them.

Nia and Aidan were still in the kitchen, but Theo was on the floor, a little circle of people around him. He'd been walking for a few days and everyone was keen to see it. Anna picked up her plate and took a bite of sourdough and when she looked across to the corner of the room, she saw Steve. It hadn't occurred to her that he might be here, that he might still be with Nia's colleague. Chloe, was it? When he saw her, he smiled, and Anna smiled back and put a hand up in a sort of wave. The last time she'd properly seen him, at Nia's fortieth, she'd been drunk and made a fool of herself. She wondered whether he and Chloe were married now. She felt oddly nostalgic for the days she had spent with Steve when the children were young. The way he'd made her feel. Understood. Important.

'I was just thinking about the day he was born,' Nia said.

Anna hadn't noticed her approaching. She thought back. Nia had been so scared about him coming early. And now here they were, a year later, and Theo was a perfectly healthy little boy, walking and climbing and making train sounds.

'I'm so glad you were there,' Nia said.

'Me too. But I'm glad Aidan arrived when he did, too.'

'Agreed,' Nia said. 'But listen, I don't know whether I ever really thanked you for that.'

Anna batted a hand. 'For what? I didn't do anything.'

'You always do that,' Nia said. 'But you were there, just when I needed you. And you can't pretend that's nothing.'

Nia walked away, scooped Theo up and patted his padded bum, and Anna thought about what Nia had said. She did have a tendency to minimise things, she thought. To think the things she did weren't very much. She cast her eye around, found Thomas, who'd wandered off and was now chatting to Sam. She spotted Edward, talking to a friend of Aidan's and drinking a beer. Her family didn't look like Nia's, but they were still her family.

About twenty minutes later, Edward found her. 'Shall we make a move?' he asked.

Anna nodded. She knew she had to say something to Steve before they left. To clear the air. While Edward rallied the boys, Anna sought him out. She was relieved to see that he was standing alone.

'Hi,' she said.

'Hi, Anna.'

'I forgot that you were sort of connected to Nia.'

'Strictly parties only,' Steve said, and his voice was soft.

Anna looked at him, really took him in. With anyone else, she would have been scared to make eye contact for so long. She wasn't even sure she would do it with Edward, and that struck her as painfully sad. She had missed Steve, in every sense. Missed seeing him, missed out on being with him.

Chloe appeared from somewhere and put an arm around his waist.

'Hi, I'm Chloe,' she said.

'I'm Anna,' she said. 'Old friend of Steve's. From years ago.'

'A different life,' Steve said.

And Anna nodded and said her goodbyes, because Edward was standing by the door looking at his watch, and she thought she might cry.

On the walk home, Sam did a silly impression of a little boy who'd been at the party and it made them all laugh. Edward suggested they order a Chinese for dinner, and when Anna raised her eyebrows, he smiled.

'What? You can't expect us to get by on a bit of bread and cheese.'

'Please, Mum?' Sam asked, looking up at her. 'I'll share duck pancakes with you.'

'Okay,' she said, holding up her hands as if in surrender.

They had their traditions. Whenever they ordered Chinese, she and Sam had duck pancakes and Thomas and Edward had spring rolls. They would eat it in the living room in front of an American sitcom. And afterwards, the boys would go to their rooms and Edward would put on some music and they would talk. And she wasn't sure whether it was enough, but for now, it was what she had.

31

NO

Friday 5 June 2015

Sarah stood with her hands on her hips, looking around.

'This place is gorgeous,' she said.

Anna smiled. She loved the flat she and Ben had bought together. It was part of a Victorian terrace, and none of the walls were straight, as she'd discovered when tiling and wallpapering. But the way the light flooded through the front windows in the afternoon was breathtaking, and there was a small, square garden that she liked to sit in on warm evenings, and they'd filled the rooms with colour and art. It had made her wonder why she'd never put this kind of love into any other home she'd lived in. She thought it was connected to her state of mind. She was happy and in love, and she wanted to reflect that in her surroundings.

'Thank you. We love it.'

Sarah was over from New York for a week and Anna was so happy to see her. At the airport, they had hugged for a long time and Anna had found it difficult to let go. They caught up regularly on the phone, but she hadn't seen her friend, hadn't been in the same room as her, for years. Everything about Sarah was comforting, her smell, her smile. And now she was in Anna's home, the home from which Anna had called her at least once a month since she'd moved in, and it felt wonderful.

'What do you want to do?' Anna asked. 'Do you want to sleep?'

'No, I need to get on London time. But I don't think I'm up for anything too full-on until tomorrow. Can we just catch up, have dinner here?'

'Of course.'

'Oh, I have a book for you,' Anna said, picking it up off the coffee table and handing it to Sarah. 'I might have told you about it. I worked on it last year and just fell in love with it, but I don't think it was published over in the States. It's so good on friendship and deciding whether or not to have children, and I knew I had to get copies for you and Nia.'

'Thank you. You know, when we met I was so sure I wouldn't have children but I thought you would, despite what you said. Do you ever regret it?'

Anna loved the way Sarah cut straight to the heart of things. She always had, and Anna was pleased she still felt like she could, despite the distance between them.

'Not really,' she said. 'There's this part of me that wonders about how it might have been, to be a mother. But I get a view into parenting through Ben, and I get to be a stepmum to his daughters, and that feels like a privilege, most of the time. I just don't think it would have been right, for me. I think a lot of women just do it because their body tells them to, or because it's what people do, and I didn't want to do it without really knowing it was the right decision. And I never did.'

Sarah drank her coffee, nodding. She was taking in what Anna had said. She would respond when she was ready.

'And how is it, with Ben's girls?'

Anna thought about how to answer this. It wasn't easy, but when it was good, it was really good. She felt a closeness with Stella that she still hadn't reached with Tess, who was having a rocky time with puberty and seemed determined to take everyone down with her.

'If you're their parent, they just love you, don't they? It's biology. I mean, you see those documentaries, about parents who've done nothing for their children, who've treated them appallingly, and they still love them, still crave their parents' love. If you come in as a step-parent, you've got nothing. You're the one who isn't their mum, or isn't their dad. Plus they associate you with their parents' split, even if you didn't meet them until afterwards, like Ben and me. So if they end up liking you, it feels like a real achievement. And I think they like me, most of the time.'

'And do you like them?'

Anna smiled. She thought about the time she and Stella had gone swimming in the sea on an Easter break to Cornwall, the way they'd huddled together afterwards for warmth and shared a flask of tea. How it had felt like nothing else she'd ever known. About the way Tess switched from pre-teen rage to pure joy and back again, how she talked passionately about the environment and animals. How she'd turned vegetarian the previous year and stuck to it, despite finding it hard. Anna admired her dedication, her enthusiasm, her energy.

'I really do,' she said. 'They make me so hopeful, about the future.'

'What do you mean?'

'Just that the future's in good hands with people like them and their friends. They're all so passionate and liberal.'

'Ah, but isn't that just being young?'

Anna thought about that. She wasn't sure she remembered how she'd felt at eleven, or thirteen.

'Maybe.'

There was an easy silence, and Anna watched the specks of dust in the air. She finished her drink and went to the kitchen to get a packet of biscuits. When she returned, Sarah spoke again.

'Alex wants us to look into adoption.'

Anna was surprised. Sarah was the same age as her, and she always thought of them as too old to become parents. But she remembered that Alex was a few years younger. And that adoption didn't necessarily have the same restrictions, when it came to age.

'And you?'

'I want her.'

Anna nodded. 'Enough to go down that road?'

Sarah shifted a little on the sofa, tucking her legs underneath her. 'That's what I'm trying to work out. I know what it entails, and I've always said I didn't want to. And I don't want to do it just to keep her. It wouldn't be fair. So I'm talking to everyone I know who's a parent or' – she gestured to Anna – 'a sort of parent, and I'm trying to figure things out.'

Anna let out a big breath. 'I hope it works out. Whichever way you go.'

'Well, Alex is pretty set on it, I think. She'll do it with or without me. So it's just down to whether or not I can.'

Anna realised then that she didn't know what Sarah's reasons were for not having children. They'd just told one another, when they first met, that they didn't think it was for them, and that had been that.

'Is something holding you back?' she asked, then. 'I mean, I often wonder how much my reluctance to do it was linked to my relationship with my mother. The worry, that I'd be cold and distant like her. But you're close with your parents, right?'

Sarah was silent, and when Anna looked up again, she saw that her friend had tears in her eyes. She crossed the room, pulled Sarah into a hug.

'I was pregnant, once, when I was sixteen. I hadn't figured out that I was gay back then, or at least I hadn't admitted it to myself, and I had this boyfriend for a year or so in high school. I got pregnant, and my parents said they wouldn't support me having an abortion, and my boyfriend was clearly not going to be involved, and I sort of resigned myself to this life of teenage single motherhood. And then I lost the baby, in the fifth month. And I had so much guilt, because I hadn't wanted it, and I felt like I'd made it happen. I had to go through labour, all that. And I just said to myself, back then, that I'd never put myself through it again. I think it was partly about feeling I didn't deserve to have a child, and partly about knowing I couldn't go through something like that again.'

Anna had learned that sometimes there was nothing to say, so she just held her friend while she cried.

'God, I wasn't expecting to bring all of this up with you,' Sarah said, at last.

'I'm glad you did, though.'

'Who knew I was such a mess, underneath it all?'

Anna smiled. 'Now, this one I know. We're all just as messy as each other. Some of us hide it well, but you don't get to our age without having been fucked up by something or other.'

'Oh yes, and what's your thing?'

Anna shrugged. 'Distant mother, no dad, couldn't commit to having children, fell in love with a man who wasn't available.'

'I wondered whether we'd talk about David.'

'How is he?' Anna asked.

She found that, now she was happy with Ben, it was really okay to ask. She didn't really care what the answer was.

'David's David,' Sarah said. 'He's married now, and his wife's about twenty years younger than him.'

It had taken Anna a long time to get over David, but she had. She didn't feel jealous of this young wife, didn't think for a second about going over there, on the pretence of visiting Sarah, to try to see him. Sometimes, she thought that if she hadn't spent those years in New York, she would have been a lot happier. And it was probably true, but she wouldn't have Sarah in her life either, and she might have been ready to settle down years before meeting Ben, so she probably wouldn't have him. Everything was connected to everything else. You couldn't just pull one strand out without the whole thing coming unravelled.

There was the sound of a key in the door, and Ben came into the room and smiled at them both.

'You must be Sarah,' he said, going over to hug her.

Afterwards, he came to Anna and she stood up and he kissed her. 'Anyone ready for a glass of wine?'

He went to the kitchen to open a bottle and Sarah did that thing that female friends do, where she quietly communicated her approval of a friend's partner.

'You seem settled,' Sarah said. 'No, not settled, more... I don't know, peaceful, I guess. Like you've found it.'

'Found what?'

'You know, "it". The secret. The answer. That feeling you talked about. So much for Nia's psychic.'

Despite her better judgement, Anna had thought a lot about Magda since meeting Ben. She'd got it right for Nia, after all. One big love and one child. So why not Anna? There had been the tragedy, which could have been her marriage falling apart or could have been falling in love with David. But now she had Ben, and he didn't fit the profile, didn't work in food or have a name beginning with J, but she was certain about him. She shook her head. She couldn't tell Sarah what she was thinking.

And then she laughed, because if she pushed aside those ridiculous worries, Sarah was right. There were problems, like what Tess's mood swings would be like when she next came to visit, or how she was going to get any publicity for some awful book she'd been landed with, or the weight that seemed to be steadily creeping on as she neared fifty, but none of them were big enough to really worry about. She was happy.

32

YES

Sunday 5 June 2016

The boys had been shut up in their bedrooms all day and Edward was watching news coverage about the upcoming referendum on TV. They hadn't discussed it, the referendum, and Anna was almost certain that Edward was going to vote Remain like her, but there was a part of her that didn't dare to ask, in case she was wrong. In case she discovered that she'd built a life with someone who held such opposing views to her. How was it possible, she wondered, to not truly know who someone was after so many years? In the beginning, there were lots of long talks about politics and big ideas, and then you got older and got so caught up in work and family and home life that there was no longer space for any of that. People changed, didn't they? People grew inward, became more conservative, more concerned with their own family unit and less about the wider world. Who was Edward, now? Who would he be, when she cut him loose and he was out in the world on his own again?

Anna felt restless. Had felt that way all day. She'd done some cleaning and been for a walk, and it hadn't helped. She picked up her phone and called Nia.

'How's the birthday boy?'

'Loving life. Currently trying to eat something he found in his shoe. Happy anniversary, by the way.'

'Thanks.'

'Any plans?'

'Family dinner. I feel like this is going to be our last one.'

'Fuck. Call later if you need me.'

'Looks like you were right all along, about us not fitting.'

'Anna, you've made a life, a family. If something works for a time but doesn't last forever, that doesn't mean it was a failure.'

'And yet, here we are.'

Nia didn't say anything for a long moment.

'Thanks for coming to the party yesterday.'

Theo was two and Nia and Aidan had hosted another party at their flat the previous day. Anna thought back to last year, to cajoling Thomas into going. This time, she'd gone alone. She'd bought Theo a toy farm complete with wooden animals. It had made her try to remember that stage with her boys. Running around and starting to speak and constantly wanting to do things they weren't yet able to do. It had had its frustrations but the cuddles had been incredible. She envied Nia, in a way. But there was a part of her that was glad all that was behind her, too.

After the call was over, Anna went upstairs to get changed. She spent longer than usual doing her makeup and she wasn't sure why. She'd known for a couple of months that her marriage was over, but she hadn't sat down with Edward and made it formal yet. She didn't know whether he knew too, whether he was just waiting for her to be the one to say it. And the fact that she couldn't tell, that said a lot. She looked in the mirror and saw a middle-aged woman. One of her worries, in making this decision, had been whether she'd ever find anyone again. But in the end, she'd decided it didn't matter. Staying with someone you didn't love any more because you might not meet someone else was too sad to contemplate.

She'd asked herself when it had happened a lot. Because she had loved him, and now she didn't, at least not in the same way, and not enough, and at some point she must have stopped. Had they become too comfortable? Too willing to show one another their grumpiest, most unkind sides? Or had it just not been enough love in the first place to last through the years? Sometimes she thought about that kiss with Steve, and the time they'd spent apart after Edward's dinner with Fran. Perhaps they'd never fully come back from that. She knew, deep down, that she'd never quite let go of the way she felt about Steve.

Ten minutes before the booking, they gathered in the hallway, coming from different areas of the house, doors closing, footsteps on the stairs. Anna was glad to see the boys, and had a brief flashback to the days of them talking to her through the toilet door and wanting to sit on the worktop while she made lunch. Then, she had longed for some time to herself. Now, it seemed, she had too much of it. They walked to the restaurant, Thomas and Sam ahead, talking about a video game they both played. Edward reached for Anna's hand and she let him take it. In the early afternoon, it had felt like summer, but now it was evening and it was chillier than Anna had expected.

She tried to focus on the evening ahead, on making it nice, one to remember. She hoped that Thomas would be on good form, as his mood could determine the whole course of the evening. She hoped, too, that Edward would be funny and light, the way he could be. The way he used to be when the boys were younger.

Edward ordered bread and drinks and when they all had a glass in front of them, he lifted his.

'Happy anniversary,' he said.

'Happy anniversary,' Anna replied.

Seventeen years had passed since they'd promised to love one another forever, and Anna thought they'd made a pretty good stab at it. They'd made a home, taken care of each other, and created these two wonderful people who would move away from them and live their own lives, perhaps do incredible things she couldn't even imagine. She turned to her boys, their heads close together, a joke on Sam's lips. Eleven and slightly awkward, he was always looking up to fourteen-year-old Thomas.

'Sam has a girlfriend,' Thomas announced, and Sam gave his brother a shove and went a little red.

'She's just a friend,' he protested. 'We're doing this project together and...'

Thomas laughed. 'Sure, a project.'

The waitress brought the basket of bread Edward had ordered then, and they all reached for it at the same time, and laughed. It was an ordinary dinner, in the end. One of so many that they'd had over the years. Sam pushing his plate to one side because there was cucumber in the salad, and then being talked around. Thomas finishing everything the others left and washing it all down with about a gallon of Coke. Anna was always the one who held it all together, kept the conversation going, resolved any disagreements. It was tiring. She was glad when it was time to leave.

On the short walk home, Anna felt stuffed and lethargic. She was walking beside Thomas, with Edward and Sam a little way ahead. Sam was telling Edward something, using elaborate arm movements.

'Did I tell you about this party next weekend? At Harry's?'

Anna knew what he was doing. He could have brought this up when they were sitting around the table, but he'd waited until he had her on her own. Over the years, she'd tried hard not to let this happen. To present a united front. But there were countless decisions, every day, and you couldn't consult one another about every last one. Gradually, it had become a thing, that the boys came to her rather than Edward, when they wanted something they thought might not be allowed. How would it be, Anna wondered, if she and Edward weren't even together? How wide would this wedge grow?

'I don't think you did,' she said.

'It's a birthday thing, about twenty of us. His mum will be there.'

Anna wasn't naïve. She knew to translate this as thirty or forty kids, no parents, plenty of alcohol. She remembered what it was like. And she didn't want him to miss out, didn't care about him getting drunk and being sick and all of that. She just worried. About drunk teenagers, unprotected sex, consent, drugs. She would talk to Edward.

'I'll talk to Dad about it.'

Thomas looked at her imploringly. 'Please Mum, everyone is going. I just don't want to miss it.'

Anna felt her heart crack a little. She remembered it all. The feeling of being left out if you missed one party, the way friendships and relationships could change overnight. You could miss one night out and miss that chance with the girl or boy you'd liked all year. It was fraught. And she knew Edward was much more likely to say no. But she had to run it past him. They were still a partnership.

'I know. I get it. I'll talk to Dad.'

Thomas and Sam both disappeared to their rooms as soon as they got home. Homework, Xbox, social media. Anna felt like she was losing them. Edward went to the kitchen and poured them both a glass of wine, brought it through to the lounge. He handed her one and then chinked his against it, and a few drops fell onto the wooden floor, and Anna decided against cleaning it up immediately. They sank into the sofa.

'Seventeen years,' Edward said.

Anna hoped he wouldn't make that joke, about getting less for murder. He didn't.

'Yes,' she said. 'Do you think we knew what we were signing up for?'

Edward looked at her, his face serious. 'I don't think we had any idea. But I wouldn't change it.'

Anna wasn't sure she would, either. She knew in her bones that their marriage was over, was just waiting to feel strong enough to talk to him about it, to start making those decisions about who would live in the house and who would move out and how they would divide up their time with the boys. But despite knowing all that was to come, she didn't feel regret about the years they'd spent together. She had loved Edward. In a way, she still did. It just wasn't enough any more. But they'd had a good life, a happy one, and she didn't know what she would have had otherwise. Couldn't know.

Without expecting it, Anna felt close to tears. She saw Edward notice.

'What is it?' he asked, leaning forward and brushing the first tear from her cheek.

Did he know? It belonged to both of them, this marriage, and she found it hard to see how it could still be alive and well for him, when it was all but dead for her. But perhaps that was part of the reason why it needed to end; they simply saw things too differently.

'I'm not sure,' Anna said. 'I just feel overwhelmed, somehow.'

Edward nodded. He stood up, put his glass of wine down on the coffee table, took hers, too. And then he sat again, closer to her, his arms around her. Anna remembered when they had just seemed to fit, but now it felt a bit awkward, a bit uncomfortable. She lifted her head, and Edward kissed her, and for a moment, it all melted away. All the doubt and uncertainty. She pretended that they were different people, that they had a different life ahead than the one she knew was right.

When Edward pulled away, they looked at each other without accusation. Anna felt like Edward was trying to see inside her, trying and failing to determine what she was thinking. It wasn't so long ago that he would have been able to tell.

'Remember that Christmas Eve when we were wrapping presents until almost midnight and Sam came downstairs, half asleep, and you threw a blanket over everything and managed to get him back upstairs without him suspecting a thing?'

Anna smiled. 'Yes.'

'That's the kind of mum you are. Calm under pressure, always thinking of what they need, what will make them happy. I admire it so much.'

Anna was taken aback. It wasn't that he'd never complimented her mothering, but he'd never said this. She didn't know that he thought about this kind of thing, that it took up space in his mind.

'Thank you,' she said. 'I don't know why I always worry that I'm not doing well enough.'

'You shouldn't. You are.'

She wanted to say something back, about how he was a good father, because he was, but she didn't want it to seem like she was saying it because he had. She would save it for another time, when he wasn't expecting it, and she would surprise him the way he'd surprised her.

'I'm going to go to bed,' she said. 'I'm tired.'

'I'm going toooooooooooooooooo bed,' Edward sang.

Anna laughed. It was something he'd done so much in the early years, singing her words back to her as if they were power ballads. She couldn't remember the last time he had done it.

Edward reached for the remote control. 'I'm going to stay up a bit, I think.'

Anna went upstairs and stood outside her boys' bedroom doors. She could hear them in there. Sam was playing a game, she thought, and Thomas was talking to someone, probably about the party. She'd forgotten to mention it to Edward. She got ready for bed and lay there in the dark, her eyes wide open. She had been tired when she'd said it, but like so often happened, the act of going upstairs and undressing and brushing her teeth had woken her. She went back over the evening, over the things Edward had said. And she resolved to talk to him, soon, about splitting up, about going their separate ways after all these years of walking side by side.

33

NO

Sunday 5 June 2016

Anna gestured to the barman for another and grimaced at him as she raised the shot glass and knocked it back. She felt hands on her shoulders and jumped, but when she turned, it was just Nia.

'I've been looking for you,' Nia said, her face full of concern.

'Where?'

'Well, I called your mobile, and then I went to your flat, and then I thought I'd try some of the local eating and drinking establishments. And here you are.'

'Here I am.'

'Do you know what time it is, Anna?'

Anna looked at her watch. 'Yes. It's twelve twenty-five.'

'Bit early for shots, don't you think?'

Nia gave the barman a stern look and he held his hands up as if to say it was nothing to do with him. He was young, late twenties or just about early thirties.

'Oh, guess what?' Anna squealed. 'This is Julius!'

Nia smiled tightly. 'Oh yes?'

'Another please, Julius,' Anna said.

The barman looked from Anna to Nia and back again.

'No,' Nia said sharply. 'I'm taking her home.'

Anna wanted to protest but didn't have the energy. She slid off the bar stool and felt suddenly much more drunk than she had when she'd been sitting down.

'Have you eaten anything?' Nia asked.

Anna shook her head.

'Right.'

When they were at the door, Nia's arm hooked firmly through Anna's, Nia turned and looked at the barman again.

'If she comes in again, don't let her get this drunk.'

It was a five-minute walk back to Anna's flat, and she let herself be pulled along the Balham streets by Nia. They didn't say much. At Anna's front door, Nia helped her find her keys and they went inside. Once Anna was settled on the sofa, Nia looked through the fridge and then said she was going out again.

'I'm just nipping back to Sainsbury's to get you some food. Don't go anywhere.'

Anna had no intention of going anywhere, but soon after Nia left, she found that she was crying. Had she cried in the bar? Had she told that young barman everything? How she had thought she'd finally found her happy ending with Ben, only for him to have a heart attack and die on her less than four years later? She had no idea. All she remembered was heading out for a quick walk and then feeling herself pulled towards that bar, where she'd drunk with Ben a handful of times. She'd thought perhaps she'd go in for some lunch, but once she was inside, sitting on a bar stool, she had known. She'd gone in for one reason and one reason only, and that was to search for oblivion.

It seemed like no time at all had passed before Nia was back, a bag of shopping in each hand. She talked to Anna as she unpacked the bags in the kitchen.

'Milk, tea, biscuits, bread, cereal, soup, cheese, eggs, potatoes, carrots, salad. This should keep you going for a bit. What would you like now, for lunch? Shall I make you a sandwich?'

Anna stood up and went through to the kitchen. 'Why were you looking for me today?'

'What do you mean?'

Anna shrugged. 'I don't know. I just... Don't you have things you should be doing, with Jamie and Cara?'

'Don't do this,' Nia said, pulling slices of bread from the packet she'd just opened. 'Don't shut me out.'

'I don't want to be a burden.'

'And you're not.'

They didn't talk much while Nia made sandwiches and tea. They carried them into the living room, sat down on the sofa.

'Have you thought any more about going back to work?' Nia asked. 'Have they been in touch?'

'No,' Anna said.

She thought about going back to the office. It was unimaginable at the moment. All those people there who relied on her, who expected her to make decisions and know what she was talking about. To focus. To sit at her desk for an entire day and not scream or cry or throw things. She wasn't ready.

'I can't do it,' she said. 'I can't imagine being able to do it.'

'You will,' Nia said, reaching out and touching Anna's arm. 'You just need more time, that's all.'

Anna put her plate down on the floor, the sandwich untouched. She saw the way Nia looked at her, the worry there. She knew she had lost weight, that she was drinking too much, that she wasn't dealing with things. But how did people do it? How could they stand to be in their own skin, all day, every day?

'Do you ever think about what Magda said?' Anna asked.

Nia raised her eyebrows. 'Of course. Do you?'

'I always thought the tragedy she mentioned was my marriage breakdown, but that wasn't tragic. Not really. I should have known there would be something else. She meant this.'

Nia looked at Anna for a long time. 'I thought you didn't even believe any of it.'

'I thought I didn't. But look how many years it's been, and it's still hanging over me.' She paused. 'I might just go to bed.'

'Please don't,' Nia said. 'I'm here, I have the whole afternoon. We could watch an old film or talk or just sit here in silence but please let me be here with you.'

Anna was moved by Nia's gesture. She'd known, hadn't she, that Nia was the best friend she could wish for? Somehow, Nia was going to pull her out of this hole, or do her very best to. Sarah had offered to come over too, and though Anna had said no, she thought often of the offer, of what it meant to her to have people who loved her, despite not having the one she wanted the most.

'*Sex and the City*,' Anna said.

'What?'

'Let's watch *Sex and the City*. I have them all on DVD. I haven't seen them for years.'

Years ago, before their lives had got serious, Anna and Nia had often spent Sundays together watching TV and eating junk food. They would wear their comfiest clothes and drag the duvet from the bed of whoever's flat they were at, and settle down for the day. Anna wanted to regress, to revert, to forget everything that had happened between those easy days and these hard ones. But no, that wasn't quite true. Because she didn't want to forget Ben altogether. She just wanted to forget that she had loved him, and he had died.

Nia dug out the DVDs and put one on, and almost immediately Anna felt like a different version of herself. A version who had believed that things were simpler, that she would marry Edward and stay with him forever. That life would work out. For a couple of hours, she sat there, her best friend at her side, and allowed herself to pretend that she was still that person. And then the DVD ended, and when Nia turned to her and asked if she wanted to watch the next one, she shook her head.

'You know that thing I always used to talk about, that happiness I was looking for and didn't know what shape it might take or whatever?'

Nia nodded.

'I didn't have that with Edward. And once I realised I didn't, I knew I had to end it. And then I was stupid enough to think I might have it with David, even though anyone with half a brain could see he was a player and he was never going to be faithful to anyone. I was so naïve. But with Ben, I really think I had it. I really think that was it. It wasn't perfect, obviously, but it was pretty damn close.'

'It was,' Nia agreed. 'It shone out of you.'

'So why did I only get to have it for a few years? It's not fair.'

Anna knew she sounded like a child who hadn't got her way, but that was how she felt.

'It isn't fair,' Nia said. 'But I'm starting to think that you don't only get one chance, one soulmate, one shot. I mean, look at you. You could have had a future with that guy James you went on one date with, or you could have stayed with Edward, or you could have met Ben much earlier, and had a life with him. Or you could have it again, in the future, with someone you haven't even met yet. I know you don't want to hear that, because you're not ready to move on, and that's fine. But one day you will be, and you might just meet someone completely different from Ben, who isn't better than him but who shows you a different way to be happy. And then there's me. I mean, if I wasn't with Jamie, I might have ended up with that hot friend of Ben's.'

'Aidan?'

'Ah, yes. Dreamy Aidan. I wonder what he's doing right now.'

Anna smiled despite herself, and then she took a deep breath. She hoped Nia wouldn't hate her for what she was about to say. Hoped Jamie wouldn't, either. Telling Nia this had seemed unimaginable a few years ago, and now it seemed like nothing.

'That guy, James...'

'Yes?' Nia asked. 'Oh my god, you've seen him again, haven't you? Do you know where he is?'

'I do,' Anna said.

Nia's eyes widened and Anna suddenly felt very sober, and wasn't sure she was doing the right thing.

'Please don't be angry with me,' she said. 'It's Jamie. James is Jamie. The first time I met him, when I was back from New York to see you and meet Cara for the first time, it just didn't seem right to tell you.'

Nia's mouth was hanging open. 'What the fuck?'

Anna couldn't tell whether she was angry or just surprised. She waited.

'All these years, I've been hoping you'll run into him again, hoping you might get some kind of fairytale ending out of it, and the man in question is my partner?'

Nia started to laugh and then Anna did, and it felt so good, to be laughing, the kind of laughing that hurt a little after a while. Nia put a hand over her mouth, trying to pull herself together, but it was impossible, and she gave in to it again, and the two of them sat there, side by side, uncontrollable, for some minutes.

There were tears streaming down their faces, and for once, Anna thought, they were not borne of sadness.

'And Jamie knew? I mean, of course he knew! That bastard!'

Anna thought back to that day in the kitchen, when Nia had been so strung out and stressed about new motherhood, how she and Jamie had decided to keep it between them.

'God, he's going to kill me for telling you,' Anna said. 'We made a deal.'

'So, let me get this straight. You've kissed my partner?'

Anna remembered the date she and Jamie had gone on. It felt like a million years ago.

'I'm so sorry,' she said. 'I have. But just the once, and it was, like, a different life. Are you angry?'

'No,' Nia said.

And Anna loved her friend so much for the fact that there hadn't even been a second of hesitation.

'But I don't want you to have a fairytale ending with him any more,' Nia added. 'If you don't mind.'

When Nia went home, she hugged Anna on the doorstep. 'Don't go out and get drunk on your own. I know I don't know what you're going through, but please let me help you. Just call me, okay?'

Anna nodded. She felt better than she had that morning, when she hadn't been able to see a way through. She felt a little lifted, and that was down to friendship, and she was going to remember it. 'Thank you,' she said. 'For finding me, feeding me, all of that.'

'For not minding that you've kissed my husband?' Nia asked, her eyes bright.

'This is going to run and run, isn't it?' Anna asked.

'You'd better believe it.'

The flat felt empty again after Anna closed the door, but not desperately so. She had some toast and tea, and she read a chapter of a book she'd had on the go for ages. And just as she was thinking about heading upstairs to bed, at half nine, her phone rang. It was Ben's daughter, Stella.

'Hi, Stella.'

'Hi. I just wanted to say hello, see how you're doing.'

Anna felt her heart tighten like a fist in her chest.

'I'm okay, Stella. Are you?'

'Yeah, sort of. It's just, it's hard, isn't it? I've been thinking about him all day, and you. How happy you made him.'

There was a pause, and Anna thought Stella might be crying.

'He loved you so much,' Anna said.

'He loved you too.'

And then they both said nothing, and Anna could hear Stella's music playing in the background, and she realised that she missed the noise and bustle of the girls being in the flat.

'How's Tess?'

'Up and down. She got her nose pierced and Mum freaked. Can you imagine what Dad would have said?'

Anna thought about that. She thought he probably wouldn't have liked it. He'd struggled with his girls growing up, the way she imagined all parents did. But what did any of it matter, in the end? What did a piercing matter, or a tattoo, when at any moment, you could lose someone?

'Sometimes,' Stella went on, 'I wish he'd had something like cancer, and we'd known, had some time to say goodbye, you know? And other times I think it's better that it happened the way it did, no notice, no time to prepare. Because he was himself right up to the end, wasn't he? Not some ill, deteriorating version of him.'

Anna couldn't speak.

'Anna?'

'Yes, Stell?'

'Do you think we could get together sometime? Go for a coffee or see a film or something?'

'Yes,' Anna said. 'Yes. I would really like that.'

34

YES

Monday 5 June 2017

Anna had had a good morning. She had two new clients and was due to work on some big upcoming releases. It was really starting to work well, her little enterprise. Sometimes, she wished she'd done it years earlier, but then she stopped herself and tried to focus on what had gone right. She'd found the courage to do it, and perhaps all the knockbacks she'd suffered from those publishing jobs had led her here. She was happy, making up her own rules and hours and not having to spend time on the Tube getting to an office in town. She felt free, in a way.

When it got to lunchtime, she closed her laptop and got her things together and took the bus to Nia's.

'Hey!' Nia opened the door and ushered her in, and Anna went through to the living room, where Theo was sitting in front of the TV, watching a cartoon about dogs that appeared to be performing some kind of rescue.

'Theo!' Anna said. 'Happy birthday!'

He didn't turn from the screen. Nia swept into the room, picked up the remote and switched it off, and Anna saw Theo's lip start to wobble.

'How old are you, Theo?' Anna asked.

He showed her three fingers. 'Three,' he said. 'I watch *Paw Patrol.*'

'Later,' Nia said. 'Anna's come to see you.'

Anna took the present she'd brought from behind her back and Theo's eyes lit up. It was a big box, wrapped in bright spotty paper. She handed it to him and he tore at the paper.

'What is it?' Nia asked in a whisper.

'Toy laptop,' Anna said. 'Hopefully not too noisy.'

Meanwhile, Theo had got into the present and was trying to open the box. Nia got down on her knees to help him while Anna watched on.

'Shall I make some tea?' Anna asked.

'No, I've bought prosecco. It's a celebration!'

Anna thought about saying no, that she had to work in the afternoon, but there was something so deliciously decadent about the idea of having a glass or two of prosecco in the middle of a Monday. Especially when it was her wedding anniversary, and she was still adjusting to the fact that she was no longer married. So she smiled and let Nia go to the kitchen for the drinks.

Theo's party had been at the weekend. For the first time, Anna hadn't gone. He had his own friends now, from pre-school, and they'd gone to a soft play. Nia had invited Anna, but said that the place was hell on earth, so Anna had arranged to see them on the day itself. For the next twenty minutes, they played a few party games and did a bit of dancing, and Anna felt nostalgic for those early birthdays with her boys. It had always felt so hard at the time; she'd been so tired and had always been stressed about the cake or the arrangements. She wished, now, that sometimes she'd just invited Nia over for an impromptu disco. After a while, Nia put the TV back on for Theo and he settled down, and Nia sat beside Anna on the sofa, poured them both a second glass.

'Is it weird, today?' she asked.

Anna was touched that Nia remembered the significance of the date. The fact that her son had been born on Anna's wedding anniversary meant that the date was an important one for both of them, in different ways.

'Sort of. I mean, not really. I just keep thinking about what we'd be doing if I hadn't left. Another dinner, another year gone. It was really time, but it's still sad, I guess.'

'How many years would it have been?' Nia asked.

'Eighteen.'

'Christ, how are we old enough?'

They laughed, but there was something underneath the light-heartedness. They were forty-seven. It was an age Anna couldn't even have contemplated when she stood there promising forever to Edward, and yet here they were, and she still felt twenty-three sometimes, still felt she was waiting for an adult to tell her what to do.

'Half the mums I know have Botox, and I'm the oldest of the lot of them,' Nia said.

Anna raised her eyebrows. 'Are you tempted?'

'Am I bollocks. How are we supposed to fight the fact that women aren't allowed to age if we go along with it?'

Anna grinned. She loved this woman.

'So we'll just grow old, shall we? And they can all just accept it?' she asked.

'Too bloody right.'

Every time Nia swore, she lowered her voice to a whisper, but it seemed there was no need. Theo was oblivious to anything going on around him.

'What the hell is this, anyway?' Anna asked, gesturing to the screen. 'I don't think it was around when mine were little.'

Nia did a little shudder. '*Paw Patrol*. It's like crack. I don't get it but he cannot get enough of it. Still, at least we've moved on from *Peppa Pig*. I was ready to lose my shit with that one.'

'So what are the plans for the rest of the afternoon?'

Anna glanced at her watch, saw that she'd been gone for an hour and a half. She should probably get back, and yet. She was having such a nice time.

Nia shrugged. 'I'll take him to the park, and then when Jamie gets home, we're going to go to Pizza Express.'

'Do you want some company, for the park bit?'

'I thought you had to get back to work?'

Anna shrugged. The prosecco had made her feel carefree and light. 'There have to be some perks to running your own business, don't there? I make my own hours.'

What she didn't say was that she was often at a loose end in the evening or at the weekend, so there was no shortage of time in which she could slot in extra work.

Nia brightened. 'We would love that, wouldn't we, Theo?'

She poked him gently on the shoulder, but he didn't turn. Anna laughed.

'Well,' Nia said. 'I would love that, anyway.'

It was a short walk to the park. Anna couldn't remember how long it had been since she'd pushed someone on a swing or caught someone coming down a slide. It had all seemed quite tedious at the time, she remembered, but now it was lovely. Now it wasn't her everyday.

'I used to love coming with you to do this with your boys,' Nia said, her eyes on Anna.

'Did you? I always used to imagine you had somewhere better to be, but you were doing it for me.'

'Well, I was doing it to keep you company, but it was wonderful, too.'

'It's so hard to appreciate it, at the time,' Anna said.

Nia nodded. 'I already get that. I feel like I barely remember the baby days, the way he would snuggle in so close, look at me like I was the whole world.'

'And then they're teenagers, and all they do is grunt.' Anna laughed.

'How is it, really?'

The boys had taken the split hard. They blamed Anna, because she was the one to instigate it, and Edward had done nothing to stop them. She'd wondered, in the days leading up to her bringing the matter up with him, whether he would offer to move out, to let her and the boys keep the house. But he didn't. He said that it was her decision, and she could go, and though they had split custody, Anna was very aware that Edward's house was their home. Still, she had known there would be losses. She had resigned herself to that.

'Sam is coming around,' she said. 'You know what he's like, he's a puppy. So full of love, he can't stay angry. But Thomas, I don't know. There's this distance, and I'm really trying, but he's a fifteen-year-old boy, so the last thing he wants to be doing is spending time with me, even if I hadn't taken a sledgehammer to his family unit.'

Nia tilted her head to one side. 'Don't be hard on yourself,' she said. 'It can be a nightmare with teenagers at the best of times. You'll never know how much of it is about the split and how much is just hormonal.'

Anna nodded. She knew it was true, but it was hard to make herself remember it.

'What about Edward?'

What about Edward? When she'd told him, he had been shocked, claimed he'd had no idea it was coming, that he thought everything was absolutely fine between them. For days, he'd tried to talk her around. And then, when she'd made it clear he wasn't going to be able to, he'd said some awful, spiteful things. Things you couldn't just forget.

'He's seeing someone,' Anna said.

The words felt strange in her mouth. The boys had told her, and she'd made a point of not reacting, in case that was what they had wanted.

'Wow, that's pretty fast,' Nia said.

Anna had known that Edward wouldn't stay single for long. He was attractive and he had a good job, a nice house. There was nothing really wrong with him. And he didn't like to be alone, so it had been obvious that he would find someone. And he had. Anna knew nothing about her, not her name, not what she looked like. And she felt no jealousy or resentment. Not when it came to Edward, anyway. The thought of this stranger spending time in that house with Anna's boys was a different matter.

'I guess it's fast, but good luck to him,' Anna said.

'Have you given any thought to putting yourself out there again?' Nia asked.

Nia wanted Anna to go on dating apps. She'd offered to help her create her profile, find some good photos, all of that. But Anna didn't feel ready. She believed she would be, one day, so she wasn't worried about it. But for now, she was enjoying getting to know herself again. Finding out what she liked to watch on TV when she didn't have to agree with anyone else. Buying herself new clothes without a thought of what Edward, or anyone else, might think.

'You'll be the first to know, when I'm ready,' Anna said.

Nia nodded. She didn't push, and Anna appreciated that. She was pushing Theo on a swing, but just then he started kicking his legs and when Anna asked if he was ready to get out, he said yes. She slowed the swing down and helped him out, and he ran over to the roundabout. Anna folded her arms and watched him spin around, in his own world. He seemed to be good at playing by himself, which was good because Nia had said they weren't going to have any more.

'God, he's so lovely,' Anna said.

Nia followed her gaze. 'Isn't he? I feel so lucky to have him, after meeting Aidan so late in the day.'

'We're both lucky,' Anna said.

And it was true, in so many ways. They had safe, warm places to live, enough to eat. They had their boys. They had their friendship.

'There's still time to get luckier,' Nia said, her eyes creased with smiling.

'What do you mean?'

'Well, you're single now, right? So there's still time to meet the man Magda saw for you all those years ago.'

Anna shook her head. 'I'll be sure to be on the lookout.'

She'd never told Nia, but that evening when they were twenty-two had haunted Anna. It wasn't that she was a believer, but it was a strange thing to have hanging over you as you navigated through your life. Your best friend sure you'd committed yourself to the wrong man, because he didn't have the right name or the right job according to a backstreet psychic. She didn't mind Nia joking about it, but she did wish they'd never gone to see Magda at all. That she'd never had half an eye on a different future.

'I'm going to make a move,' Anna said.

'Okay. Thanks so much for coming with us. Oh, and Anna?'

'Yes?'

'Aidan and I have this wedding to go to in September. They've invited Theo too but, let's face it, we'll have a much better time without him. I was wondering whether you might have him for us.'

'Sure, I'd love to, if I can. Whose wedding is it?'

'My friend Chloe.'

'And Steve?' Anna asked. She felt a little like she'd been slapped, tried to keep her voice level.

Nia clapped a hand to her mouth. 'Shit, I forgot you knew him. That you two were—'

'Nothing. We were nothing. Send me the date, okay?'

Anna hugged Nia, and on the way out of the park, she tried to hug Theo, but he wriggled out of her grip and giggled, and she settled for blowing him a kiss. She walked home. It wasn't all that far, from Clapham South to Tooting Bec, and the lightness the prosecco had brought on had gone and she knew it could turn into a headache. The fresh air would do her good. She thought about Steve, about how hearing he was getting married was a blow, even when she hadn't seen him for a long time and knew he was in a committed relationship with Nia's friend. Perhaps it would always be like that, with him. Perhaps they could have been something, in another life. But not in this one.

When she was about halfway home, near Balham Tube station, Anna saw a pair of children's sunglasses and recognised one of the dogs from the programme Theo had been watching earlier. She picked them up and rested them on a brick wall, hoping the owner would come back and see them. She took some deep breaths, concentrated on the feeling of the early summer sunshine on her arms and face. Every so often, it disappeared behind a cloud, and each return felt like a promise of good days to come.

35

NO

Monday 5 June 2017

Anna looked at the woman in front of her. Jade. She was twenty-three, well-spoken, well-educated, keen. She had a degree in English Literature from a good university. She was the best candidate Anna had seen that day. But there was one more to go. She stood up and showed Jade out of the room, pointed her back in the direction of reception, and then she spent a couple of minutes gathering her thoughts before calling the receptionist to ask for the final candidate to be sent up.

While she waited, Anna finished her coffee and stood up to look out of the window. They were on the fifth floor, and she looked down at the busy Soho street below, the people like little Lego figures. When she heard a knock, she turned around and called for the candidate to come in. She had to hide her surprise when a woman of around forty entered the room. Every other interviewee had been in their early twenties.

'Hello,' she said, walking back over to the desk. 'I'm Anna, Head of Publicity, thanks for coming in.'

The woman reached out a hand and shook Anna's. 'Julia, nice to meet you.'

Anna asked the same questions she'd asked the others, and Julia answered well. She didn't have experience, but then neither did any of those younger women. But she seemed to have done her research, to know what the job would entail and to be interested. What Anna really wanted to know was what she'd been doing for all those years since she'd graduated. Probably being a mum, she guessed. She wished she'd looked more closely at Julia's CV.

'Is there anything you want to ask me, or discuss?' Anna asked, as she always did at the end of an interview.

Julia bit her lip, swallowed. 'Sort of. I just wanted to say that I know most people go for this sort of job almost straight out of university. I know I'm not your typical candidate. I've been raising my three children for the past fifteen years and now that they're a bit older, I want to reach out for the career I had planned before they came along.'

Anna nodded. She wasn't sure what to say. And then suddenly, she was.

'Do you think there are any skills that you've developed over your years as a mother that you could bring to this role?'

Julia smiled. 'I do. Parenting teaches you about multi-tasking. Clearly the specifics are very different but once you've changed a baby's nappy while also talking a four-year-old through putting his socks on and listening to a six-year-old read his school reading book, you're not really fazed when someone asks you to do a couple of different things at once.'

Anna laughed. 'I can imagine.' She liked this woman, she realised. She could imagine working alongside her.

'And resilience, too. Teaching a child to read or use the toilet or tell the time can be pretty soul-destroying. One day you think they're getting it, the next you're back to the beginning. I'm used to having to keep trying until I get things right.'

'Great,' Anna said.

They both stood up, shook hands again. Anna sensed that Julia had something else to say, and she nodded encouragingly.

'I hope you'll give me a chance. I really feel like I could be a good fit for this role, and I would give it my all.'

'Thank you,' Anna said. 'It was really nice to meet you.'

All afternoon, she thought it over. Jade would fit in better with the rest of the team, simply because of her age. But she really felt that Julia would be better at the job. It was a gut feeling, but that's what she had always gone with in the past. By the time she left for the day, it was decided. She sent a quick email to HR before leaving, asking them to make the offer.

On her way out, she said goodnight to the receptionist, Bryony.

'Interviews go okay?' Bryony asked.

'Yes, great, thank you. I think I found the right person.'

'Perfect. Have a good evening.'

Anna felt a shiver of sadness. Sometimes, when she'd had a busy, productive day, she forgot that she was going home to an empty flat. And when it struck her, often as she turned the key in her front door, she had to fight against a wave of dread, had to force herself to make something more than toast for dinner, to go to bed earlier than one in the morning. It was a struggle, still.

She made her way to the Tube, let herself be pushed along by the crowd. Down the escalator, onto the hot, busy platform. She stepped onto a train, jostled her way to the middle of the carriage. A teenage boy touched her arm.

'Would you like to sit down?'

Anna looked at him, smiled and shook her head. She used to worry, when that happened, that the person offering must think she looked pregnant. Now, she worried that they thought she looked old.

She stole a look at the boy who'd spoken. He was sitting beside a man who was probably his dad, and they were chatting, their heads close together. Anna felt a twinge of recognition, and something else. She put her headphones on and turned on an audiobook, but she wasn't really listening to it. She was watching this man, the way he was carefully explaining something to his son, the way they were interacting as if they were the only people there. Without warning, the man looked up and caught her eye for a moment, gave her a half smile, and Anna felt something tugging at her, felt her insides soften. She had a sudden memory from years ago, of standing outside the flat she'd shared with Edward, on her way to see Nia just after Cara had been born. She'd picked up a toy dropped by a little boy who was walking with his dad, and she'd felt a strange kind of connection there. She'd forgotten about it afterwards, because she'd got caught up in meeting Cara and also in discovering that Nia's Jamie was her James. She did the maths, based on how old Cara was now. Could it be the same father and son? Was that crazy?

When Anna changed to the other branch of the Northern Line at Kennington, the father and son did too. But they went past Clapham without getting off, and Anna pushed the thought away, decided she was being ridiculous. At Balham, she made her way to the doors, and saw that they were doing the same thing. She followed them up the escalator and out into the light, carefully stepped over a pair of kids' sunglasses that were smashed on the pavement. And then they turned into a shop, and she carried on.

Once she'd let herself in, flicked on the kettle and made tea, Anna had a look through the post that she'd brought in from the mat. A gas bill, a couple of leaflets, and something that wasn't for her. It was addressed to John Murphy. Not the previous owner. And then she noticed that it wasn't just the name that was wrong, but the address. It was for next door. She grabbed her keys and went down her front path and up the next one, and just as she was about to push the envelope through the letterbox, the door opened.

It was him. The man with the son from the Tube. He ran a hand through his sandy hair, and Anna took a moment to really look at him, his broad shoulders and his beard and his crinkly eyes.

'I'm Anna,' she said. 'I live next door. I...' She gestured towards the envelope in her hands. 'This is yours. Or... for someone here.'

He smiled, reached out a hand to take it, and in the transfer, their fingers touched and Anna felt like she'd had a small electric shock.

'Thanks, it's mine,' he said. 'New postie, he seems to get a bit muddled up. I'm Steve.'

'Steve? But...'

He folded his arms, looked at her, waiting.

'Sorry, I just thought the letter was addressed to a John.'

'Oh, that. Yes, I go by Steve. Middle name.'

Anna grinned, couldn't help it. She imagined telling Nia she'd met her handsome neighbour and his name began with J.

'Did I see you on the Tube just now?' Steve asked.

'Yes.'

'And you're my next-door neighbour?'

'Yes.'

'I've only been here a couple of weeks. It's just me, and sometimes my son, Luke. Is it just you, next door?'

It seemed like a blatant attempt to find out whether she was single. To her surprise, she found that she didn't mind.

'Just me.'

'Well, have a good evening.'

Something in her didn't want to leave, but she forced herself to. Back up one path, down the other. Since Ben, there had been no one. And she'd thought that was just how it was, now. She'd thought that side of her life was over. But there was no denying that there was something there, with Steve, with her neighbour. She felt a little shiver run through her at the thought of it. Here she was, feeling a bit like a teenager with a crush, feeling like she sort of knew this man who she'd almost certainly never met, or definitely only met in passing. It was exhilarating, and scary, and nice.

Anna let herself back into her flat and leaned back against the door. Took a deep breath. And then she went into her kitchen and started making herself a salad for dinner. A little later, once she'd eaten and she was sitting on the sofa with a book in her hand, she called Nia.

'Hey,' Nia said.

'Hey yourself. Guess what happened today?'

'You finally pitched that book idea I keep telling you about, the one about my boss and Ellen? *Fifty Shades of Dull Office Romance.*'

Anna laughed. 'Are they back together?'

'Oh, who the hell knows? I've given up trying to keep track. But I do have a lot of material, you know, for the book.'

'I did have a good day at work, actually. I found a new publicity person.'

Anna thought back to the interviews, to Jade and Julia and the other girls she'd seen, all preened and out to impress. It seemed like a long time ago.

'That's good,' Nia said. 'But I don't think that's why you're calling.'

'No, you're right. On the way home, I met my new neighbour, and I think I might have a crush on him.'

Nia laughed. 'No one thinks they have a crush. When you have a crush, you know.'

'Okay, I have a crush on him.'

It was a big thing to admit, and Anna knew that Nia understood that.

'That's exciting!' Nia said. 'What's his name? Tell me it's Jeremy.'

'This is the bit you won't believe. He goes by Steve, but he's really John.'

'And what does he do for a job?' Nia asked, her voice a bit squeaky.

'I don't know that yet.'

'Did you invite him round for coffee?'

'No.' Did people actually do that? Was anyone bold enough? Probably. 'I just wanted to tell you.'

'I'm glad you did.'

'It feels a bit like a betrayal, of Ben. Tell me it shouldn't.'

'It shouldn't,' Nia said.

'It doesn't make me miss him any less.'

'I know.'

They stayed on the phone for another ten minutes, talking about Cara and what Jamie was cooking and whether Anna was free to join them for lunch on Sunday. She was.

'You sound excited,' Nia said, just before they ended the call. 'It's nice.'

'It is nice,' Anna said.

After they'd hung up, Anna sat for a long time, thinking about Ben, about Steve. About falling in love, and how much it could end up hurting, but how it was worth it for those moments of pure joy. That feeling.

36

YES

Tuesday 5 June 2018

On the day that would have been her nineteenth wedding anniversary, Anna received her divorce papers. They dropped onto the doormat when she was making herself a sandwich for lunch, and she sat at the kitchen table, somehow unable to open the envelope, for about ten minutes. And then she tore it open and found that she was crying. And she wasn't sure why. She'd never once doubted her decision to leave her marriage, but she didn't regret the years she'd spent in it, either. There had been a lot of happiness, and then there wasn't, and she'd left. It was as simple, and as complicated, as that. Still, almost two decades, and a promise broken. She thought back to who she'd been on their wedding day. How much she hadn't known.

There were the boys, too. Each time she looked at them, and thought about the possibility of not having them, of having no children, or different children, she shuddered and was glad. It hadn't been easy, raising them, and it had taken a long time for them to accept her decision to leave their father. For the first year, at least, they had been frosty with her, had only come to her for the agreed times and rarely contacted her in between. But they had softened, eventually, and she had answered every question they asked and they had come to an understanding. They missed her being at home, but they wanted her to be happy. And she was.

Thomas was sixteen, Sam thirteen, and Anna was confident that they were good people, and she was immensely proud of that. Twice a week, they would arrive after school, with big hugs for her, and they would go through her cupboards and eat all her cereal and make round after round of toast. And the flat would come alive. It wasn't that she was lonely when they weren't there. But she loved it when they were. The anticipation of their arrival, each Monday and Friday evening, felt a bit like falling in love.

The previous afternoon, her heart had lifted when she'd heard the scrape of the key in the lock.

'I missed you,' she'd said, leaving her deluge of emails and standing to hug them. They were both several inches taller than her, and they rested their chins on her head when she held them. And it always brought to mind an image of them as babies, tiny and cradled in her arms. She remembered lifting Thomas when he was seven and thinking she wouldn't be able to carry him for much longer, and now he could lift her. It was scary, how fast it all went. Everyone said it, and she'd resented it when she was in those dragging, early days, but now her sons were almost adults, and she saw that it was true.

'How are Dad and Helen?' she'd asked.

Edward had met Helen about seven or eight months after Anna had left. Helen hadn't had children, and the boys often complained about her not understanding something or other.

Sam had rolled his eyes. 'Helen's redecorating,' he'd said.

'Where?' Anna had pictured the house, the colours and wall-papers she and Edward had chosen.

'Everywhere. She's giving it a new lease of life, apparently.'

Anna had smiled tightly. She didn't care what happened to that house, but it was her sons' home, the place where they'd grown up, and she hoped Helen would be careful with their feelings when it came to updating it to suit her tastes.

'What does Dad think?'

Thomas had turned from where he was standing by the kettle. 'I think he just does what he's told.'

'And how's school?'

Thomas was doing his GCSEs, Sam just finishing year nine. They were both doing okay. Sam had struggled, over the years, with friendships more than academic issues, but things were more settled now. He had two best friends, one boy and one girl, and the three of them seemed to be kind to one another, to have each other's best interests at heart. For Thomas, things had been easier. He was into football and had always had a crowd of other boys around him. Now, he had a girlfriend, Lauren, and Anna liked her a lot.

'Only a few exams left,' Thomas had said. 'Lauren's going to come over here on Saturday if that's okay. We're going to revise together.'

'Of course. And you, little one?' Anna had asked, turning to Sam.

Sam had screwed up his face. He hated it when she referred to him being the baby of the family. But he was, and he always would be. 'Fine,' he'd said.

Anna hadn't been sure whether that was the whole story. If it wasn't, whatever was troubling him would come tumbling out at some point, she was confident of that. He was an open book, and they were close, and she loved that he confided in her. About six months ago, he'd told her that he thought he was gay, and she had kissed his forehead and thanked him for telling her, and that had been that.

It was hunger that brought Anna back to the present, dragged her from her thoughts of her sons. She glanced at her watch. Almost one. She had a look in the fridge and didn't much like what she saw there, so she decided to take herself out for lunch. There was a new café near the common that she'd been meaning to try.

As soon as she stepped inside, Anna recognised the man behind the counter, or thought she did. Was it really? Was it possible? There was a queue, and Anna craned her neck this way and that to get a better look, all the while trying to make sure he didn't notice her. It was James. One-perfect-date, didn't-call James. It was. She was sure of it. She pulled her phone from her pocket, sent a message to Nia.

> I've found James.

James?

> THE James. Perfect James.

WHAT? WHERE?

> That new café by the common. He works there.

IN FOOD!

> Oh my god, yes!

AND?? What happened?

> He hasn't seen me. I'm still in the queue. What should I do? I feel like I can't breathe. Should I leave?

> DO NOT LEAVE. This man is THE ONE. He
> must be!

Anna laughed and slipped her phone back in her pocket. She couldn't believe Nia was approaching fifty and still talked about there being a 'the one' for everyone. Although, Nia had met Aidan late in life, and they were blissfully happy. Anna didn't believe in 'the one', but she believed in being happy, in taking chances, in constantly working at your life to make it the best it could be. She was at the front of the queue. She raised her eyes, looked at James.

'Hi.'

'Hi,' he said, his voice friendly. 'What can I get you?'

So, he didn't remember. Anna was more disappointed than she'd expected.

'Brie and bacon panini please, with salad. And a coffee. Latte.'

James nodded and told her how much it came to, and she paid him, her fingers brushing his. Did she feel something? Warmth, connection, electricity? Did he?

'I'll bring it over,' he said.

Anna took a seat and messaged Nia again.

> He looks a bit like Peter Andre. I didn't notice
> that last time.

> Maybe you could be his mysterious girl.

Anna smiled and turned her phone over. She had sat down at a table for two in the window, and she watched people going past. Jogging, walking dogs, hurrying to appointments. It was almost summer, and she was her own boss, setting her own hours, and it felt good. She allowed herself to remember the date she'd gone on with James, when she'd not long finished university and felt like life was all still ahead of her. When he hadn't called the next day, or the next week, or ever, it had stung. It had stung more than it should have done, and until she'd married Edward, and sometimes after, if she was honest, she'd looked for him in crowds, on the street. Wondered about him. Where he was, who he was with. Why he hadn't wanted to see her again.

The café started to empty out. By the time James brought Anna's order over, there was no queue and only a couple of other tables were occupied.

'Here you go,' he said, putting her cup and plate down on the table a little too hard. He smiled, didn't step away when she expected him to. 'Listen,' he said, 'I'm sorry, I was frantic before, but you seem really familiar. Have we met?'

What to tell him? If she told him the truth, would it be embarrassing that she had remembered and he hadn't? She decided she didn't care.

'It's James, isn't it?' she asked.

'I go by Jamie now.'

'Okay, Jamie.' She tried to make the adjustment in her brain. 'I'm Anna. I think we went on a date a really long time ago.'

He reddened slightly and put one hand to his mouth. 'Anna! I'm so sorry. I remember now. The bus, the Thames, dinner.'

Kissing, Anna thought. *There was kissing, too.*

'How are you?' he asked.

How did you sum up more than two decades of life in a brief conversation?

'I'm really well,' she said. 'I have a little business, publicity for publishing companies. I have two teenage sons.'

She stopped, feeling foolish. Had he wanted to know these

things? Had it sounded like she was trying to show off about what she had?

'That's great, Anna,' he said.

'And you? You were in finance, weren't you? This is quite a change.'

'It's what I always wanted to do. And last year, I thought, fuck it, it's now or never. I made enough money over the years that I have a bit of a cushion. But this, this is great. I get to talk to people, make people food; it's so much better.'

Anna nodded, and then there was a pause, and she felt awkward, felt sure he would say goodbye and go back to his place behind the counter.

'I lost your number,' he said.

'What?'

'I lost your number. I didn't deliberately not call. I was desperate to call, in fact. I looked for it everywhere. But it must have been in my pocket and gone through the wash or something. I'm sorry.'

Anna shrugged. 'It doesn't matter now,' she said.

But what if it did? What if her whole life might have been different? And his?

'Can I take it again now?' he asked.

She looked up at him, puzzled.

'Your number. I mean, I know it's probably not the same one. But maybe I could take you out again. I mean, if you're single? If you'd like to?'

Anna felt a smile creeping over her. She felt it inside and out. She took a pen from her bag and wrote her number down on her napkin, and she handed it to him. There was something in the gesture that made her feel like she was back there, in her early twenties, with everything to come.

'Thanks, Anna,' Jamie said, turning to leave the table. 'I'll call you. Oh, and can I get you something for dessert? On me?'

On the walk back to her flat, after a delicious piece of carrot cake, she felt light and fizzy. She didn't need a relationship; she knew that now. She was happy enough with her work and her sons and her peaceful home. All of that was the feeling she'd searched for. But still, there was nothing quite like the thrill of a connection like that, of the possibility of something coming to be. It would, or it wouldn't. And either way, that was just fine. She was exactly where she should be, exactly who she should be. And all the paths she might take in the future?

Well, she thought with a smile, when she reached them, she would know what to do.

37

NO

Tuesday 5 June 2018

Steve handed Anna a mug of coffee and they sat down opposite one another at the table. He bit into his toast.

'I should hear about that new job today,' he said.

'The shop chain refit?'

'It's not shops, it's restaurants.'

'Restaurants?' Anna asked.

'Yes. Why?'

Anna couldn't tell him, could she? She couldn't say that when she was twenty-two, a psychic had said that the love of her life would have a name beginning with J and would work in food. No, she couldn't. Or wouldn't. And she still wasn't sure she believed in any of that, not the way Nia always had, but she couldn't help but feel like this was some kind of message. Some kind of validation.

'Nothing, I must have got confused. Let me know, will you?'

'I will.'

Anna reached for her phone and composed a quick text to Nia.

> Steve might be about to start refitting restaurants. Does that count as working with food?

Nia replied almost straight away.

> Close enough!

Steve reached across the table and took hold of Anna's hand, lifted it to his mouth and kissed it.

'What was that for?'

'I'm just happy,' he said.

Anna was happy. It had taken her a while to trust it, to trust him, to not dismiss it as too good to be true, or too soon after Ben. But she'd got there. She knew that it might not last forever, or that something might happen to change the way she felt about him, but right now, she was happy, and she wasn't going to let worrying about the future change that. She'd been thinking about something, and she was ready to put it into words.

'I have a question for you,' she said.

And just like that, she was nervous. What if she'd misjudged it, and he wasn't as serious about her as she was about him? But no, it was impossible. He'd said he loved her first; he'd made himself clear at every step.

'Oh yes?'

'I wondered whether you'd like to move in together.'

He stopped, then. 'Here?'

'Well, I've been thinking about that. I don't mind whether it's here or your place.'

Steve snorted. Anna's flat was nicer. She'd spent more time

decorating it and choosing furniture and coordinating things. Her garden was a little bigger, too. They almost always stayed at hers. Steve had started keeping some of his things there. But Anna had noticed that he always went home (sometimes with her, sometimes without) when Luke was coming over. And she wanted to be sensitive to that. If Luke was happier in the flat next door, she could live with that.

'I mean, we're practically living together anyway,' Anna said, and then stopped, realising that she sounded like she was trying to talk him into it. She didn't want to have to talk him into it. She only wanted to do it if he wanted to.

'Why would you want to give up your place for mine, though?' Steve asked.

'Because you're there. And I thought maybe it would be better for Luke.'

Steve laughed. 'You know I only go back to mine when Luke's around because I don't feel like it's fair to inflict an enormous man-boy on you.'

Anna let out a long breath. 'I really like Luke, you know that.'

'I do, but I don't think you fully understand how much he eats. Anyway, we're getting off topic. I would love to live with you, Anna.'

She felt something inside her start to unravel. 'You would?'

'I would. Of course I would. Do you think I like living alone?'

Anna didn't answer that straight away. Was it so obvious that living with someone was better than living alone? She'd always quite liked living by herself. Until now, when there was someone in her life who she wanted to be with all the time, who she missed even when she knew he was at the other side of a single wall.

'I didn't know,' she said. 'You've never said.'

'Let's ask Luke what he thinks, and then we'll sort it out.'

'Okay then.'

It had been so simple. No argument about whose flat it would be, about whether it was too much or too soon or not enough. Things with Steve were like that. Just simple and right. She thought briefly of her marriage. How young she'd been. How wrong. And then that disastrous relationship with David in New York, followed by the happy years with Ben. She'd never thought she would find it again, after losing him. But here they were.

'What time do you need to head off?' Steve asked.

Anna looked at her watch. 'Soon. Ten minutes.'

It was so tempting to say she'd spend another hour with him, be a bit late. She was the boss, after all. And he was his own boss. He ran a small building company and had a handful of people working for him. Enough that he could sometimes take the morning or afternoon off on a whim. But she had meetings she needed to go to.

'While we're asking things, I have one too,' he said.

'Go on.'

'Why did you never have children? I mean, did it just not happen for you or was it a conscious choice? You're so good with Luke, and with Stella and Tess.'

Anna thought it was strange that he'd brought this up at the breakfast table, but she didn't mind. It made her think he'd probably been wondering about it for a while.

'With Edward, it was one of the things that we broke up over. He wanted to, I didn't. And after that, I don't know, I had a series of not-quite-right relationships, and by the time I met Ben, it was too late, and he'd already done it, of course. But having Stella and Tess in my life has been wonderful.'

Steve nodded. 'Any regrets?'

Any regrets? Anna saw what Steve had with Luke, what Ben had had with Stella and Tess, and it seemed like a kind of magic, but not one that she wished for, for herself. She was content with what she had, what she'd chosen. She saw Stella about once a month, Tess slightly less often. She loved them both fiercely, but she didn't wish they were hers. Their mother had been generous enough to welcome Anna into their lives, to encourage her to retain her place there even after Ben's death.

'I've been so lucky in so many ways,' she said. 'I love my career, and I got to spend some years in New York, and I have a home that makes me happy, and I'm in love with someone who treats me really well.'

'I hope that's me.'

Anna laughed. 'I'm happy. I'll never know whether I would have been more or less happy if I'd led a different life.'

'That's true. I just think, sometimes, what a great mother you would have made.'

Anna wasn't sure what to do with a compliment like that. It was so different to anything she'd been complimented on before. Was it true? Would she have done a good job of mothering, if she'd gone down that road? She hoped so. The fact that she'd decided against it proved that she wouldn't have entered into it lightly. Parenting was as serious as it got, and she would have tried to give everything to it.

'It's great that I get to spend time with Ben's girls, and with Luke,' she said. 'I know all the hard parenting work is done but it's so nice to be a small part of his life.'

'Not so small,' Steve said.

Anna was thinking about something that she hadn't thought about for a long time.

'Have I told you that I think we might have met before? I mean years ago. When Luke was a little boy. I was standing on a street in Clapham, and I picked up his toy rabbit. Does that ring any bells at all?'

Steve's eyes widened a little. 'I'm not sure. I mean, he definitely had a rabbit. A tatty-looking, grey thing, but he was always dropping it. I don't remember...'

Anna was a little disappointed, but she tried not to let it show. She shook her head. 'Ignore me. I should go. I'll see you later, for dinner?'

'Sure.' He leaned in and kissed her lips.

All afternoon, while she was in meetings and reporting to her manager on the team's recent work and going through her emails, her mind was on Steve. Nia was a firm believer in everything happening for a reason, but Anna never had been. She thought it was all pretty random, and things could have gone a different way for her. For all of them. She couldn't help wondering, sometimes, how things might have been if she'd met him then, if that had been him. It would have meant no Ben, of course, which was tough to imagine. But she might have spent all those years with Steve and Luke, the years of losing teeth and learning to ride a bike and falling in love for the first time. Life was strange, with its twists and turns, its blind alleys and its long stretches of straight, clear road.

Anna's phone beeped with a message from Steve.

> Got the job.

She smiled and told him she was proud of him, and then she sent a message to Nia.

> Guess who's moving in with her boyfriend like someone in her twenties?

> Congratulations!

> You think we fit, right?

> You two definitely fit. Two spoons in a drawer.

> Good, because he got that restaurant refit job.

> I knew Magda wouldn't let me down.

Anna smiled and turned her phone over so she could finish off her work.

She'd left the office for the day and was walking to the Tube when her phone rang. She answered without checking who it was, and when she heard Steve's voice, she found herself smiling.

'I remember,' he said. 'It was on the street where we lived, Hazelbourne Road. I'd had a terrible night with him, with Luke, and I was just trying to get through the day. We were out walking with nowhere to go. And then you called out and I remember noticing how pretty you were, how kind of you it was to help. We were always losing things, in those days. Socks and dummies and these little cars he insisted on carrying around with him.'

Anna was silent. There was a lump in her throat she couldn't swallow away.

'Are you there, Anna?'

She focused very hard on keeping her voice level. 'I'm here.'

'What's wrong?'

'What if we'd met then? What if we'd had all those years?'

Steve was quiet. Anna thought she might have lost him, but then he spoke again.

'Me and Theresa were still hanging on then, just about.'

'Oh.' Anna felt stupid. She hadn't thought of that.

'It's got to be enough that we have each other now,' he said. 'You mentioned all those years, but what about all the years ahead?'

Anna stopped in the middle of the street, causing someone to bump into her back and call out something rude. She ignored him. Steve was right, of course. They had lots of years ahead. And they were settled, in their work and their homes. But more than that, they were settled in their bodies and their personalities. They knew who they were, what they wanted. If they'd had that chance, years before, it was quite possible that one or other of them would have messed it up, somehow. And then they would have nothing.

'It is,' she said. 'It is enough.'

'Good,' he said. 'Now, are you on your way home? I'm about to start making you dinner.'

Anna told him she'd be there as soon as she could, and ended the call. And all the way back, she didn't open her book or put her headphones on. She just thought about what she'd had in the past, what she had now. It was easy to forget to be grateful. It was easy to think about roads not taken. But the fact was, all the small and big decisions she'd made had led her here. And if she could go back, and change something, everything else might fall apart.

Life was like a house of cards, in that way. At once fragile and unbelievable. Why hadn't she been able to see it before? She was exactly where she should be, exactly who she should be. And all the paths she might take in the future?

Well, she thought with a smile, when she reached them, she would know what to do.

* * *

MORE FROM LAURA PEARSON

Another book from Laura Pearson, *Rollercoaster*, is available to order now here:
https://mybook.to/RollercoasterBackAd

ACKNOWLEDGEMENTS

This book has been a long time in the making. I wrote a lot of it during the pandemic, squeezing in an hour or two of writing each day around homeschooling my children. For various reasons, it hasn't seen the light of day until now. I'd like to thank Kate Evans for all the love and effort she put into it in those early days.

Huge thanks, as always, to my editor Isobel Akenhead and my agent Jo Williamson, and the whole Boldwood team, for helping me to breathe new life into it and finally bring it to this point.

Massive thanks to my writing buddies, particularly Lauren North, Nikki Smith and Zoe Lea, who have seen me through all my disappointments and my triumphs. Day after day of messages and voice notes. This wonderful and trying job would be so much harder without you. And speaking of messages and voice notes, thanks as always to Jodie Matthews, Abi Rowson and Lydia Howland for being the best.

Thank you to my family for all the support. My dad, my late mum, my sister. And my in-laws, who read all my books and are brilliant champions. Thank you to Paul, always.

And a final thanks to my children, Joe and Elodie, for being understanding when I have to shut myself away or am distracted because my head is in a book. I wanted to show, with this novel, that there's more than one way to have a complete and fulfilling life. I believe wholeheartedly that you can achieve that with or without having children, and that there are more routes to a happy ending than you can count. But you guys are mine.

ABOUT THE AUTHOR

Laura Pearson is the author of the #1 bestseller *The Last List of Mabel Beaumont*. She founded The Bookload on Facebook and has had several pieces published in *The Guardian* and *The Telegraph*.

Sign up to Laura Pearson's newsletter to read a free short story!

Visit Laura's website: www.laurapearsonauthor.com

Follow Laura on social media here:

- facebook.com/laurapearson22
- x.com/laurapauthor
- instagram.com/laurapauthor
- bookbub.com/authors/laura-pearson

ALSO BY LAURA PEARSON

Boldwod

Boldwood Books is an award-winning fiction publishing company seeking out the best stories from around the world.

Find out more at www.boldwoodbooks.com

Join our reader community for brilliant books, competitions and offers!

Follow us
@BoldwoodBooks
@TheBoldBookClub

Sign up to our weekly deals newsletter

https://bit.ly/BoldwoodBNewsletter

Printed in Dunstable, United Kingdom